Published by Haunt Publishing
www.hauntpublishing.com
@HauntPublishing

ISBN (paperback): 978-1-9162347-8-9
ISBN (ebook): 978-1-9162347-9-6

Cover design by Zuzanna Kwiecien:
behance.net/zuzannakwiecien

Typeset by Laura Jones:
lauraflojo.com

# THE GINGERBREAD MEN

## JOANNA CORRANCE

HAUNT PUBLISHING

# CONTENT NOTE

abandonment; alcohol (reference); blood, gore; confinement; death; gaslighting; manipulation; mind control; misogyny; murder; physical abuse.

To mum and dad,
thank you for a childhood of
magic and imagination

# CHAPTER 1

I decided to leave my fiancée on Christmas Eve, the very same day that I had proposed to her.

We stood beneath a snow-filled sky at the Christmas market in Edinburgh, hot drinks clasped in our gloved hands and glowing from the thrill of our recent engagement. Eleanor, my fiancée, was choosing new baubles for our Christmas tree which, on her insistence, had been erected at the end of November. I had tried to explain that the needles would fall off and that by Christmas Day we would be left with balding branches and a clogged hoover. If it were up to her, she would probably have kept the tree up all year round.

There was no hesitation. I made my decision in the seconds between her putting down a matte bauble and picking up a glossy red one, as she deliberated over which would suit our tree's garish aesthetic better.

When people spoke about leaving their long-term partner, it was usually after months, or even years, of painful deliberation, after the fighting had become too much or the indifference too lonely. It wasn't like that for me.

Oblivious, Eleanor continued to chatter away, radiating her usual rosy-cheeked chirpiness. She had recently qualified as a children's art therapist, which had only seemed to enhance her sunny demeanour. Her family, all headmistresses or doctors in niche specialities, had the kind of relationships you see in nice, family-friendly films. I knew that was meant to be a good thing, but it could leave me feeling a bit inadequate.

1

Our boots had sunk into the snow, which was grey and slushy from the grit and hundreds of stomping, dirty soles. On either side of the path was crisp, untouched snow that had fallen during the day. Rows of identical wooden huts lined the path, decorated with gold fairy lights wound through holly. Eleanor clasped her paper cup of hot chocolate in one mittened hand and gestured with the other at some shiny, metallic baubles in their boxes, still debating the appropriate level of garishness. It seemed that, when it came to Christmas, the uglier the better. From late November onwards, our flat would be filled with tat, the kind of things we would never be caught dead with in our household at any time outside the festive season. I went along with it despite my feelings on the matter. We had planned to revisit the subject once I had moved in properly, when I was certain she would have come around to my way of thinking.

I had only just handed in my notice on the lease for my grubby one-bedroom on the outskirts of Edinburgh, and I was in the process of moving the few furnishings that belonged to me into Eleanor's Stockbridge flat, which had more room between floor and ceiling than it did actual floor space. Things had been moving in the direction of a proposal for some time and, given that I had already been unofficially living with her, Christmas Eve had seemed as good a time as any to finally formalise it. Thankfully, she was delighted to be engaged and didn't seem to mind that I couldn't afford a proper ring. Apparently, her grandmother had promised her hers anyway. We had planned to bring up the topic of the ring when we made the announcement the following day over Christmas dinner at her grandparents' house. They lived in a beautiful old Victorian building, within walking distance of all the galleries and parks. They were the kind of people who, when you commented on what an amazing place it was and in such an incredible location, would bristle and say, "Bought it for pennies back in our day," but any sense of discomfort about their own wealth was notably absent when it came to the lavish spread on the dinner table and the number of professionally wrapped gifts under their ceiling-high Christmas tree, which had evidently been put up and decorated by their hired help. Tomorrow, the house would be glittering with tinsel and wealth. It would be my third Christmas with them.

I knew exactly how her family would react when we announced our engagement. There would be a barely noticeable flash of concern quickly followed by gasps and congratulations; the popping of Champagne corks would come just a moment too late. Eleanor wouldn't notice the apprehension, but I would notice everything. When Eleanor's mother first met me, her eyes had lit up and she commented on "what a handsome chap" I was. Her gaze flickered curiously from me to her daughter and Eleanor pretended not to notice. Eleanor's mother was of a generation that seemed to think it was acceptable to openly label people as "plain." Later, when she asked me about my background and what I did for a living, she had smiled thinly.

"Eric." Eleanor waved an orange mitten in front of my face, obscuring my view. She hadn't noticed that, throughout the entire debate about matte versus gloss, I had been staring at the woman standing several feet behind her.

The woman was younger than me by a few years, perhaps the same age as Eleanor. She blinked a flash of powder blue and curled her dewy lips into a small smile that brightened her rounded cheeks, which flushed in the cold air into two almost comically pink circles. She was startlingly doll-like, with a face that looked like it was made of delicate, glistening china. It was as eerie as it was entrancing. I glanced behind me, wanting to make sure she wasn't looking at someone else, and when I turned back her smile had widened, exposing two slightly too-large canines, one a little snaggled. Strangely, it only enhanced her appeal.

With the grace of a dancer, she peeled off a grey glove and extended her open palm. Her index finger curled and beckoned me towards her.

"*Eric*," Eleanor repeated, irritably brushing a curly blonde strand from her eyes and tucking it back beneath her hat. "Are you listening to me?"

Glancing down, I blinked back to the present and placed a hand on her padded arm.

"Eleanor, I'm sorry." I wasn't actually sorry, but it seemed like the right thing to say. Ignoring her bemused expression, I removed my hand from her arm and walked past her without looking back.

The entrancing woman stood by the mulled wine hut with a small, triumphant smile. The strange combination of the thrill and the wickedness of what I was doing only drew me in further. She stood by a steaming vat of mulled wine and, as I got closer, a rich, woody, Christmas smell washed over me: spices, ginger and nutmeg. I was intoxicated.

Wordlessly, she took my arm and led me away.

# CHAPTER 2

I spent very little time reflecting on what I had done; in fact,
I spent more time thinking about why I *wasn't* thinking
about what I had done. An ex-girlfriend once accused me
of being selfish and ended the relationship only a few months
in. She said that I was so wrapped up in my own thoughts
that I forgot to consider the thoughts and feelings of anyone
else around me. I remembered thinking at the time how unfair
that comment was. Everyone was selfish in their own way; it
wasn't necessarily a character flaw. I liked to think of it more as
self-preservation.

Her name was Cornelia, which I only remembered because
she told me its Latin origin was "horn" and we'd drunkenly
snorted with laughter as I christened her "horny Corny." It
stuck in my head by virtue of being such an unflattering nick-
name. Cornelia said that she was initially drawn in by the glam-
our of being with an aspiring writer; she liked the idea of life
with a tortured artist, sitting in little cafes drinking espressos
and, once I'd made it, being invited to highbrow parties with
other "creative sorts." By the time she left, she said I was "nothing more than a selfish dreamer surrounded by unfinished proj-
ects and unfulfilled ideas." When I said that she was the one
being selfish for leaving me because I didn't meet her unrealistic
expectations, she rolled her eyes and slammed the door as her
final parting shot. That break-up hurt, although mostly my ego.

I didn't come from a family of creative people and often
wondered if that was where the perceived selfishness came

from. Because the thing was, if you didn't feel as though you belonged anywhere, it was easy to become introverted, desperate to find where you were really meant to be.

My father was the owner of a small but respectably profitable floor-fitting business. He was the kind of man who endeared himself to others with his jolly and louder-than-life exterior. Like me he was handsome, but in a rugged way that I hadn't inherited, the kind of handsome that accompanied ungroomed facial hair, a roll-up in hand and a charmingly cocked smile. When he introduced himself, people would notice the warm boom of his voice before they even registered his name, their hand clamped submissively between his giant paws. Outsiders never really understood why we didn't get along, and even when I tried to explain, nobody ever really got it. My father's vocabulary consisted of many grating catchphrases, and he liked to punctuate his sentences with phrases like "at the end of the day" and "the point I'm trying to make is" to make himself sound more business-like, but he overused them to an infuriating extent. One of his more recent inappropriate filler words was "literally." During a recent telephone conversation he was describing the fright he got when my stepmother organised a surprise party and everyone jumped out at him, and he told me that he "literally shat himself." Literally?

I always thought my mother would have been creative if she hadn't been so stifled. When I was young, she would tell me made-up stories, which I presume is where my love of writing came from. They had been good stories too. As the years went by and my father's affairs became less discreet, she became quieter. Creativity was deemed a pointless pursuit in my family, the kind of activity that would make the neighbours raise a bewildered brow. My father was the only person I had ever heard say "I don't like music," and the older I got the more bizarre that statement became to me.

My father had wanted a strapping lad to join the business and watch sports and play golf with. We did try to bond on a number of occasions but, somewhere in between reluctant trips to the pub and events at book festivals, we realised that where he found me pretentious I found him overwhelmingly banal.

It was difficult to find the words to explain my upbringing, since it was hardly as though I was mistreated or neglected in any way. It was more a case of not fitting quite right, being an odd jigsaw piece in our puzzle of a family and neighbourhood, and their attempts to make me fit only warped my edges and folded my corners so that, even when I left home, I still didn't really fit in anywhere, no matter how hard I tried.

# CHAPTER 3

"**D**elia." She presented me with her hand as we stopped by the kerb. Her voice was unexpectedly deep, and she pronounced her name *Dee-leh-ahh*, dragging it out at the end and letting the sound of it linger. It was almost like someone was doing a voiceover whenever she moved her lips. She effortlessly hailed a taxi with a graceful wave of her hand. When she gave the driver the address, one I didn't recognise, he looked surprised and examined her cautiously, as though assessing whether she was good for it. After a moment, he shrugged and the taxi pulled away from the kerb – not, however, before his gaze shifted curiously over to me, then to Delia and finally to our intertwined hands.

"Eric." I lifted her hand and, without even thinking, kissed it gently, surprising even myself. I was never someone who kissed people's hands; I had always felt it was the kind of thing reserved for men of a certain age after a few too many. I flushed, resisting the urge to fully breathe in her spiced scent.

"You know, I wouldn't normally do this kind of thing," I said.

"What kind of thing?" She smiled impishly.

"You know." I fumbled my words. Her head cocked to one side, a dark lock falling in slow motion from the bundle of hair pinned precariously in place. She tucked it behind her ear with the other rogue strands. I imagined that if I ran my hands through it they would glide like silk. "*This*."

"Who was that woman with you?" she asked. "Your wife?"

"No." I replied too quickly.

"Then who?"

"Just a friend."

"She looked nice."

Since it wasn't a question, I turned to the window and watched the newly falling snow. It touched the glass in soft, fat flakes, stark against the inky darkness of the evening. Tall buildings stood on either side of the manicured streets, decorated with shining white squares like advent calendars, office workers bustling frantically behind them, trying to clear their desks before Christmas Day. I'd always thought Christmas Eve was a holiday for most people, but I supposed not. I'd made up lies about sick family members to get out of holiday shifts at the restaurant.

"It's Christmas Day tomorrow," I said, purely to break the silence.

"It is."

They felt dreamlike, our conversations; they were stilted, like we were reading from a script. Her facial expressions never quite matched what she was saying.

"Don't you have plans?"

"I do."

I didn't enquire further, from fear she might change her mind and stop the taxi, asking me to get out once she remembered she had other things to be doing.

"So, where are we going?" I was surprised that it hadn't occurred to me to ask before getting into the taxi.

"My hotel." She replied, slowly turning her head to look out her window. We were no longer facing each other. I wanted desperately to tug on her hand, which I was still holding, and pull her towards me.

"Oh." I was struck by a sudden disappointment, but I did my best to hide it. "So, you're just here on holiday?"

"No. *My* hotel." She turned to face me. "I own it."

"You own a hotel?" It was difficult to hide my scepticism.

"That's what I said." Her voice became a little sharp. "Why? Does that surprise you?"

"No, *no*, of course not." I said hurriedly. "Is it a family business?"

"Kind of." She swivelled her whole body to face me, then withdrew her hand from mine to loosen her scarf, revealing a strangely tantalising flash of throat. Her smile reappeared. "Do you often follow strange women to strange places, Eric?"

"You're not strange."

"I'm not." Her voice was low and level, making it difficult to tell whether it was a statement or a question.

Several hours went by in a peculiar, comfortable silence. Occasionally her hand would drift towards mine and toy with my fingers before gently pulling away and returning to her lap. The roads became less groomed and the taxi rumbled uncertainly, making unhappy noises on the icy surfaces. Without streetlamps, there were only the taxi's headlights illuminating several metres of country track before us.

Eventually, just as I was about to ask how much longer we would be, the road rose towards a glorious building up ahead. Rich orange light pulsated behind each tall window, the structure like a decorative lantern with a candle burning inside. A cloak of snow was draped over the roof like thick white icing, bunching precariously over the high gutters and giving the structure the appearance of a grand gingerbread house.

"You own *this*?" I asked, marvelling at a building that was neither a castle nor a mansion. It was something in between, but I wasn't sure what the word for it was.

"I own this," she parroted, seemingly oblivious to my astonishment.

The taxi rumbled to a halt at the entrance, having navigated the wide, sweeping driveway from which the snow had been swept aside, no footprints in sight, as though it had been cleared specially for us. Leaning forward towards the scratched plexiglass screen that separated us from the driver, Delia slipped a wad of notes through the gap. The driver didn't bother counting them. I pretended that my attention was elsewhere, refraining from offering the scant contents of my wallet.

"Thanks." The driver stashed the notes in the glove compartment and hopped out of the taxi, coming round to Delia's side and opening her door. He took her arm and helped her to the ground as though she was too frail to do it herself. I bristled as he touched her, despite the fact that he was lumbering and bald and of no threat to me.

"You have a good night now." He nodded his head at her and turned to me as I came round. He lowered his voice for only me to hear. "Creepy place this, aye?"

I frowned and didn't reply. Instead, I let Delia reach up and touch my cheek, examining me for a moment. Her nails were painted a pearly pink, so delicate you could be forgiven for thinking it was their natural colour, effortlessly elegant like the rest of her.

"Come on." Dropping her hand, she let it fall into mine, and we walked together towards the entrance, up wide stone steps to a large archway and a black wooden door with long glass panels. A man watched us from the other side and opened the doors for us. He was dressed in a smart white shirt and well-fitted dove-grey trousers that hugged muscular thighs. His face was narrow in a way that made him look condescending, with a long, pointed nose that flared at the nostrils as though he was always surrounded by an unpleasant smell.

"Good evening, Delia." His chest swelled and he turned his narrow eyes in my direction, his face wearing an expression I struggled to gauge.

"Henry." She slipped her coat from her small shoulders, clearly expecting him to catch it. He did. "How are you?"

"Well, thank you," he said, as though releasing a long-held breath. He turned to me, his posture relaxing slightly. "May I take your coat, sir?"

Shrugging off my weathered waterproof, I thanked him and handed it over. He pinched it between thumb and forefinger, placing it in the same hand as Delia's coat and holding it far from his body as though it repulsed him.

"Busy night?" Delia asked, oblivious to his quiet rudeness as

11

she handed him her scarf and gloves and pressed her bare hands against her flushed cheeks, relaxing into the warmth. He shook his head and she smiled, pleased. "It's so lovely to be home."

As she strode ahead, I followed her over an uneven slate floor sunken with age. The yellow walls were lined with antique chests and shelves home to stuffed birds. A taxidermy peacock perched on a particularly ornate chest, beak agape as though mid-shriek. Its luxurious train of greens and blues tumbled down, the feathers not quite touching the floor. Somehow, the chandeliers that lined the ceiling managed to look tasteful rather than tacky, flashing with the bright colours of the birds and casting a diamond-like scattering of light across the floor. The entire place was heavy with Delia's scent and I found myself running my hands over the polished surfaces in the hope the aroma would stick to me.

She turned to me with wide, unblinking eyes.

"A drink?"

# CHAPTER 4

I had always been of the view that it was lonelier to be in the company of the wrong people than it was to be completely alone. There were times when I had found myself in a bar surrounded by people and one of us would ask a question, another would answer and then they'd either ask the same question back or hurriedly come up with another question. Then the sequence would repeat. I often wondered if that was how those people conducted their day-to-day conversations, or if they felt the same way I did, and if we were just too incompatible to connect on any level. My heart would sink and, after false proclamations that we, "have to do this again sometime", I would leave, deflated.

In contrast to the tantalisingly quiet taxi journey, once we were in the hotel Delia lit up, perhaps with the fresh confidence of being on her own territory. She started to speak much more, expressing herself with vibrant enthusiasm and animated gestures as she talked about nothing in particular. Words tumbled with ease out of my mouth, and the conversation spilled naturally into literature, music and film. She shared my love of jazz, snorting with laughter when I told her how as a teenager I went through a phase of sitting on my windowsill at night, smoking one of my father's roll-ups, playing loud jazz and wishing I would have an existential crisis – not understanding the meaning of "existential" but thinking it sounded very sophisticated. My father eventually told me to cut it out because his friends could see me on their way home from the pub and it was becoming embarrassing. The

13

story delighted Delia, who I noticed had a wonderfully endearing quality of looking like she was on the verge of laughing when she grinned, eyes brightening and nose wrinkling. It was a real grin, not like the seductive smile offered to me back at the Christmas market. It made me feel clever and funny.

We sat in comfortable armchairs by a tall window that looked out into the inky darkness as a storm swirled around us. It was too severe to be anywhere in the vicinity of the Central Belt. Before I could ask where we were, which I guessed was somewhere up in the Highlands, a tired-looking waiter appeared, stifling a yawn as though he had just woken up. He wore the same white shirt and grey trousers as the doorman. Delia ordered for us.

"So, you're a writer, Eric?" She resumed our conversation, leaning back in her chair and precariously holding the slender stem of her glass.

"Yes." I paused. "Although I work in a restaurant as well. I was going to quit though – I *am* going to quit – you know, to pursue writing full-time." I didn't mention that it was Eleanor who would support me to do that.

"That's so wonderful." She looked at me with a genuine fascination that filled me with warmth. "This area is such a great place to write. You know, we've had writers come here on retreats before – they *love* it!"

She chattered easily, showing a genuine interest in the novel I was yet to make any real progress with. The way she spoke about it made me feel like I could do it – like I *had* to do it.

As the bottle on the table diminished and the waiter appeared as though by instinct with another, I had to fight my decreasing inhibition and growing desire to blurt out how wonderful it was to speak to someone who understood my passion and made me feel like the person I wanted to be. Her presence was addictive. If we couldn't be lovers then we had to be friends; I couldn't accept any less. The very idea of not being in her company gave me a jolt of panic.

She rose, draining her glass.

"Come on then," she said, extending her hand towards me. She grinned again. "Let's go upstairs."

# CHAPTER 5

I awoke in the hotel on Christmas morning to an empty bed. For a moment I was surprised to not find myself beneath familiar, mauve bedsheets, surrounded by decorative cushions, Eleanor beside me in her faded tartan pyjamas. Instead, I emerged from an immaculately pressed white duvet that felt like it had never been slept in, and fumbled about blearily, half wondering if Delia was hidden somewhere in the bedding. There was a faint trace of her scent on the cold side of the bed, which she had obviously left some time ago. I shut my eyes to jumbled memories of falling against plump cushions and piles of clothes discarded on the parquet floor, images which all seemed strangely distant as I tried to recall the warmth of her in the crook of my arm. At least I could remember her soft breath in my ear as she slept, lapping like the distant sea. I had watched, between a gap in the heavy camel curtains, the snow drifting by the bay window in the darkness until I slipped into a sound sleep.

A knock startled me.

"Merry Christmas, sir." The door swung open and an immaculately groomed man in the now familiar uniform of white shirt, grey trousers and black apron barged in, pushing a rattling trolley which held a silver tray. He placed the tray on one of the coffee tables and marched briskly over to the curtains, whipping them apart. A brilliant white light filled the room and forced me to cover my eyes. Outside, the thickness of the snow concealed the landscape.

16

"Merry Christmas," I replied uncertainly, tugging the duvet up higher to cover my bare chest. "Where's Delia?"

"Downstairs, preparing for the Christmas party," he replied, eyes brightening ever so slightly at the sound of her name.

"Oh." I felt suddenly awkward. "I should see her before I go, to say goodbye."

The waiter smiled pleasantly.

"But, sir, Delia said you would be joining us this evening. We laid an extra place at the table."

I perked up instantly, trying to hide the delighted smile twitching at the corners of my mouth.

"It begins at seven, but drinks at the bar for half six." With a brief bow, the waiter retreated.

As he left, another member of staff appeared at the door, a man slightly older than me. He looked unsure, opening his mouth as though he'd forgotten what to say. The waiter stopped him, placing a hand on his arm, and firmly guided him away, taking care to close the door behind him.

Rising from the bed, unashamedly naked, I moved to the tray on the coffee table and gingerly lifted the lid. I was greeted by the warm steam of a freshly prepared breakfast: a sliver of pink smoked salmon laid over peppered eggs. Beside it was a flute of orange juice bubbling with Champagne. I sipped it delicately, lowering myself into the cream armchair and letting out a satisfied sigh.

By the time I finished breakfast it was nearly the afternoon. I checked my phone, which was close to being out of battery, and was relieved to see that there was no signal, which meant no messages and therefore no need to face any backlash. Not yet at least.

It was unlike me not to be up, washed and dressed long before that time, since I had always been a morning person by nature. Even when I covered late shifts at the restaurant, I would still wake up at 6:30am ready for my jog, regardless of the weather. Eleanor would brag to her friends about my commitment to fitness, and they would roll their eyes in the direction of their cumbersome counterparts, slouched in their seats and stooped from their desk jobs.

The thing I had always liked about the morning was how quiet it was. In early summer, during that peaceful hour when the nightlife has come to an end and the commuters are not yet rushing from their door to catch their trains, I would jog round the Meadows as it glistened with fresh dew. It was an hour during which I could be completely alone with my thoughts. That was one of the things Eleanor liked about me; she said that it was endearing how quiet and thoughtful I could be, lost in my head even when we were in the company of her loudest friends. In truth, I always felt that their volume compensated for their lack of personality. She said she reckoned it was what made me such a good writer, the fact that I observed and absorbed. She didn't seem to mind it when I became quiet and antisocial. We did have a disagreement once about me prioritising my morning runs over the household chores, but thankfully Eleanor agreed that she had the time to do them in the morning before she left for work. We were both in agreement that it was much better to return to a clean house rather than having to pick up the chores after a long day.

Peering out the window, I decided that the weather was too extreme even for my obsessive morning routine. Although the sunlight glittered on the white ground, in the distance I could see dark snow clouds moving in rapidly. Another storm was on its way. I pulled on my jeans, which had looked smart when they were freshly washed and pressed but were now slightly loose with wear, hanging unflatteringly around my thighs as though they were too big for me.

I pulled my woollen jumper over my head. It was one of the nicest pieces of clothing I owned. Eleanor had knitted it for me. She had insisted on making most of my winter wardrobe when we got together, which I didn't mind. Around that time, knitted patterns and a more homely look had become fashionable and

I became inadvertently trendy. I touched the sleeve, pausing in a sort of sadness for just a second before forgetting what had distracted me and blinking back to the present.

Out in the corridor it was unnervingly quiet. The soles of my shoes padded gently against a jute carpet which ran the length of the wooden floors and turned sharply down the stairs. I almost swerved into another of Delia's employees, an older man who stood quietly by the banister several steps down, holding a spray can and a yellow dusting cloth and polishing the wood. He turned his head slowly to acknowledge me, giving a curt nod before going back to his work.

"Merry Christmas, sir," he said, raising a wiry eyebrow at the banister. "Can I help you?"

"Just looking around." I paused, wondering if I could substitute my run. "There isn't a swimming pool or a gym, is there?"

"No, sir." He resumed his polishing. "No pool or gym."

"Damn." I murmured, moving past him. "Never mind."

"See you tonight, sir," he said, keeping his gaze fixed on the banister.

# CHAPTER 6

When I was young, my family always did the usual Christmas thing. We had the big tree and the sparkly tinsel in red and green that wrapped around the window, just like everyone else on our street. There were the overzealous neighbours who would transform their immaculate square of grass into a fake winter wonderland, with life-sized models of reindeer, flashing lights and an inflatable Santa Claus who would sway ominously in the breeze. I remembered looking at those gardens and thinking that there was something depressing about them. It wasn't that we didn't live in a nice part of town; in fact, our suburban estate was considered quite desirable. Each identical brown new-build was spacious inside and had brand-new central heating and neat square lawns which were easy to maintain. In summer, the women, pale from winter, would drag out their deckchairs and sit in the sun where they would burn, like vampires.

For as long as I could remember we had a plastic Christmas tree. My mother was obsessively clean, constantly hoovering or neatening up after my father, making up for his messy nature. My father often rolled his eyes fondly and teased her about her fussiness, but he would be the first to comment if standards slipped. So, we had a plastic tree to avoid messy pine needles littering the carpet. When I complained that it didn't smell like it was supposed to, she hung one of those little scented cards that you dangle in the front of cars. Pine fresh.

Being an only child, I was always overindulged when it came

to presents. Back then, I thought Santa wriggled through the impossibly narrow slots of our gas stove and dropped off the presents under the tree while I slept. Every year I left a mince pie out for him and a carrot for his reindeer.

One Christmas I got up first thing and put on the Christmas jumper my mother had laid out for me – it had a picture of a snowman on it and real bells that jangled when I moved. Peeling back my curtains, I was disappointed to see the glistening grey of the wet tarmac street rather than the crisp white I had seen in every story and film about Christmas. But never mind; Christmas was all about the presents.

I bounced down the stairs and held my breath at our lounge door before entering. I would feel and shake all the boxes before my parents came downstairs to see if I could guess what they were. I always thought it must be rubbish being a parent and having to pretend to be happy for the children, with their piles of presents, when all they ever had was one or two small parcels for themselves.

That morning, the sight beneath our tree was disheartening. A couple of metallic baubles had fallen on the cream carpet and rolled sadly on their side. There were no presents. By the gas fire, my carrot and mince pie still sat on their plate. I reached out, but the stove was cold to the touch. Normally my mother would have it fired up hot and ready to start the day, insisting that we all had a hearty breakfast before we could start unwrapping. I started to cry.

A rumble outside at what my mother would call an "unreasonable hour" distracted me and, wiping my eyes, I peered between the slats of the white Venetian blinds to see my father parking up on our drive and striding towards our house with a large black bin liner slung over his shoulder. I rushed to the door and waited for the turn of his key and the click as it swung open. My handsome father, tall and proud, still in his clothes from the previous night, stepped inside. His mucky boots left dark, damp imprints on our pale carpet. He dropped the sack on the floor and a polka-dot-wrapped box tumbled out along with other gifts of assorted sizes. They were so well wrapped that they had to have been done professionally, like in chocolate shops, so perfect-looking that it seemed a shame to tear into them. My heart leapt and I squealed in delight.

I asked him why Santa hadn't brought the presents, already on my knees and shaking the parcels. My father paused before widening his mouth into a grin, the kind that cocked up on one side and created a charming dimple in one cheek. His voice boomed as he explained that poor Santa was too big to fit through the slats in our heater. That made sense. When I asked about the mince pie, he assured me he would get it to Santa before the day was over.

As we carried the presents to the tree, I heard a soft padding behind me and turned to see my mother standing in the middle of the stairs. She was still in her fluffy white dressing grown, and her dark makeup from the night before hadn't been washed off. It circled her eyes like shadows. She was wearing an expression I hated, where her nostrils flared and her lips were pursed tight.

She demanded to know where he had been, white knuckles pulling the lapel of her dressing gown against her chest, as though she was worried it might slip off. I glanced at my father's face; his charming smile faltered a little. Her voice wobbled through her anger.

"Maggie." His voice became sweet and smooth, like treacle. "Come on, it's Christmas Day. Let the wean open his presents. Don't spoil it for him." He turned to me. "That's what you want to do, isn't it, Eric? Open your presents?"

I nodded enthusiastically, looking pleadingly at my mother. I remembered being annoyed at her, feeling sorry for my dad who had been out all night helping Santa. After a moment of hesitation she agreed, following us into the lounge and taking a seat on the sofa. She pretended to smile as I tore open my gifts, even though her eyes glittered with tears. I wondered if she was upset about the footprints my father had left in the corridor. When he handed her a small box that he plucked from his pocket, she tossed it ungratefully aside. I went over to hug my father to make him feel better. As I burrowed my head into his chest, he smelled of his usual cigarette scent, something that resembled my mother's nail polish remover and something unfamiliar. It was like a candied cherry scent. I inhaled it, enjoying the sweetness.

Our dinner was quiet that night. The only sound was from our CD of modern Christmas tunes, which we played every year. Later, when I was asked to put the wrapping paper in the bin, I saw my mince pie and the reindeer's carrot sitting at the bottom. I huffed furiously, hoping that Santa didn't think I was as ungrateful as my bad-tempered mother. I wouldn't really understand what had happened that Christmas until years later.

Delia's Christmas party couldn't have been more different from those of my childhood. The bar glistened with gold and smelled of citrus, spices and pine. It glowed with warmth from the open fire. Green and gold were scattered across surfaces and crept up and around curtain rails, casting tiny lights across the floors and walls like golden confetti. I stepped over rich red antique rugs to a ceiling-high Christmas tree decorated tastefully in delicate gold baubles that looked as though they might shatter at the slightest touch. There was no sign of garish tinsel or mismatched colours, just a perfect combination of gold, green and red, all softened by the intentionally low lighting.

An excitable buzz filled the air and I found myself in a sea of white shirts and grey trousers. I sensed the other party guests running an eye over my jumper and jeans. The power shower in my en suite had stripped me of my old smell, and I had spritzed myself with a miniature glass bottle of scent which sat by the sink. I now felt like a completely different person. I felt expensive. Infuriatingly, however, it meant that when I put on my old clothes I felt that my cleansed and preened body didn't belong inside them. I squirmed, the fabric suddenly itchy and unclean.

As I moved deeper through the gaggle of guests, I recognised the doorman from the previous evening, Henry. He lurked near the wall with a glass in hand, holding it close to his face. His narrow eyes scanned the room and paused on me before he gave a brief nod of recognition. I didn't like him.

The conversation in my immediate vicinity quietened as I made my way towards the centre of the commotion, where Delia was perched on a bar stool, laughing in delight at something the man next to her was saying. Looking around, I realised that, other than Delia, there were only men at this party.

"Eric!" she exclaimed, turning her attention from the man, mid-sentence. He frowned in my direction before returning to his drink, pretending he had not just been snubbed.

"Hi, Delia." Her scent was so strong that I imagined I could find her in a crowded room blindfolded; it complemented the scent of pine and citrus beautifully. As I looked at her, I found that my memory didn't quite capture her face properly. My mental image of her was blurry, with inaccurate facial proportions. With her almost pointed ears and spiky canine that poked out when she grinned, she seemed more like a beautiful fairytale creature than a woman.

She was leaning over the bar, its warm wood the colour of gingerbread. Sequins draped her body and trickled over the floor, oozing around her like liquid gold. With glimmering green emeralds hanging from her ears and bright red nails, I realised she matched her decorations perfectly.

"You look beautiful."

"George," she said to the man next to her, ignoring my compliment, "would you mind giving Eric your seat? He doesn't know anyone else here."

George stood up without question and gestured for me to take the bar stool. Although he smiled politely, I could see that his jaw was clenched.

"I'm so happy to see you! How has your day been?" She reached out and planted a kiss on my cheek, not bothering to wait for my response. "Sorry I had to leave so early this morning. I had lots of party planning to do, and you looked so peaceful."

"That's alright." I shuffled in the stool, unable to relax while other men hovered around me. I straightened my spine and sucked in my stomach. "Thank you for inviting me. Sorry I'm underdressed."

Delia smiled and shrugged.

"Are your family here?"

"No." She shook her head and took a sip from her flute. "It's a staff party. We do it every year. It's so much fun."

"So, everyone here works in the hotel?"

"Yes." She nodded as a drink appeared before me in a matching flute, frantic with gold bubbles. Delia watched me carefully as I lifted it to my lips and sipped tentatively.

Champagne. I had learned to distinguish Champagne from Prosecco and Cava during the many dinners with Eleanor's family, when they would "bring out the good stuff." Eleanor's mother Elspeth used to play a little game with me where she would turn to me before anyone else and ask what I thought of the drink without showing me the bottle. Nobody else registered it, but I knew exactly what she was up to. At first, I couldn't tell the difference and I hated her for showing me up like that in front of Eleanor and the rest of her family, but before too long I was grateful. I learned that Champagne had a thicker, creamier taste, whereas Prosecco was sweeter than Cava, which was dryer and lighter.

"Mmm," I nodded in approval. "Champagne, lovely."

"It is! Isn't it?" Delia agreed, satisfied.

Thank you, Elspeth.

25

# CHAPTER 7

Delia took her place at the head of the dinner table. I had expected more guests to arrive, some women perhaps; however, the table remained dominated by men and commanded by Delia.

"You only employ men?" I asked eventually.

"Yes," Delia replied, slipping a fork between her lips and assessing the quality of the meat. A splotch of cranberry sauce stained the corner of her mouth and she dabbed it gently it with her white napkin. It left a blood-like stain on the fabric.

"Why?"

She shrugged, smiling – a childlike glimmer.

Frowning, I turned back to my meal and pierced one of the fat pigs in blankets, so hot that the sausage swelled taut within the glistening bacon. It steamed and deflated as my fork went through it; I half expected it to squeal.

The long rectangular table was heavy with platters of food, and lined with tall, slender candles dripping wax over candelabras surrounded by holly wreaths. The staff were bringing out the food before flinging off their aprons and resuming their positions as guests. I served myself a ladle of sweet roasted vegetables in gravy, potatoes crisp with goose fat and a slice of the large stuffed bird nearest me.

It wasn't like any work party I'd ever been to; everyone was very relaxed with one another, like old friends reunited. There was none of the usual banal work chat woven among polite conversation, the norm at work events I'd experienced.

Delia was so absorbed in conversation that she ate very little throughout the evening. Many times I watched her pick up a bite of food just to answer a question or start a new conversation, only actually eating the food several minutes later. Everything she did seemed inexplicably thrilling, each movement like part of a ballet routine, effortless and graceful, keeping to a gentle rhythm. I found myself drifting along, albeit with far less grace.

"Is everyone staying here?"

"Of course." She nodded. "I couldn't expect them to travel home in this terrible weather. Everyone tends to stay over the winter period. Otherwise they probably wouldn't be able to get back." She gestured at the frosted window and the wall of snow that rose halfway up the glass pane, dividing it into black and white. "The bad weather means we get lots of cancellations and sometimes no guests at all. I like the company."

I nodded slowly, hoping that her aversion to anyone travelling in bad weather extended to me. I wasn't ready to leave just yet.

"So where are you from originally?"

"Around the area," she replied vaguely. "The hotel has been in my family for quite a while."

"And do your parents still work here?"

"No." She shook her head and seamlessly changed the subject, gesturing with her hand. "At one point this place was falling to pieces. It wasn't even safe to go upstairs. Woodworm, I think. The entire place needed treated. New floors, walls replastered, the whole lot. Thankfully, they managed to restore some of the original features, like the cornicing and the ceiling rose." Her hand began to glide around her, palm open as she gestured at the ceiling. "It would have been a travesty to lose them. Don't you think they did a splendid job?"

I nodded.

"You know, this room wasn't actually red a few days ago!" She beamed and pointed to one of the oldest of her staff, who sat smiling pleasantly among the chatter. "It was blue. Edward repainted it for me. I just thought that for Christmas we simply *had* to paint it red. Isn't that right, Edward?"

The old man nodded, his grey-blue eyes surveying the vast, crimson room.

"Of course, we'll want to change it back after Christmas." She smiled at him charmingly, and he raised a wiry brow in her direction, giving her a silent telling off. They both broke into a knowing grin and returned to their meals, the old man rolling his eyes amusedly.

Once we had finished the meal and pulled our crackers, Delia rose and we followed her into a room with yet another Christmas tree, this one standing over a mound of perfectly wrapped gifts. Our crackers had contained little golden paper crowns and we all wore them like kings.

I accepted an offer of coffee, even although I didn't particularly want one. The question had seemed like more of a formality; the drink was simply handed to me, having already been made, and I felt it would have been rude to decline. It was carefully presented on a little duck-egg saucer, and there was a small, warm gingerbread man beside the cup. My stomach was taut from food and wine, and I found that just the thought of biting into it made me feel a little nauseous.

The fire was set and crackling. It flickered a pleasant amber light across the polished surface of the coffee table, where I placed my untouched drink and biscuit. Sinking into the deep green of a tartan armchair, I peered at the red walls around me and wondered if the old man had been told to paint this room specially for Christmas too. I watched as the hotel staff filed in, some finding seats while others formed standing clusters and talked among themselves.

"What shall we listen to?" one of the men asked, fussing with an old record player in the corner. He looked directly at me.

"Got any jazz?" I suggested.

"Delia hates jazz," he replied tartly, selecting a record of his choice. I frowned in confusion, but before I could reply Delia swept past me and sat down on the chair nearest the fire. My attention strayed, moving from Delia to one of the oil portraits in a gilt frame, which was hanging from the dado rails by thin gold wires. The subject was an old woman staring down at me with watery blue eyes paled in blindness, her lined face dragged into a frown and her hunched body draped in black, blending into the dark background.

"That's my grandmother," Delia said after a few moments, nursing a large glass of red which had rouged her lips. "I was actually named after her." She sighed. "Hideous, isn't she?"

I didn't reply out of fear of offending her.

"I keep meaning to take her down and put her in storage. But I can never quite bring myself to do it."

"Why not?"

"She's part of the house. It would feel a bit like disrespecting my history if I were to take her down simply because she's unpleasant to look at." Brightening, she bounced to her feet and strode towards the tree. "I got you a gift." As she hesitated over the boxes, I wondered if she was going to pick one at random, but when she plucked a small, navy box from the pile, I noticed that the brown paper tag had my name on it. She dropped it in my hands, a heavy thing, and I felt myself flush as all eyes turned on me.

"But I didn't get you anything."

"How could you have?" she said, smiling. "The weather was too bad to get into town."

Carefully untying the ribbon and easing the paper apart, I opened the box inside and found it stuffed with strips of brown paper padding, the kind you find surrounding expensive gifts. It enveloped a little glass bottle, which had a gold lid shaped like a polished pebble. I removed the lid to reveal a small nozzle. A cologne.

"Go on!" Delia clapped her hands excitedly. "Try it!"

I pressed the nozzle and closed my eyes, clouding myself in the scent. It was similar to Delia's aroma but more masculine, a gentle smokiness to it. It smelled of everything I loved: church incense, damp forests, that Christmas aroma that transported me back to the market and my first glimpse of Delia, her hand extending to beckon me over. When I opened my eyes, I saw her watching me anxiously.

"Do you like it?"

"I love it."

Slightly lightheaded, I got to my feet and planted a kiss on her lips. Out of the corner of my eye I saw Henry watching, shaking his head as though in disapproval and dropping his gaze to the floor.

"I'm so glad!" She clapped her hands in delight and returned to her chair. The room had fallen silent around us. As I surveyed the men around me, I wondered fleetingly how Delia had managed to go out and buy me such a personal gift in the snowy weather.

★★★

"Did you know," said Delia, clunking her glass on the coffee table and addressing the room, "that Eric here is a writer?"

Murmurs of interest.

"Won't Eric be perfect for our evening game?"

The murmurs increased, now mutterings of assent. I looked around uncertainly.

"What game?"

"Oh, we play it all the time, especially when we have guests." Her eyes flashed a brighter blue, like siren lights. "You have to tell a story in front of the fire. And whoever tells the best story wins. It's kind of a running thing. You can tell any story you want, but we seem to have found a favourite in scary stories, haven't we?"

The room collectively agreed, echoing Delia's reaction.

"Go on, Eric!" Her eyes glittered. "Tell us a story."

Through the fog of wine, I shook my head and awkwardly fumbled an excuse.

"It's your profession, is it not?" she pressed, stretching a sharp-toothed smile. "Come on, *frighten us!*"

I had made the mistake of holding my breath in my nervousness; when I finally spoke, I sounded ragged and breathless.

"I can't." I shook my head, cheeks burning. "I don't have a story."

"Everyone has a story."

"I can't just make one up on the spot."

"But you're a storyteller!"

I wished she would stop pushing me. I could see her lips turn down in disappointment.

"No, really, Delia." My smile was awkward and forced. The eyes of the room seemed to burn right through me.

"Tell you what," the old man Edward interrupted, sensing my discomfort. "Why don't I take a turn tonight? It's been a while and I think I have a good one."

I flashed what I hoped was a grateful look in his direction.

"Yes please, Edward!" After a flicker of disappointment that had momentarily soured her features, Delia resumed her pleasant, dewy smile. "This is exciting." She turned back to me, clamping a warm hand over mine. "Edward's stories are always splendid. They're usually about ships or the sea and always *really* scary. Perhaps next time, Eric, when you have a better feel for it."

Edward got to his feet and walked towards the fire, his stride slowed by age. As he turned and stood in front of the flames, framed in orange and gold, he spread his hands welcomingly, gathering the attention of the room which buzzed like static in excited anticipation.

"Good evening."

His previously unassuming voice had become a thunderous sound, like the blast of a ship's horn or the waves of a storm exploding against rocks. His eyes darkened in the dim light.

"Tonight's story I call 'It Waits in the Waves.'"

# CHAPTER 8:

## IT WAITS IN THE WAVES

There was once a young fisherman who lived on an island where the winters were as long and dark as the summers were perpetually bright. Good-looking and likeable, the fisherman was popular with the locals, many of whom were keen to introduce their daughters to him. Contrary to common belief, his fishing trade was a lucrative business.

At the dances held in the community hall, young women would flock around him, encouraged by their nearby parents. The fisherman's family were the traditional sort, telling him that it was about time he settled down with someone suitable to start a family of his own, and they were so generously forthcoming with their suggestions. However, the one woman the fisherman truly wanted was never at the dances. His family struggled to understand his fondness for her; to them, she didn't fit the mould, wasn't what they imagined for their son.

Each morning she could be found down by the rocks, stripped bare of most of her clothes and submerged in icy cold water at the shoreline. She didn't pin her hair elegantly or wear pretty dresses; rather, she let her hair hang loose over her shoulders, the sun glistening in the grooves of her strong body. The fisherman would watch as she pulled herself out of the water, tense against the cold breeze, before covering herself with a towel as if only just realising how exposed she was. One morning she caught the fisherman watching her and challenged him to jump into the frothy frozen waves with her. Goose-pimpled and shivering, they emerged and wrapped themselves in each other's arms. The fisherman went home that night with the memory of her etched in his mind, and from then on he joined her every morning. After one particularly long trip away on business, he returned to hear the woman say that she had truly missed him. The fisherman wasted no time, and they were married that very month.

The fisherman's mother ensured that the bride was perfect for the wedding day, binding her long golden hair tightly in a gypsophila cage and locking her body in a severe white gown with barely enough room to breathe. That night, as the fisherman released his bride's body from its restraints, she gasped in relief and they both laughed, promising one another that they would never change for anyone.

One morning, as the fisherman left for a few days' work, his wife escorted him down to the harbour, wishing him a safe trip and kissing him. The fisherman glowed with a warm pride, as she was the only fisherman's wife to come to say goodbye to her love. The only other woman there was the old sailor's daughter, who had been minding her father since his wife had taken to bed ill. She hugged her father and wished him a safe trip. The fisherman waved at his wife, who blew kisses in his direction. They continued to wave until vanishing from each other's sight as the boat disappeared into fog.

Late one night, when the freezing fog hung suspended above the surface of the eerily still water, the fisherman stood on deck with the old sailor, peering over the guardrail and smoking cigarettes. The white hairs around the old sailor's mouth were tobacco-stained and the tips of his fingers yellow-tinged. He smelled of salt and smoke. As they stood in comfortable silence, the fisherman listened to the wind.

"Do you hear that?" he asked. Just above the breath of the breeze floated a high, mournful voice.

Lifting his lamp, the fisherman swung it from side to side, the flame reflecting off the frozen fog. Below, he could sometimes make out the black edges of rocks protruding from the water.

"Pay no heed, lad." The old sailor shook his head. "Sea ghouls is all."

"Sea ghouls?"

"Aye, water monsters. Most of them are harmless, sad souls lost at sea, destined to float without direction until the day the oceans dry up. But others, monsters from the deep that crave destruction, they prey on mortal men like us. Best left well alone."

"You're mad, old man."

The fisherman waited for the old sailor to return to his bunk before clambering into the small rowing boat nearby. He could hear the sad cries for help above the wind, unable to make out the words. If it were his wife, he hoped that someone would do the same for her.

"Where are you?" He called into the night, bringing the small boat close, until it bumped against a wall of rocks. "I'm here to help."

"Come closer," a faint voice called from the rocks ahead. "I can't move. I'm frightened I'll slip and fall."

"Don't worry, I'm coming." The fisherman removed his thick woollen gloves and, snatching his lamp to guide him, threw himself onto the rocks.

"Thank you," the voice breathed. "I've been alone here for so long."

"There's nobody else?" the fisherman asked, searching the darkness in his orb of orange light. "What about your crew?"

"No crew. I am alone."

The fisherman's lantern illuminated a pale back, the ribs and spinal column protruding, and a head of long black hair falling wet and thick like oil. She stood, facing away from him, naked.

"My God." The fisherman pulled off his waxed coat and rushed towards her, hoping to wrap it around her shoulders with his free arm. But his bare hand touched the side of her shoulder and he recoiled at once. Her flesh was cold and wet, slimy to the touch. He stepped back, his sphere of light still containing her, and she turned her head slowly, very slowly, until she faced him. Her skin seemed to stretch over her skull, pulled at strange angles as though it didn't fit. It was grey in places, rotting away.

She smiled a terrible smile, a smile that stretched from ear to ear, far too wide for the face it split.

The fisherman screamed, dropping his lamp, which shattered on the rocks. Stumbling away, nearly blind in the foggy darkness, he threw himself back into his boat. From the rocks he heard a quiet scrambling and, in the faint light, glimpsed her slink silently into the water, her pale body disappearing into the deep dark without leaving so much as a ripple. He rowed as fast as he could back to the fishing boat where another lamp, swinging on deck, offered him a guide. He glanced behind him desperately between strokes, and saw a slimy black head with that dreadful smile emerge from the water before disappearing back under.

She was coming for him.

Screaming for his crew, he saw them appear above deck, coming to his aid, hauling him back onboard and setting sail at once at his insistence. The old sailor watched him with narrowed eyes but said nothing.

Several days later, they returned to harbour. The fisherman peered out to see his wife waving to him through the fog, which was now pierced by the rising sun. She wore a loose white shirt that billowed in the breeze and slacks rolled up at the ankle. The old sailor's daughter stood nearby, waiting patiently, wrapped warm in a thick coat over her frock. The fisherman startled when he glimpsed a ripple in the water, a slick, dark head approaching the harbour wall. The fisherman cried out, waving his arms in warning, but his wife saw her husband beckoning her and stepped closer to the edge. A thin hand reached up out of the water, which was dark with a layer of glistening fuel coating the surface, and snatched at her ankle, tugging hard. The fisherman watched as she slid on the algae-covered stone and disappeared into the water. He cried out, prepared to throw himself in to rescue her but, before he could, he saw her break the surface and propel her body towards the harbour wall, reaching for the hand of the sailor's daughter, who gripped her and pulled her up.

The fisherman came to shore and gathered his shocked wife in his arms, all the while peering fearfully down at the water. The sea ghoul was nowhere to be seen.

That same night, after his wife had cleaned herself up, she began preparing dinner. The fisherman watched her in the kitchen as she gutted a fish for the stew. With a steady hand she sliced open the silver belly and dipped her fingers inside the cut. Pulling out the innards, she stuffed them in her mouth and chewed noisily.

The fisherman's wife stopped going for her morning swim, and though she answered the fisherman when he spoke to her, she didn't sound quite like herself, her voice shrill and ill-fitting. However, dinner was served each night and the house was kept immaculate; in fact, she had even started filling vases with dried herbs and flowers so that the house smelled fragrant. The fisherman's mother was delighted, and expressed relief that her daughter-in-law had finally settled into married life.

Each time the fisherman spent days away, his wife was even more changed on his return. She had stopped greeting him at the harbour, and when she wasn't doing housework she would sit for long periods doing nothing, just staring. One night he returned home late and all the lights were on. His wife stood by the window, staring out with glassy eyes. When she saw him she smiled, her mouth stretching into that wide and terrible smile.

The fisherman began coming home less and less, preferring to hide away in the local pub until closing time, and sometimes he didn't come home at all. One morning, despite a feeling of dread, he had no option but to return to the house; he had another long sail ahead and needed his bags. It was so early that the sky was still dark, but the lights were all on as usual. As he opened the front door, he was greeted with a dreadful smell that even the herbs and flowers couldn't disguise. It was the scent of everything horrible about the sea: sulphurous seaweed, damp, caustic salt, rust, congealed rot. His wife emerged from a shadowy corner, her smile still splitting her face from ear to ear, her skin pulled strangely across her brow and cheekbones. In places it had an unhealthy blue tinge.

"This skin is no good anymore," she muttered, pushing past him. "I need a new one." She flung open the door and vanished into the sleepy streets. Snatching his bags, the fisherman followed her, picking up speed and watching her lurch towards the harbour, her limbs moving at strange angles beneath her nightdress. She reached the harbour wall, where the old sailor's daughter was waiting for her father to finish checking the ropes. Oblivious, her doll-like face was serene as she watched the rising sun.

"No!" the fisherman roared, accelerating to catch up with his wife – no, not his wife, the dreadful sea ghoul wearing his wife's skin. "Get on the boat!"

The sailor's daughter looked up, bright blue eyes widening in fright at the distorted body readying itself to leap on her. She hesitated and accidentally bit her lip, her unusually sharp canine drawing a bead of blood, which trickled down her chin. This excited the sea ghoul into a frenzy, and it launched itself towards her, stark against her porcelain skin.

"Beautiful skin," it gurgled.

The sailor's daughter sprang onto the boat, evading its grasp. The fisherman reached the sea ghoul and snatched the frilled collar at its neck, pushing it violently forward over the harbour wall. It turned to face him as it fell, still smiling its hideous smile, and disappeared beneath the water with an unnaturally soundless splash. The fisherman clambered onboard and waved at the old sailor, who was still readying the ropes.

"We have to get away!" the fisherman cried. "It wants your daughter's skin."

"Father?" The girl turned to the old sailor, who remained on land. He grimaced.

"It wants your skin," he repeated. "It won't stop until it has it, and as long as you are here it will be waiting."

The girl glanced from her father to the fisherman.

"Get far away from this place. Both of you." The old sailor waved his hand, as though he had foreseen long ago such a fate for his precious daughter. "You, lad, brought this upon my daughter. It is your responsibility to look after her. Get to warmer waters where the sea ghoul can't pass. Get far away and never come back."

The boat's engine began to rumble, and the fisherman and the old sailor's daughter vanished into the mist without another word.

In the years to come, the island became known for the sea ghoul that haunted the harbour, waiting for the girl to return. Each day it rotted a little more, until, too weak to move, it gradually disappeared beneath debris and sewage, where it would remain, waiting until the oceans dried up, waiting and smiling its terrible smile.

# CHAPTER 9

I awoke with a start the day after Boxing Day. I had my first shift back at the restaurant that evening.

Although it was still morning, if I remembered the taxi journey correctly it would take at least several hours to get back to the city. Fumbling with my tangled clothes and pulling them on, I was relieved to find that the wallet in my jeans had several notes in it as well as my credit card, glossy and unused. Eleanor had told me to get it to improve my credit rating, but she generally discouraged me from using it day to day. I wasn't as organised as she was when it came to finance. Her rating was, of course, perfect, so she tended to put her name down for most things.

My jumper's fabric had the unpleasantly soft texture of clothes due a wash. I snatched the glass bottle of cologne that Delia had given me and spritzed it generously over myself, feeling that familiar rush of pleasant warmth and a faint longing to hear her trickling laugh and low voice. Oddly, I still couldn't picture her face as I should, and the image conjured by my memory certainly didn't do her justice.

Although Delia had spent the previous night with me, she was gone now. The morning before that, Boxing Day, I awoke to find her in the chair by the bedroom window looking out at the snow. She was perfectly made-up and wrapped in an elegant silk dressing gown. It was difficult to imagine her bleary eyed, with smudged make-up and tousled hair; she always presented herself pristinely.

I grimaced at the thought of returning to the restaurant. It felt like a distant and unpleasant memory that I had rightly discarded, and I felt cold and deflated. My job had never been like Eleanor's; nobody would return from holiday and ask their colleagues with genuine interest what they had been up to. At my work, nobody really spoke about personal things, and with good reason. Our manager, Patricia, listened to everything that was said within the restaurant's four walls, and if you were smart you kept your mouth shut. You didn't want to be caught out in your inevitable lie about why you couldn't cover the Christmas shifts. I would have to make a point to look sad about my sick relative when she asked me about my holiday. Patricia's memory was so sharp that I swore she must have had a little notebook documenting everything we ever said. She was the kind of woman who, if you were recanting an event or telling a story, would pick out inconsistencies or exaggerations made for dramatic effect and confront you mid-sentence. For Patricia, stories were factual and nothing more. She would call you out and you would be left stumbling over your words, desperate to finish and missing the punchline, your story falling flat on the bare facts.

Some people probably considered Patricia to be good-looking; she was long and thin as though she had been stretched, and had an absurdly large chest for such a small body. She always pinned her bronze "manager" badge just over where her nipple ought to be. I always made a point of averting my gaze, wanting her to know that she didn't have the desired effect on me. Her jaw did a strange thing where it jutted out ever so slightly too far, too subtle for anyone to notice unless they'd spent a significant portion of time being berated by her while that jaw clacked up and down, up and down, up and down. We didn't like each other. Because of my bus times, I always arrived just as my shift was starting, and she would glower at me with two pencilled-in eyebrows as I wrapped my black apron around my waist. She would say, "If you arrived fifteen minutes before your shift, like everyone else, then we wouldn't be paying you for faffing about when you're supposed to be working." Every single time. I would smile and apologise. Sometimes I would feign interest in her personal life, but she could see through it, immune to my charms. Rolling her eyes, she would march away, slender heels click-clacking on the floor, alerting the others that she was approaching, and they would spring to attention.

After a while, I noticed that the restaurant owner only hired good-looking people, which I supposed was a compliment of sorts. Once he had hired them, it was Patricia's job to beat any complacency out of them. The students never lasted long under Patricia's reign, and we were left with a core team of what I called "The Aspiring" – aspiring actor, aspiring singer, aspiring artist, aspiring model, or like me, aspiring writer. The flexibility of the job gave us the freedom to pursue our dreams, which always seemed just out of reach. The Aspiring would often slope in from an audition, an interview, a casting, sighing deeply and hoping that the next time would be better. Occasionally, some-one would make it, and they would triumphantly hand in their resignation. We never followed it up to see how they got on, mostly out of jealousy. None of us interacted socially, which was strange, given how much we had in common. It was probably because we all knew we couldn't get what we wanted out of each other.

I took a roundabout route to the front entrance of the hotel to try to find Delia, but she wasn't in any of the places I was familiar with. I tried her office door handle, which was the solitary door on the small landing leading up to the first floor, but it was locked. Henry was sitting in his usual spot at the desk in the alcove by the entrance, fussing over papers and squinting like he needed glasses. I got the feeling he knew he was being watched before he looked up; he quickly tucked his documents into a drawer, tilting his head so he could look down his long, narrow nose at me.

"Morning." He rose to his feet, nodding his head at me, a pretence of politeness. He spoke slowly, careful with his words. Before asking me what I was doing, he plucked my coat from the rail by his desk and brought it to me. "Going somewhere?"

"Yeah, I have to go to work. You seen Delia?"

He shook his head.

"Just, I want to say bye." I paused. "I need to give her my number, or something."

"I could pass on a message," Henry suggested, faux helpful. "You could leave your number with me."

I checked my watch. The morning was catching up on me.

"Yeah, alright then." I took the offered paper and pen and scribbled a hurried note, with my phone number, email and full name just to be sure. "Give this to her as soon as you see her?"

"Of course."

"Okay. Well, thanks." I took a step towards the door. "Best route to the bus stop?"

"Take a right at the end of the drive and walk for two miles. You can't miss it." Henry strode past me and opened the door; the gesture strangely emasculating. I caught him looking down at my impractical brogues as a gentle flurry of snow swept over us. "The bus will take you to the railway station in town. Be quick though; it gets dark early here."

I had been away on a ski trip with my school when I was a teenager. I saved up by doing weekend shifts as an assistant for my dad's flooring company, with the agreement that if I could save up half then he would cover the rest. I couldn't recall actually making that much, or working that much for that matter, so I assume he put in more than his share. My father was big on physical activity and keeping fit, but he couldn't fathom why you would pay to go abroad to do it. When I got off the bus in the mountain resort, it was the first time I'd seen snow unmarked by city grime. I was entranced. The way the sunlight reflected off every snow-covered surface made it look like glitter ran through the white. The snow was so heavy that it softened the edges of the small-town buildings; it was like a little gingerbread village. I felt like I was in a dream. It was my favourite memory.

Outside the hotel, I paused to admire the rolling hills of pristine white beneath the heavy sky. The sun peered through gaps in the clouds and cast glittering spotlights in the distance.

As advised, I turned right at the end of the drive. My socks become instantly wet, the snow soaking through my leather shoes. It didn't take long for the chill to set in, and I was shivering. With no buildings to act as windbreakers, or heat pumping from open shop doors and street vendors' portable stoves, I was at the mercy of the cold wind. It whipped sharply at my skin, which had become raw and pink, stripping away any trace of Delia. Her comforting scent vanished in the winter gusts. Each step became increasingly arduous, like I was being chased in a dream and the air was thick as treacle. I glanced behind me, a little spooked by the reality of it all, how isolated I was. The silence made it seem even more plausible that someone might be watching or following me. The only sign of life behind me was my lone thread of footsteps on the single-track road. They would soon be covered.

I must have been ascending because it was getting colder and the snow was starting to fall more heavily, the sky gradually darkening even though it couldn't be too far into the afternoon. I was starting to panic about making my shift on time, so I picked up my pace, marching determinedly on. At least the walk would give me time to think.

I paused to consider what I would do after my shift that evening, and where I was going to go. It seemed absurd that I hadn't even considered the practicalities of going back after what I'd done. I'd given up the lease on my flat and all my things were at Eleanor's. With any luck, she would still be at her grandparents for the holiday, and I could let myself in with my spare key. I might even stay the night while I sorted out my situation. I could pack up my belongings and leave before she came back, which meant I could avoid any uncomfortable confrontation. The city was big and there was a good chance we wouldn't run into each other again if I knew the places to avoid.

I told myself that I didn't want to see Eleanor hurt. I tried to ignore the fact that even though I couldn't see it, she still would be. I had picked up that trait from my family, who had always avoided any awkwardness or the airing of dirty laundry at all costs. We were a family who never faced our issues; we just let things simmer beneath the surface, everyone knowing the truth but nobody wanting to say anything. Even at my mother's funeral, when I was old enough to understand what was going on, I couldn't bring myself to say anything to my father and, likewise, he couldn't bring himself to say anything to me. The subsequent deterioration of our relationship was worth it not to have to face the truth.

I remembered it clearly. The funeral "after-party." I knew that wasn't what it was supposed to be called, but I could never remember the proper name for it. It was held in the kind of place my mother would have hated, a windowless bar that smelled stale and sweaty. The indoor smoking ban hadn't long come into force and the ingrained smell of cigarettes was fading away to reveal the true unpleasant reek of those kinds of establishments. I wrinkled my nose, not wanting to sit on the faded soft furnishings and choosing a more sanitary wooden stool instead. The people around us were mostly my father's friends. Their wives had put up a front of being my mother's friends too, but they weren't really. My mum had never been one of them. They were loud and shrieking, clucking and fussing around each other, picking at things like a flock of hens, ruffling their stiffly styled hair and nosing in on conversations with feigned concern for the benefit of future gossip. Thankfully, at the funeral after-party they had the decency to keep their voices at a reasonable volume and look at least a little sombre as they drank the wine. Their funeral outfits were all respectable on the face of it, but when you looked closely you would notice that they were just a little too short, a little too tight in strategic places, their height elevated by little black shoes with sharp heels, which stabbed the ground around my mother's grave.

The men were worse; they lurked in the shadows, nodding their heads at my father and offering empty grunts of condolence as he stooped over his pint. My father put on what most would have called "a brave face," but I knew him well enough to know that there was no bravery to it. He smelled of that cherry sweetness that had become familiar to me over the years, the scent that belonged to a woman who everyone around us at my mother's funeral was friendly with. Fortunately, she at least had the decency not to show up that day.

I paused as I reached the bus stop, my clothes soaked through from the wind-whipped snowflakes that thawed on my skin. Perhaps I was being too hasty. After all, I didn't know what the future held with Delia. I had only just met her, and I might never see her again. I didn't have to tell Eleanor what had happened between us; I could make something up to explain my absence over Christmas – she would be angry, of course, but I knew her well enough to know that her anger never lasted long. Reassuring myself that I could still rebuild my life, I perched on the pale grey bench at the centre of the Pyrex box, which offered at least a little shelter from the wind. The snow swirled around, as though trapping me inside, and the wind made a high whistling sound as it rushed through the gaps in the shelter. There was a timetable board pinned up beside me, but the frame was empty. Shuffling forward on the plastic bench, I sat as close to the edge as possible, always wary of getting too comfortable at a bus stop. Back in the city, they were home to all sorts of unhygienic horrors; chewing gum stuck to the back of my trousers wasn't even the half of it. The longer I sat there, the more aware I was of the unpleasant plastic smell of bus stops, and I instinctively pulled Delia's small glass bottle from my pocket, spritzing the air around me.

In the middle of planning the lies that I would tell Eleanor on my return, it occurred to me that if I resumed my relationship with her, I would likely never see Delia again. My stomach lurched at the thought, and I realised that I hadn't asked Henry for the hotel telephone number. I didn't even know what the hotel was called, let alone where it was. I pictured Henry's lofty expression and wondered if he would even bother passing on the message. He wasn't to be trusted.

A low rumble caught my attention and I turned to see a small country bus bumping and jerking over the uncleared road towards me. It slid to an uneasy stop and the door clicked and juddered, hissing like it was releasing steam. An older woman sat in the driver's seat dressed in a blue uniform. Her eyes were magnified by thick lenses and her hair would once have been a vibrant red but had faded with age into a wispy perm of strawberry blonde.

"Room for one more." Her smile stretched and for a moment, all I could picture was Edward's horrible story about the smiling sea ghoul. The driver gestured behind her at the seats, which were all full bar one. Elderly women with thick coats and large handbags perched on their laps all stared back at me with that curious look that local folk gave strangers. They all smelled old. I half expected them to all break out into those awful smiles that Edward had described so vividly.

"Going to town?" The driver raised the part of her brow where eyebrows ought to have been. I hesitated.

"Do you know what the hotel just up the road from here is called?"

"There's a few I can think of. It's very popular up here with the tourists in the summer months." She grinned an immaculate row of false teeth. "Not so much this time of year though. You're lucky there's even a bus coming by today. All the other drivers called it a day – they don't have my stamina." She nodded over her shoulder. "These ladies need their day in town."

There was an unpleasant tittering behind her.

I approached the bus, pausing before I stepped inside. Even if I did manage to find the hotel's address, if Delia thought I had left without saying goodbye then she might not want to speak to me again. The thought pained me.

"Will you be back later?" I asked.

The driver shook her head.

I hesitated again, my mind racing, picturing my return to the city, sneaking into Eleanor's flat like a squatter. Then where would I go? The more I thought about it, my job didn't seem worth going back for; I could always get a job in another restaurant. What was waiting for me back in the city wasn't the life I wanted for myself. I stepped back.

"Sorry, wrong bus," I said.

"Suit yourself." The driver shrugged and closed the door. Before it shut fully, she called out to me. "Better get back sharp, sonny boy. It gets dark early here. You don't want to get lost in the night."

Although I knew she was being helpful, I couldn't help but imagine, as night fell, the bus coming to a halt and those tittering old women tossing their handbags aside and creeping out, grinning those stretched smiles and wandering the night. I shuddered and quickened my pace in the direction of the hotel.

# CHAPTER 10

"**E** *ric!*"
A tear-stained face appeared at the door of the hotel, dark circles around her eyes, makeup smudged. By that time, my head was throbbing from the cold and my eyes were bleary, my eyelashes almost frozen together. I squinted to make her out properly, her dark hair tumbling over a silk, mustard-yellow blouse, bright against snow and pale brick. In my blurred vision she looked like a long wasp, which, just for a moment, made me recoil. I was relieved when, as I approached, her wasp-likeness vanished and her features came into focus. I rubbed my eyes, wiping shards of frost from my lashes and eyebrows, blinking rapidly.

"I had a meeting with my accountant this morning." Her voice was nasally. She sniffed loudly and I realised that she was still crying. "I had to go into town early and when I came back you had gone." She ran the back of her yellow sleeve over her eyes, leaving a black stain. "Is this how you treat women? You get what you want, and then you leave without a word?"

"No, Delia."

"Did you only come back because you couldn't catch a bus?" Her voice trembled. "Because if that's the case, you can leave now. Walk to another hotel for all I care!"

Henry appeared behind her, beneath the dim glow of artificial light. His features were taut, anxious.

"Delia." I got close enough to snatch her upper arms, causing her to jump slightly. "I had a shift at work. I'd lose my job

48

if I didn't turn up. But I got to the bus stop, and I realised that I didn't want to go. I want to be with *you*, Delia." I paused, my brain whole seconds behind my words. "I know we've only just met, but I've never met anyone like you. I think you're *wonderful*."

Her face softened.

"You do?"

"Yes." I nodded emphatically, clutching her hands in mine. "I left a message with Henry. Did he not give it to you?"

Henry froze behind her, casting me a wide-eyed look. Releasing my hands, Delia went from being crumpled and snivelling to snapping straight and whipping around, the suddenness catching me off guard. She was momentarily wasp-like again. Her eyes met Henry's and as she took a step towards him, he retreated.

"You watched me sob for the past hour and you didn't say *anything*?" she hissed. Her voice had lost its low lull. "Why would you do that, Henry?"

"I'm sorry." He mumbled towards the floor. "I forgot."

"No, you didn't," I snapped. "You haven't liked me from day one and I'm sure I can guess why that is. I've seen how you look at her."

Henry shook his head, still staring at the floor.

"No, Eric, it's not like that. Let me—"

"I hate you!" Delia screamed, with a force that made me jump back in fright. Without warning, she snatched a vase from one of the antique bureaus and hurled it in his direction. It missed by several inches and shattered in an explosion of pink and orange shards. "Get out of my sight."

As he turned to walk away, she took a deep, steadying breath and held up her hand.

"No, wait," she called after him.

He paused and looked over his shoulder with a glimmer of something that could have been hope or fear; it was impossible to tell.

"Clean this up."

Snatching my hand, she swerved me round the shards of broken glass. I cast Henry a smug look, finding myself as pleased as I was perturbed by her unexpected flash of violence.

# CHAPTER 11

The conservatory had become my favourite part of the hotel. From what I could see, the space went largely unloved during the winter months. Tired and neglected, its rattling glass was foggy from the condensation that trickled down to the terracotta tiles on the floor, making them slick and hazardous. The longer I spent there, the mistier the glass became. Little round iron tables were scattered evenly, so cold that when I touched them the flesh of my fingertips became briefly stuck to the metal.

When Delia was working, it had become my morning routine to collect my coffee from the bar, wrap up in one of the tartan throws from the living room and stroll into the conservatory with a notebook I had pilfered from reception when Henry wasn't looking. So far, I had managed to write my way through three of them. I would sit on one of the small, hard chairs and peer through the misted glass at the jagged white landscape, surrounded by silence. The cold kept me alert and filled me with an energy that I didn't get from the sleepy cosiness of the living room or my bedroom. My pen would scratch furiously on paper until I sat triumphantly before a completed, handwritten chapter. The absence of any distractions, commitments or night shifts had given me the push I needed to focus in a way I had never managed back at home. I would need to get it typed up and saved. It made me anxious knowing that the only copy of it was loosely scribbled inside a flimsy notebook, but, unfortunately, the hotel didn't have computer access for guests. Once I was finished, I would ask Delia if I could use the laptop in her office.

I imagined that in summer the conservatory would be spectacular, with the doors and windows pulled apart and the sunshine radiating against glass, iron and tiles. I fantasised about pulling off my socks and walking barefoot over the warm, rough floor, gathering my books and coffee and strolling out into the gardens, which I pictured as being beautiful and blossoming. Delia would be lazing in the sun, shielded by a wide-brimmed hat and a long, floaty summer dress.

Nevertheless, there was still something magical about sitting alone in the glass room surrounded by the white of winter. The coffee thawed my hands and throat, and left a dull warmth in my stomach to counter the cold. Once I returned to the warmth of the main hotel, I would feel a pleasant sleepiness, like I had earned a good rest. My eyes would droop lazily, and I would sink into one of the armchairs, sometimes falling asleep until dinner. Wholesome exhaustion. The last time I'd had that feeling was on one of Eleanor's family holidays. I'd been surprised to discover that, other than for skiing, such a well-off family didn't regularly go abroad and instead congregated at a little holiday cottage on the west coast, the kind of place that was frayed at the edges and felt a little damp on arrival, not warming until the heating had been on for several hours. The bedrooms were poky and the porch inevitably filthy once everyone had stripped off their outdoor gear and abandoned it to hang, musty-scented. They arrived one vehicle after another, grandparents, parents, siblings, all weighed down by picnic baskets, tartan blankets and thermos flasks. During the day we would go to the beach, which was all ragged shoreline and freezing, frothing waves. The whole family, including the grandparents, would change into their swimming costumes and run towards the water, bracing themselves for the big submergence. I recall standing there, still in my T-shirt and trunks, as the sea lapped my feet, the water so chill it spread a dull pain up my legs. Eleanor's family were in the water by that point, encouraging me in, her brother veiling his mockery with disingenuous words of support. Even the grandparents were bravely churning up the water, doing the breaststroke with confidence. I stood on the edge watching them stare back at me, their looks suggesting that unless I did it I would never be one of them, which of course, back then, I was desperate to be.

"Come on, Eric!" Eleanor had smiled at me, her pale, freckled body shivering several feet away.

Tensing everything, I let out an animal cry and charged towards them, hearing them whoop in delight and praise. As I dropped beneath the surface I felt the rush of the cold stripping me bare, and experienced a silence louder than the day-to-day rumble of cars and beep of electronics, a strange wave of calm. I slept soundly every night I spent at that little cottage.

Those holidays with Eleanor and her family were nothing like the package holidays of my childhood, which were spent sweltering by a tiled poolside and sprawled on deckchairs while my parents drank colourful cocktails, with limitless access to sugary drinks and the kind of buffet snacks my mother forbade at home. We would return home heavier, bloated and burnt, more weary than refreshed.

I blinked, surprised by movement outside catching my attention through the foggy glass. My hand jerked, spilling hot coffee down the front of my knitted jumper. I swore, patting it cool. It would no doubt leave an angry red mark on my skin.

Two figures, it was impossible to make out who, were standing in the snow several feet from the conservatory. There was a flicker of orange light between them, followed by a loud shrieking laugh. I approached the door and turned the old, rusting key in the lock. The handle was stiff from age and the hinges wailed long and mournfully as I pulled it open, letting the lying snow tumble across the tiles. Up ahead, Delia and Edward were huddled close, heads dipped as they smoked a cigarette and blew into their free hands to generate warmth. Delia burst out laughing again, presumably at something Edward had said. She noticed me just as her head tossed back in that delightful way it did when she found something genuinely funny, laughing a rich belly laugh.

"Eric!" she exclaimed mid-laughter, puffing out an icing-sugar cloud of smoke and condensation. Edward glanced at me, smiling in recognition.

"Eric," he parroted.

"What are you doing in the conservatory?" She approached me, cheeks pink from the cold wind as she planted a soft kiss on my cheek. "It's horrible in there! Whole thing needs pulled down and rebuilt."

"I was just getting some writing done." Her pleasant, spicy scent was slightly tampered by the smell of tobacco. "It's nice in the conservatory." I glanced back at small glass structure beneath a heavy ceiling of snow. "It must be amazing in summer."

Delia didn't reply, instead turning back to Edward.

"Edward's just been telling me some of the funniest stories from when he worked at sea. We're meant to be having a work meeting, but we're both terrible for getting distracted, aren't we, Edward?"

"Certainly are." He inhaled deeply and blew out a fine plume of smoke before gesturing at me with his packet. "Apologies, Eric. Do you smoke?"

I shook my head. "Body is my temple and all that." Delia and Edward cocked their heads as though they didn't understand the saying. "No, I don't smoke," I clarified.

"Quite right. Dirty little habit. I only ever do it when *he's* about." Delia nudged Edward to reassure him that she was joking. "You know, Eric, if you find yourself at a loss for things to do, you really ought to join Edward's little afternoon tea club. Would that be alright, Edward? I know that since Callum retired it's been a little quiet for you and Sandy. I think you would all get along wonderfully!"

"Of course," Edward said, assessing me carefully before committing. "It's at two o'clock on Wednesdays. We would love to see you there."

"Yeah, sure," I replied non-committedly, desperately thinking of a way to steer the subject away from the invitation. "So, Edward, you worked at sea? Navy?"

"No, fishing."

"Ah, I guess that was the inspiration for your fireside story a while back?"

"Perhaps." He shrugged, flicking his cigarette into the snow and indicated the notebook under my arm. "Hopefully we'll be hearing your story before too long?"

"Not for a while yet. I'm still a fair bit off finishing my novel." I tucked the little book more firmly between my arm and torso, frightened it might fall and be swept away by the wind. Edward opened his mouth, presumably to enquire more into my novel, but he was cut off by Delia who was frowning in my direction.

"What's that on your jumper?"

"Oh." I glanced down at the dark-brown stain. "I spilt coffee on it."

"It'll need laundered." The statement was directed at Edward. "Would you be able to find Eric a spare shirt while this is cleaned?"

"Of course." He nodded obligingly. "I'll get housekeeping to sort the stain."

Reaching forward, Delia touched the fabric.

"I hope it isn't permanent," her voice trickled. "It's such a lovely jumper. Where did you get it?"

I frowned, glancing at the hand-knitted pattern, and shrugged.

"I don't remember."

She smiled.

"It really is lovely." She discarded the remainder of her cigarette, which sizzled for a second in the snow before the little light flickered and died. "Well boys, got to run." She brushed her fingers tantalisingly against mine. "Busy day."

"Do you want to have lunch with me later?" I asked hopefully.

"I'm afraid I can't." She pulled a face, appearing genuinely disappointed. "But I'll try and make dinner. Honestly, it's chaotic at the moment." Spinning around, she began teetering back to the front entrance of the hotel, her heels impractical in the snow. I watched her long legs and round hips, hoping that she would glance back just once. Edward chuckled after her, waiting until she was out of sight.

"High heels in the snow. What is she like?" Rolling his eyes, he clamped a heavy hand on my shoulder. His arm was thick with white, wiry hair. "Anyway, come on." He steered me back towards the hotel. "Let's get you a fresh shirt."

# CHAPTER 12

As time passed, I become increasingly familiar with the different cliques that existed in the hotel. Since the staff lived there permanently, and there were no guests over the winter months, they had to occupy themselves with extra-curricular activities on top of the day-to-day chores and maintenance. Little clubs had been established which met religiously on certain days of the week and at certain times. Edward's afternoon tea club was not an anomaly.

There was a crafts club that met on a Tuesday morning, mainly consisting of the housekeeping team, a fussy bunch who were as meticulous about their dry-flower arranging and cross-stitching as they were about keeping the hotel clean and tidy.

The kitchen staff had formed a baking club which kept them entertained outside of mealtimes. Although I had never been inside the kitchen, there was a small glass panel on the door which I could peer through and watch them mix, whisk and delicately ice, usually with a glass of wine to hand. Their creations would later be displayed in little glass cake stands in the restaurant, available for anyone who wanted one. One of the staff, an older man called Sandy, saw me peering in one day and pressed his face close too. "Mince pies," he murmured longingly. "Keep an eye out for the mince pies. They only make them around Christmas but they're definitely the best. Get snatched up as soon as they're out the oven." Then, after taking a moment to breathe in the steam from fresh bread and hot cakes, he wandered away. Sandy, I noticed, was part of two clubs, Edward's afternoon tea club and the "drinking club." The drinking club was less formal than the rest in terms of activity. The members, mostly maintenance and bar staff, would sit over a bottle of whatever whisky the barman had recommended and discuss it briefly, using the information booklets that came with the boxes. After that, they would launch into unfiltered gossip about everyone else. I edged in once, keen for a bit of company over a drink, as well as out of nosiness. However, they fell silent, making it abundantly clear that my presence wasn't welcome.

The final club I had identified was the choir. Edward seemed to oversee that one. I had smirked a little when I first saw them setting up and practicing their scales by the fire. I rolled my eyes and gathered my things, readying myself to move out of the living room and continue my writing somewhere quieter. Then they sang. Edward's voice took the lead, a deep, haunting baritone, supported by the voices of the others, which complemented his perfectly. For a moment, they were more than merely human, their voices amalgamating into something ethereal, like nothing I'd ever heard before. I found myself sitting back down, entranced by the sound, which seemed to linger in the room long after they were finished. As he was packing up, Edward told me that it was one of the songs he used to sing at sea and invited me to join, but I politely declined, not in amused contempt but because I knew I couldn't hold a tune.

The one thing all the men in the hotel had in common was Delia. They orbited her like planets do their sun, always seeking her approval and looking at her in adoration. Contrary to my initial concerns, it didn't appear that there was anything sexual in it; it was a kind of admiration I couldn't place. Respect, perhaps? Her presence demanded it.

In general, the staff were politely pleasant towards me in a way that made me feel superior and excluded in equal parts. Growing up, I didn't have that many friends, having always been wary of other people after seeing the way my mother's supposed friends had treated her. I kept people at arm's length more out of habit than anything else; however, I couldn't deny that watching the tight-knit groups around me made me feel an ache of longing for that kind of relationship. At least I had Delia.

Henry continued to irk me. He had stayed largely out of my way since he had lied to Delia about me, not even offering an apology. I watched him sometimes, the way he slinked around the hotel avoiding everyone, including Delia when he could. I could tell it bothered her and she always made a little extra effort with him, touching his arm, teasing him playfully and trying to engage him in idle chat. He would recoil each time. Watching Delia try to include and appease him made me love her all the more; in my opinion, she ought to just fire him. In the evenings when we congregated around the fire, he would lurk at the back of the room or simply excuse himself altogether.

One evening, just as I was preparing for bed, I saw something strange. It was late and Delia had excused herself, holing up in her office through to the early hours, as she often did. In her absence I had ordered a bottle of wine to the room and run myself a hot bath, dropping in a little of the bath oil which she had left on the bathroom counter. It had the same spiced scent as my cologne, splashing into the water and resting on the hot surface before drifting away with the rising steam that filled the room and perspired against the tiles. With a hint of irritation, I noticed that the cleaners hadn't replaced my towels in a few days, and I made a mental note to take a trip to the laundry room shortly to change them before Delia's lovely scent was spoilt by the smell of damp.

Later, when I had wobbled uncertainly to bed, groggy from the heat and wine and my belly still full from dinner, I heard a strange sound coming from nearby. A crunch, then a crack, followed by a heavy, huffing breath. Disorientated, I felt around in the darkness, dehydrated and clammy from the heat emanating from the rattling radiator. At first, I wondered if I had dreamed it, simply exaggerated the sound of the radiator in my sleep. Then I heard it again.

*Crunch, crunch, clink, huff, huff.*

Swivelling round, I got to my feet, wary of turning the lights on once I'd realised that the sound was coming from the window. I felt my way towards the sliver of silvery light between the curtains, I wrapped my fingers around the velvet and pulled it gently back. Adjusting my eyes to the darkness, I peered outside at the movement in the snow down below. Near the woodshed, a dark figure was stooped with a spade in hand and its back to me. The spade crunched into the snow and clinked against frozen ground. The figure bent down, breathing heavily, and fussed with something over the hole in the ground before hurriedly filling it up again. Its head turned side to side to check that no one was watching, and the lights from the entrance window caught the profile in a dim, yellow glow. The outline of the long, pointed nose and sharply jutting chin was unmistakable. Henry patted the ground flat in front of him and shuffled back to the hotel through the falling snow, which was thickening by the minute. I stayed by the window several moments longer to watch the night, which was now uncannily still. When nothing stirred, I shuffled back to my bed, still in a half-drunken stupor, and woke late the next morning, with a dull head and a vague recollection of the night's events. I felt something else too, something that I'd later identify as a sinking feeling of discomfort that had nothing to do with the hangover.

# CHAPTER 13

A fight had broken out among the hotel staff the previous day.

Apparently there had been a mix-up in the laundry room and one of the kitchen assistants had taken the wrong apron. The offending party had spilt a berry jus down the pale blue front of it, and "that kind of stain would never come out" according to the chef, who was upset because he had taken considerable time to adjust the straps and hem specifically for his height. I watched gleefully as the drama unfolded.

The chef had pointed furiously at a purple-blue stain on the front of the apron, saying he recognised it from the baking club the previous week when they had been making blueberry tarts. At that point I snorted with laughter, but on looking around I realised that nobody else saw the absurdity of it. The audience was observing with wide-eyed concern. Insisting that it wasn't an intentional theft, the baking club turned the blame on the housekeeping team, specifically laundry, who were accused of being sloppy and disorganised. Murmurs of agreement rose from the onlookers, who all seemed to have a story about lost uniforms. Housekeeping defended their own and stepped in, arguing that they had enough on their plate without having to organise whose clothes were whose. They suggested that individuals take responsibility for their own possessions or, if that wasn't possible, perhaps they ought to just do their own laundry. Voices were raised.

As manager, Edward intervened and tried to cool tempers, encouraging solutions rather than a focus on the problems.

Eventually, the disgruntled head of housekeeping suggested that his craft club embroider initials on everyone's sleeves as their project for the week. The members of the craft club grumbled for a moment, but conceded that embroidery was something they hadn't done yet and it might be a useful skill. The following Tuesday morning, a queue formed by the craft table. As I passed, Neil, one of the maintenance men, gestured to the space behind him. "Here to get your shirt done?" he asked brightly. I raised an eyebrow, glancing down at my perfectly fitted shirt, which matched the others, and shook my head.

"Don't you think it's nice?" Over dinner that evening, I sat opposite Delia, who was prodding a venison fillet with her fork as though she wasn't sure if she was hungry. We had our usual table by the window, looking out into the darkness as fat flakes of snow drifted by in the security lights.

"What is?" I asked, nearly finished my plate.

"The initials thing." Abandoning her cutlery, she leaned back in her chair. "Some of my friends are business owners too, and they have to manage their staff – they're *constantly* squabbling. My friends say it's tedious. They spend about as much time managing egos as doing their actual job. This lot just get on with it, sort things out among themselves," she smiled, "and the first I hear of it is a solution. Exactly how it should be."

"It was pretty funny, actually." I lowered my voice, glancing around to make sure that none of the diners were within ear shot. "Two of them very nearly started fighting. Like, physically."

Delia frowned.

"Nobody likes a tattletale, Eric."

"I'm not—" I stopped myself from arguing about being unjustly reprimanded, deciding instead to change the subject. "Speaking of business, how's it going? I've noticed there still aren't any guests. With the place fully staffed, that must be taking its toll on finances?"

"Not really." She shrugged, looking away disinterestedly. "My accountant manages it all just fine every year."

"That's good." I did my best to mask my uncertainty. I was fully aware that her finances could affect my future wellbeing.

We sat quietly for several minutes, Delia looking contentedly at me, fully at ease in the silence, whereas I felt the need to say something interesting and was worried about fumbling my words. She watched me, with the trace of a smile on the edges of her mouth, in a way that said "go on, entertain me."

"Oh." She perked up in her chair. "I know what we should do this evening!" Rising to her feet and abandoning her nearly full plate, she waved her hands excitedly, a grin spreading. "A snowball fight!"

63

# CHAPTER 14

I thought I still remembered what joy felt like, but I didn't really, not in the same way I did when I was young. As an adult, what I thought was joy was always punctured by concern, be it financial, social or professional. It wasn't real joy, not like it used to be.

Children didn't have to temper the surge of adrenaline that came with excitement unless an adult told them to calm down, but adults rarely did. More often than not they took pleasure in watching that kind of untarnished joy, which they recalled vaguely from their own childhood. They would want the little person to hold on to that feeling for as long as possible because, one day, which ironically would be the day the child finally had control over their own life, they would never feel it in quite the same way again.

Something happened to me on the grounds of the hotel that evening. I felt it. I felt pure joy. We had filed out the building, chattering pleasantly, still constrained by social niceties, and as we stood with the snow up to our calves, looking up at a glittering navy sky, it was like an explosion in our midst and everyone scattered. For a moment I felt like I was in a glass bubble, the world beyond muted as I watched something I didn't fully understand. Then it shattered in an explosion of excited screams. Almost with a kind of hive mentality, I started running, heart thumping and limbs trembling in excitement. Wicked grins spread across the men's faces as they dipped gloved hands into the snow and began firing snowballs in a frantic flurry. Nearby,

Delia had lost all composure, tumbling in the snow with her wet hair clinging to her skin. A tightly packed snowball struck her on the head and knocked her to the ground, but she scrambled back to her feet grinning wildly. I let out a strange giggle that, under normal circumstances, was a noise I would have been embarrassed to make. It was like something had unwound inside me; all my muscles, which had been taut with apprehension and vague concern about the unknown, had become loose and warmed by movements that resembled a wild dance.

I twirled around, firing a snowball into the cluster of men, who were pinning each other to the ground and stuffing snow down one another's collars. Memories of my childhood, my job, Eleanor, my writing, everything that had ever caused me any angst, were forgotten, slipping away into the night.

It ended when we were too exhausted to continue. Flopping back breathlessly, we allowed our bodies and brains to reconnect. It was only then that we realised how cold it was, and we shivered. Our clothes were soaked through and the fabric was becoming stiff, freezing against our skin. Rising to our feet, we followed Delia back to the hotel. I managed to catch up with her and link her arm in mine.

It was only when I was back in my room that I realised that Henry had been nowhere to be seen at that snowball fight.

*** 

My plan had been to dig out some dry clothes, but I noticed some of the men passing my bedroom door, which I'd left ajar, all of them wrapped in their white dressing gowns, broad smiles on their faces. A man whose name I couldn't recall popped his head through the gap and gestured for me to follow. I hesitated for a second before quickly changing into my own dressing gown and joining them. We filed back downstairs, shuffling contentedly like a gaggle of white geese.

Back in the living room, the fire burned with such ferocity,

THE GINGERBREAD MEN

logs trembling and crackling, that the entire room seemed to
rumble. The bar staff, also in dressing gowns, handed out mugs
and distributed spiced hot chocolate from steaming pots. The
evening gingerbread men peered up at us from the saucers,
waiting for us to crunch contentedly on them and rest sleepily
back into our chairs, or on cushions by the fire, stretching lazily
like cats by a hearth.

I sipped a delightful combination of cinnamon, nutmeg and
ginger chocolate; even the drink seemed to have traces of Delia's
aroma to its taste. She slipped into the room in a peach silk robe,
loosely tied at the waist and swaying by her pale ankles. Peaches
and cream. Glancing around the room, her eyes met mine and
she padded barefoot towards me, placing herself on the arm of
my chair and swinging one leg over the other. Her hand crept
delicately up the back of my neck. The room fell silent.

"Shall we have a story?" she asked brightly, leaning back so
that she was pressing into my shoulder. Excitable agreement
followed. "Hmm." Scanning the occupied seats in the room, her
gaze landed on the old man Sandy, who was clasping his mug
between his weathered hands for warmth. "Sandy, it's been a
long time since we heard from you!"

Sandy bowed his head and placed his mug on the coffee
table. When he spoke, he had the low growl of a heavy smoker,
and his tight grey curls rose from his head like wisps of smoke.
The wooden floorboards creaked under his feet as he moved
towards the fireplace, the only sound in the room besides the
rumble of the fire. The men on the floor shifted aside to make
room.

"Once upon a time," he began.

# CHAPTER 15:

## THE NIGHT PROWLER

Once upon a time, vampires walked the earth. This, of course, was back when the sun was further away from the planet, too far to offer the bright daylight that now keeps us safe, and people lived in fear, forever in a kind of darkness. Predominantly women, the vampires gathered in groups, shrieking and tearing through the lands, tricking their way into houses by pretending they were being pursued, appealing for help before draining their victims dry. They stalked the darkness, singing terrible songs and dancing a beautiful, frightening dance. People were fooled into thinking they were travelling performers, and they'd emerge from their homes, curious, to investigate. By the time they realised what the visitors really were, it was too late.

As the sun came closer to the earth and the world brightened, it was the vampires who were forced into hiding. And after a while, people forgot that they ever existed. Vampires were no longer real, just the stuff of nightmares and scary stories. Nobody realised that they were still there, buried in the darkness of the ground, waiting.

One day, a young gardener was tending to one of his client's plots. They had asked for a pond to be dug beside an old stone wall, which would have beautiful views over the rolling hills and the neighbouring church grounds. The gardener had always enjoyed working in that garden; in fact, he would sometimes extend his lunch break solely to sit on the stone wall to enjoy the views, feeling the heat of the sun on his bronzing skin. As the sun went down, the gardener realised that he'd taken too long at lunch that day and hadn't completed what he'd promised his client. So, he stayed late, and he dug.

There was an unpleasant squelch when his spade hit something soft in the earth. He threw it aside and got down into the pit, crawling on hands and knees, and began pushing the soil aside with gloved hands. His eyes widened when, with a brush of his hand, the dirt slid away to reveal a pale face staring up at him. At first he thought it was a corpse, deathly pale, its eyes coated in a milky film. But a faint breath was coming from between its lips, and the body gave a gentle cough, spluttered powdery earth from its mouth – from *her* mouth. The gardener tucked his hand beneath her head and tried to gently pull her up. She was stuck in place. He wrenched her with as much force as he dared, and she came away. She seemed to have been plugging a hole to a great, cavernous space below. Rolling her limp body aside, he peered into the hole, flicking his lighter and dipping his hand inside. In retrospect, he realised that this was a foolish thing to do; you never know what kind of flammable gases are there beneath the ground. Thankfully, there was no explosion. But what he saw frightened him terribly.

There was a dark wriggling and writhing at the edges of the light. Squinting, he let his eyes adjust, and that was when he saw them. The shadowy shapes of women, moving slowly, twirling in slow motion, their voices distant and haunting. One tossed her head back and looked at him, her milky eyes catching the glint of his flame.

"Give us our sister back," she hissed. "Haven't you taken enough?"

The gardener leapt back from the hole, dropping his lighter, which plunged into the darkness.

"Don't go too close."

He turned his head sharply towards the source of the voice to see the young woman sitting upright, brushing the dirt from her body.

"They're hungry."

"Vampires!" the gardener gasped, having heard the tales. "You're one of them?"

She nodded sadly. The gardener scrambled back.

"Please." Her voice was soft. "I have never wanted to hurt anyone. I don't want to hurt you. I'm not like my sisters. While they danced in the darkness, I climbed to the top of our grave and dreamed of the world outside."

The gardener took her hand tentatively and examined her. She was pretty in a strange way, with startlingly white-blonde hair matted with dirt. Her features were small and button-like. She certainly didn't look like any vampire he had imagined. Together, the gardener and the vampire sealed the hole in the ground, the angry screams of her sisters muffled and silenced, and they walked home to the gardener's house, hand in hand, warm skin against cold.

As the sun came up the following morning, and the gardener headed out to work, the vampire pulled up a loose floorboard in the gardener's house and squeezed into the gap beneath. Both were impatient to see each other again once the sun had gone down.

Years passed, and the gardener was all but content, wondering only why the vampire would sneak out once a week just as he was falling asleep. She would carefully untangle herself from his embrace and slip out the door, but was gone only a couple of hours. When he asked her about it, she would say he must have been dreaming and kiss him gently, a metallic tang on her lips.

One night he followed her.

She danced in the empty streets, twirling and humming to herself, the hem of her dress billowing around her. The gardener tried to keep out of sight, following her into a busier part of the town, where she stopped outside a bustling pub on the square. She drifted towards a group of men, loud-mouthed and rowdy, unsteady on their feet. Their eyes wandered after her, causing the gardener to bristle with anger. One of them separated from the crowd and followed her. He wrapped an arm around her waist, and she let him, leading him to a bench in a quiet spot. She let him nuzzle into her, before pressing her mouth against his neck, taking just enough to tire the man out. Wiping his throat clean with her handkerchief, she propped him back up against the bench so that he could sleep it off.

By the time she returned home, the gardener was already back and sitting at the dining table, a lamp lighting up his features ominously in the night. The vampire jumped in surprise, but broke into a smile.

"You're up?"

"I followed you tonight." His voice trembled with fury.

"Oh." She continued smiling. "He'll be alright. I only take as much as I need."

"That's not the *point*." The gardener slammed his fist on the table, and an apple rolled to the floor. "Do you know how that makes me feel? Seeing you like that? Behaving like a monster?"

The vampire's eyes widened, and she stepped back.

"*No more*," he hissed. "You don't do that anymore."

"But I need to," she said quietly, reaching out to touch the gardener's arm. "I'll become slow, like my sisters, who feed off the worms and the rodents in the earth. Or worse, I'll fall into a deep sleep and I'll be little better than a corpse."

The gardener hesitated.

"Then have my blood." He pricked his finger and held out the bloody tip.

"That's not enough."

"You'll have to make do."

Once a week, the gardener would prick the tip of his finger and let the vampire taste his blood. Years passed, and she became paler and more tired, barely able to keep her eyes open when he lifted her from beneath the floorboards at night. Eventually, she stopped speaking.

The gardener couldn't bear the hungry look in her eye when he presented his bloody finger to her, a constant reminder of the monster she was. He began feeding her less and less, until one day he stopped bothering to lift the floorboards at all.

One night, the vampire bit into a mouse that scurried over her, and she drained it dry, gathering enough strength to pull herself up. She pushed at the floorboards, realising that the gardener had nailed her in. Wailing and kicking, she begged the gardener to return her to her sisters.

"Be quiet," he hissed through the gap. "Someone will hear you, and you know what they do to vampires."

Her finger pushed through the gap and clawed his cheek, leaving a bloody scratch on the gardener's face.

"You monster," he spat. "I should have left you in the ground where you belong."

The vampire fell silent.

The gardener came to understand that it was only a matter of time before the vampire found a larger rodent, maybe a rabbit or even a cat, something big enough to give her the strength to break through the flimsy floorboards. Angry and bloodthirsty, there was no telling what she might do. So, in desperation, the gardener returned to the place he found her and stood uncertainly outside the neighbouring church.

"Can I help you?"

The minister stood behind him. To his surprise, she was a woman, dressed in dark robes, her black hair pinned back neatly. When she smiled, a deep, doll-like dimple appeared in one of her cheeks, and she revealed a slightly snaggled canine. Her voice was soft as a lullaby. The gardener found himself telling her everything, collapsing into the grass and weeping into her robes as she comforted him. The minister vowed to help.

Together, they returned to his house and pulled up the floorboards. The gardener gagged at the stench from the rotting rodent bodies. Strangely, the minister didn't look at all perturbed when she saw the vampire and, instead, rolled up her sleeves and helped pull the limp body out. The vampire's once plump lips were pale and shrivelled, revealing her gums and pointed teeth. Both the gardener and the minister wore rings of garlic around their necks and a silver crucifix dangling at their chests.

The vampire began to move. Realising that they had been fooled into thinking she was unconscious, the gardener cried a warning.

"Get back!" He stepped in front of the minister.

"You think these will stop me?" The vampire reached forward and wrenched the garlic and the cross from the gardener's throat.

"Run!" the minister cried, snatching the gardener's hand and pulling him to his feet. They ran in the direction of the church, pursued by the vampire, who was slow in her weakness. They burst through the doors and tumbled against the pews, gasping for breath. The vampire stopped at the entrance, eyes narrowed in rage.

"She can't come in here," the minister said breathlessly, gathering herself and smoothing her robes. "We're safe."

The vampire let out a strange wail, which attracted attention from the neighbouring house. The old client of the gardener stepped outside to see what the commotion was about, approaching the vampire uncertainly to ask if everything was alright. Without hesitation, the vampire grabbed him and sunk her teeth deep into his throat. She dragged the body to the garden next door and began digging.

"Sisters!" she called, revealing the long-buried hole and pushing the body into it. It thumped heavily to the bottom of the cavern. Everything was silent for a moment. Then the terrible shrieking began. A song started to form in the cacophony as the vampires rose from the ground, hungry and filthy. They embraced their sister and wailed at each other, a strange, hypnotic tune. They started to dance around the church, cackling wildly as they twirled, and encouraged the gardener and the minister to step outside.

The minister took the gardener's hand and moved closer, her warm scent comforting him.

"It's alright," she whispered reassuringly. 'We're safe in here. You can stay as long as you like."

Together, the gardener and the minister took to the window, peering through the distorted stained glass to observe the beautiful, frightening dance.

# CHAPTER 16

I was cold when I woke up. The room around me was empty, and the fire was little more than charcoaled remains, puffs of smoke rising as though it had only just gone out. Shivering, I pulled my dressing gown tighter around me and wished I had slippers to wear. I must have fallen asleep at the very end of Sandy's story. My dreams had been of dancing vampires, drawing me in with silky-smooth voices. I was surprised that Delia hadn't woken me up when everyone was leaving.

Something was making me uneasy. It took me a moment to realise that it was because something *had* woken me up; there was a scuffling sound coming from the dark corridor outside the room. I got to my feet and looked around. Housekeeping hadn't done their rounds yet, and mugs and saucers littered the coffee tables, biscuit crumbs trampled across the rug by the chairs. As I crept into the corridor, the silvery light of the moon, which spilled from the doors of the adjacent rooms, gave it the appearance of a scene from an old black and white horror film. As I approached the stairs, and the thud of my heart seemed loud enough to wake the other occupants of the building. A floorboard creaked, and the sound of scuffling up ahead paused; whoever it was knew I was there. I held my breath. My father had made fun of me when I was little, telling me that "big boys aren't afraid of the dark." Of course, what he meant was that "big boys don't *show* that they're afraid of the dark."

Henry stood by the door of Delia's office on the first small landing of the curved stairs, fiddling with the lock and rattling the handle. He jumped in fright when he noticed me standing at the bottom of the stairs, and his mouth went from a surprised "O" shape to an infuriated scowl.

"Henry." The nervous thud of my heart steadied to an even beat. "What are you up to?"

"Working," he replied tartly, smoothing the front of his pressed shirt unnecessarily. "I needed some papers."

I raised an eyebrow, turning to the lock on the door.

"What papers?"

Henry rolled his eyes and crossed his arms.

"Why don't you just go ahead and ask me what you actually want to ask me?" His voice became smooth and composed, slipping into a kind of calm that unnerved me. I could always spot someone who reacted well under pressure; the muscles of their face would relax, their voice would become slippery and they'd lean forward in a way that was confrontational, but you would never be able to accuse them of it. As he stared through me, it felt as though he was identifying each insecurity and uncertainty. I instinctively stepped back. Henry was a man well versed in confrontation.

"Why are you breaking into Delia's office?" I tried to keep my voice equally even, but it didn't come out that way.

"To access papers for an audit I'm carrying out for Delia's accountant," he replied simply. "You're very welcome to help me with it. Besides," he paused, a smirk hovering on the edges of his lips, "it's a good way to kill a few days when you have nothing better to be doing."

I pulled myself up to my full height and stepped forward to assert myself. However, as I approached, Henry jumped back violently and extended his palms to stop me from coming any closer.

"What is your problem?" I snapped, taking another step towards him. He moved back again, as though I disgusted him, and raised an arm over the lower half of his face, shielding himself.

"Please." All confidence lost, he retreated. "Don't come any closer."

I opened my mouth to start a fresh argument but before I could, Henry circled around me and hastily descended to the corridor and away into the darkness. I stood still for a moment, baffled by the encounter, before checking that Delia's office was still locked as she always left it. I returned to my empty bedroom and fell into an unsettled sleep.

# CHAPTER 17

Sandy retired the following week.

It was less of an announcement and more a ripple of gossip that spread through the hotel, reaching me only when I queried the large delivery of helium balloons. Great pink orbs hovered around the ceiling in the dining room where the retirement party was supposed to be taking place. The whispers were everywhere.

*I heard he royally screwed up the wine order.*

*Someone told me he'd been slacking lately, spending a bit too much time at his little club in the bar, if you know what I mean.*

*No, him and Neil had been smoking inside. It's a health and safety hazard. I heard Delia going through them both last week for it. I bet he didn't listen.*

*I think Delia asked him to retire gracefully so he doesn't have to go through the humiliation of being fired. She's good like that.*

*I mean, he is pretty old.*

*Not as old as Edward.*

*True. But Edward's fit as anything. Sandy's really let himself go lately.*

*That's true.*

A series of giant, colourful letters had been ordered and tied to the curtain rail above us. It was supposed to read "GOOD-BYE SANDY" but nobody had noticed that the letter S had fallen, so it read "GOODBYE ANDY."

I joined Delia at the buffet table as she examined the selection of cakes, and peered over her shoulder at the little plate of mince pies.

"Oh, mince pies." I plucked one off the plate, still warm from the oven. "That was nice of the kitchen to make them specially for Sandy. They're his favourite."

Delia frowned.

"Are they? The kitchen always makes them at Christmas." She smiled, carefully selecting one for herself. "Such a shame Sandy will miss the Christmas party next week. It's my favourite time of year."

For a moment I felt disorientated. Christmas had felt so far away just the other day. I wondered how it had crept up on us so quickly.

"Oh, here he is!" She clapped her hands in delight, interrupting my confusion, as Sandy appeared at the door, grey and stout as he slouched through the frame. He looked exhausted, and his face was an explosion of spidery capillaries stemming from his nose. Everyone let out a cheer, raising their glasses and shouting, but not saying anything in particular. I joined in with a muffled, "Congratulations" between bites of my mince pie. Sandy was right, they were delicious. His gaze turned from us to the "GOODBYE ANDY" sign by the window and his eyes began to glitter.

"No." His lip quivered, voice barely audible above the cheers. "I don't want to go."

Delia was instantly by his side, snatching his hand and twirling him playfully as her pretty blush-pink dress rippled around her. Her smile was static. As they twirled, she leaned in close and breathed something into his ear. Sandy appeared to settle down and accepted the offer of a drink before lumbering into the throng of party guests. The merriment continued, but there were no speeches or announcements, and nobody seemed to be paying that much attention to Sandy.

A few hours later, Delia commanded silence by clapping her hands, and announced that Sandy's taxi had arrived. She beckoned us to follow her, and we naturally formed a line that reminded me of a funeral procession. By the entrance, Sandy had a single suitcase waiting on the stone step, and he picked it up with an ease that suggested there was very little inside.

We stood in the warmth of the reception area as he hovered on the porch, bracing himself against the sharp wind, fat snow-flakes beginning to settle on his head and shoulders. Behind him, a taxi shone its headlights, causing us to squint and concealing the features of the driver, who waited patiently by the open rear door. His figure was a dark outline behind the bright beams. Sandy shook his head and dropped his suitcase, turning back to Delia, a flash of fear flickering across his face for just a moment.

"Please, Delia." He clasped his hands together in a gesture of prayer. "Don't do this."

Delia maintained her impassive smile.

"Goodbye, Sandy," she said brightly.

Sandy trembled, dropping his hands and clenching them into fists.

"You *bitch!*" he shouted.

A collective gasp came from our bristling hive.

"I gave you *everything!*" he continued. "You've taken every-thing and left me with *nothing!* And now you do *this* to me?"

He stepped towards her, snatching her wrist in large, rough hands. Before we had the chance to intervene, she leaned in close to him again, using her free hand to touch his face. The wind caught her hair and whipped tendrils of it into Sandy's face. Blinking, he released her and took a tentative step back. Stumbling through the snow, he approached the haunting silhouette of the driver and allowed himself to be ushered into the taxi with no further fuss. Delia remained still on the porch, dark hair and pink fabric billowing around her in the breeze.

"What did she say to him?" I whispered to the man next to me. He shrugged.

We heard a car door slam and a crunching noise as the taxi reversed through the snow, the bright beam of the headlights getting smaller and fainter as it purred into the distance.

A few moments later, Delia turned to us, nursing her delicate wrist, which had the angry red bracelet of an emerging bruise from where Sandy had snatched her. Her smile had vanished, leaving her looking shocked and upset.

"He's crazy." She shook her head in disbelief and walked back inside, past the abandoned suitcases and our murmurs of agreement as we rushed to be the first to check if she was alright.

# CHAPTER 18

"**E**ric!"

One afternoon, as I pottered about finding excuses to delay my writing, I turned to see Edward sat by himself at a table in the empty drawing room. The early afternoon sun cast a cool yellow light over him and caught the dust particles that filled the air like a soft powder. On his table was a single glass, a bottle in an ice bucket and a three-tiered stand of finger sandwiches and pretty iced cakes. It looked inexplicably depressing for such a pleasant set-up. Edward was dressed in the usual uniform of white shirt and grey trousers, but they had been immaculately pressed and his beard had been groomed, trimmed close to outline his heavy-set face. His black patent shoes were polished to a mirror.

"Oh, hi Edward," I waved back, telling myself to keep walking past the door and down the corridor into the bar, where I'd planned to fritter away the afternoon. Instead, feeling sorry for the solitary man, I stopped. Edward's lined face stretched into a delighted smile.

"Come, join me!" He gestured enthusiastically to the armchair next to him by the little round coffee table.

"Oh, I'm a bit busy…" I said, assessing how much work I would actually get done at that time of day and simultaneously feeling a pang of guilt. "But what the hell. Alright."

"Excellent!"

I took my place, picking up the white napkin and pressing it into my lap. My papers sat on the windowsill beside us.

"How's the novel coming along?" he asked with genuine interest, glancing at the chaotic wad of notebooks. It was one of the things I liked about the old man; where most people would ask questions and wait for an answer out of obligation, Edward had a glitter in his grey-blue eyes that revealed true interest.

"Good, I think," I said hesitantly. "Well, actually, it was going *very* well for a while, all coming together. Back in Edinburgh I was always getting distracted. It was like I never had the chance to sit down and actually write – there would always be something else I needed to do. Here, I can just get on with it." I frowned in the direction of my work. "But over the past couple of weeks it's gone a bit stale."

"How so?"

"Not sure. It's like the dialogue is stilted and the scenes are getting really two-dimensional. I don't know, like it's losing soul a bit. Does that make any sense?"

"It does," said Edward, nodding.

"Maybe I just need a distraction."

"A distraction sounds like an excellent idea," Edward agreed. "A little break never hurt anyone. It sounds like you just need to have a bit of fun, and with Christmas coming up it's the perfect time for that." He rose to his feet and checked the bottle in the ice bucket. "Now, how's about I get you a glass and a plate so you can join me in afternoon tea properly?"

Glancing at the pink-and-white iced sponges, fat scones that were still steaming a little and the selection of soft sandwiches, I agreed with little resistance.

Edward was gone for longer than I expected, and on his return I could hear him talking loudly with someone from the other end of the corridor. He emerged carrying two extra glasses and two white side plates.

"Look who I found looking lonely by the front door!" He indicated behind him and Henry loped in. The corners of my lips naturally dropped, and I had to make a conscious effort to pull them back up.

"Really, Edward?" Henry sounded flustered. "It's fine, I'm happy to leave you to it."

"Absolutely not!" Edward clapped a hand in Henry's direction, missing him as he jumped back several inches. "I never see you in any of the clubs, and you look so damned miserable all the time! I'm meant to be the manager here. How do you think it reflects on me if folk are unhappy, hmm? Come on, just take a seat with us and enjoy yourself." Reaching his chair, he lowered himself gently into the soft cushions and flexed his knees, which crunched unpleasantly. He sighed deeply. Little indicators of Edward's true age always caught me by surprise; his greyness and stiff limbs were masked by a brightness and a robust physique. "In truth," he looked up a little guiltily, "since Callum and Sandy left, it's me who's been awfully lonely."

"You have the choir," Henry pointed out, glancing at the door behind him as though he was planning to escape. "And Delia, you two are like peas in a pod." There was a bitterness to his tone that I struggled to place.

"Oh, we don't talk in the same way that Callum and Sandy and I used to talk. We'd spend hours here once a week putting the world to rights. It was the highlight of my week!" He lowered his gaze sadly. "And now they're gone. I like to think Sandy will move somewhere warm. He's a gardener by trade, you know? That was what he always missed the most, being here – bright, blossoming gardens. Maybe he'll write to me sometime."

Henry looked hesitantly in my direction before huffing wearily.

"Yes, alright then." Snatching one of the chairs, he pulled it back so that it was several feet away from us, but still within reach of the table.

Edward brightened.

"So, we were just talking about Eric's novel." Reaching forward, he selected a hot scone and began lathering it with jam and cream.

"Is that so?" Henry turned to me, his voice dry. "What's it about?"

"It's complicated," I replied.

"If you ever want it to be published, you'll need to make it less complicated so you can pitch it."

I furrowed my brow, irritated, even though I knew what he was saying was true.

"It's about a young man trying to make something of himself. It's about the decisions he makes and where it gets him."

"Nice and vague. They'll be all over that."

"Piss off."

We stared stonily at each other for a few seconds before realising how absurd we both looked, breaking into an eye-rolling smile. I realised it was the first time I'd seen Henry smile properly. The long, narrow features that I had previously found ugly were pulled into something that could, I supposed, be considered attractive. Edward leaned between us and filled up our glasses.

"Weren't you involved in publishing in some way before you came here?" Edward asked, settling back with his drink in hand. Henry shrugged casually.

"Not publishing as such. I was a contracts lawyer, but I was involved in some publishing contracts and rights, etcetera. The side of things most people find boring. I was a partner in my firm."

"Then what the hell are you doing here working as a doorman?" I couldn't help myself. It made sense in an odd way that Henry had come from wealth and success; he oozed affluence, even in his standard hotel uniform. I could never quite place what that look was, whether it was postural or in his expression, but, whatever it was, it had the ability to make me feel small, inferior.

Henry raised a brow and stiffened slightly.

"I've no idea," he replied curtly, the ebb of warmth I had felt from him vanishing as his features realigned and became pinched and unfriendly.

Edward took over the conversation with well-rehearsed small talk and, despite myself, I started to have a good time. Henry thawed gradually, chipping in and offering insights into the characters that lived in the hotel and the nature of the cliques. He and Edward occasionally laughed at something I didn't understand, but I didn't want to spoil the flow of conversation by asking. Enthralled, I worked my way through a platter of colourful French Fancies and half a bottle of Prosecco before I started to feel flushed from the combination of sugar and alcohol.

I excused myself from the table and went to the bathroom, where I splashed a little cold water against my rosy cheeks and peered at myself in the gilt-framed mirror. Although the same mottled eyes stared back, I noticed that my face was a little softer around my chin and there was a small bulge over the tight waist of my jeans that hadn't been there a few months ago. It didn't help my self-esteem to see a smudge of cream from the French Fancy on the edge of my lips. Licking it away, I neatened my hair and jutted my chin out slightly to try to recover my once prominent jawline. It made me look more confrontational than attractive. I remembered someone who used to push her jaw out like that, a woman I didn't like, the thin woman who wore a bronze badge on her oversized chest. I struggled to recall her name, or how I knew her.

Normally any kind of public bathroom would make me squirm in discomfort and I would make a point not to touch anything, even in friend's bathrooms. However, everything in the hotel smelled fresh and it was clean to the point of sparkling. A selection of hand creams, soaps and scents lined the peach-coloured marble that surrounded the sinks. Rather than feeling grimy, like I usually would, I always left the communal hotel loos feeling fresh and slightly pampered. Selecting one of the glass bottles that was available in each bathroom, I lifted it to my throat and sprayed myself, aware that I was feeling flushed and potentially perspiring a little. Spices and Christmas. I inhaled deeply.

Behind me, in one of the wooden cubicles, a toilet flushed, and one of the barmen, Ricky, approached the sink, nodding to greet me. He scrubbed his surprisingly delicate hands – I had expected bar work would roughen one's hands – before leaning close to me and audibly breathing in, his mouth barely visible beneath his bushy black beard. For a moment, I wondered if I should grow a beard to hide my jowls.

"*Ahh*, peppermint. Lovely. Reminds me of the sweets my gran used to carry in her handbag, God rest her soul."

Before I could query his flawed sense of smell, he waved a hurried goodbye and returned to his post. Frowning, I gave myself a cursory sniff. Definitely Christmas spices.

Back in the drawing room, my glass had been refilled, and Edward and Henry were deep in discussion, gesturing enthusiastically from opposite ends of the table. Henry was smiling cheerfully again. Taking my seat, I leaned over in Henry's direction to pick up my glass.

"What are you talking about?" I asked brightly.

Instead of replying, Henry pushed his chair back with such force that the legs caught the fabric of the rug and shifted the table. The glasses and cake stand wobbled precariously. Clamping a hand over his mouth and nose, he rose to his feet and took several steps back.

"*What?*" I looked from him to Edward. "What did I do?"

Henry waved his free hand at me and continued to retreat.

"Please, just stay away from me." Whipping around, he strode out of the room as quickly as he could without actually running. Bewildered, I turned back to Edward.

"Seriously, what did I do?"

Still leaning back and not looking as perturbed as I would have expected, Edward sighed and rested his hands on the arms of his chair.

"I wouldn't worry about it." Shaking his head, he peered sadly out the window. "You haven't done anything. That's just Henry. He's like that sometimes. It's why I try and include him in things, to make him happier. He used to be a big deal, you know, partner of his law firm, working all day and long into the night. But he was running on fumes; there's only so much a man can do before he breaks." He reached for a violet macaron and held it to his lips. "So, he left it all behind: the career, the family. It's a quieter life for him here, but, as you can see, he still has his moments."

"He gives me the creeps." I drained my glass in one mouthful. "You know, I caught him trying to break into Delia's office."

Edward raised a wiry brow.

"Yeah," I continued. "It was the night after Sandy's story. Everyone else had gone to bed and he was picking the lock. And there was something else—" I stopped and swore under my breath as I watched Henry trudge through the snow outside the window, carrying a spade. "He's doing it again!"

Jumping to my feet and clunking my glass on the table, I rushed past a bemused Edward, whose lips were parted slightly as he delayed biting into his macaron.

# CHAPTER 19

I opened my mouth to shout at Henry, who I had followed outside, but stopped when I heard his deep, shuddering sobs. He crouched low on the ground, digging his spade into the snow at the same spot by the side of the hotel, just below my bedroom window.

"Henry?" I lowered my voice to a gentler level, trying to hide my uncertainty as best I could. It seemed absurd that I couldn't recall the last time I had seen a man cry; it made me inexplicably uncomfortable. "Henry, what's wrong?"

His spade crunched into the snow and he turned round, looking at me with bloodshot eyes, his chest rapidly rising and falling.

"She'll never stop." His voice was barely audible above the breeze. "She'll never let me go. She'll never leave me alone, no matter how hard I try." He sniffed loudly and let out another trembling sob. Tentatively, I moved forward and looked at the shallow hole he had dug in the snow. Inside, caked in ice, were multiple glass perfume bottles. Henry dipped a shaking hand into his pocket and pulled out another one, the same glass bottle of scent I had used in the bathroom. He lowered it gently into the hole, taking care not to let it chink against any of the others. Then he began filling the hole up again.

"There was a time when I just threw them in the bin," he babbled, "but she must check the bins, because they would reappear almost immediately – even the ones in my bedroom, as though she'd crept in at night and left one of them by my sink, or by my bed. Once, she even left one on my pillow right next to me as I slept." He patted the ground flat, breathless from the exertion. "Then I tried smashing them or emptying them outside in the snow, but the smell would fill the air. It would follow me inside and find me, and then I would be back to square one again. It's like we're trapped in a bubble and it fills the space around us if we let it out. The only way is to bury them."

"What are you talking about?" I took a step towards him, causing him to jump and brandish his spade warningly.

"Don't come any closer!" He clenched his jaw. "If you do, you'll ruin everything for me – I've done so well this time!"

"Alright!" I stopped and held up my hands. The wildness in his eyes was diluted with something I recognised, something terribly sad and desperate. "Why don't you put down the spade and we can—"

"What did you smell?" he demanded.

"What?"

"What. Did. You. Smell?" he repeated, isolating each word.

"From where?"

"From the bottle. The ones she keeps in the bathrooms, the ones she gives as gifts."

"Oh," I hesitated. "I suppose it's kind of spicy, smells a bit like Christmas."

"And what does that smell remind you of?"

"Delia, it's her scent."

"No, before Delia – what did it remind you of *before* you met her?" He waved his spade wildly as he spoke.

"I'm not sure – Christmas, obviously?" I paused to think. "It makes me think of an old girlfriend of mine, especially at Christmas – not *her* scent per se, but she was always lighting cinnamon candles and putting out little burners – and when we went skiing, we would go to the same chalet with her family and it smelled of mulled wine." I smiled, hoping my babbling would have a calming effect on Henry. "They were the kind of people who used the word 'winter' as a verb." My light laugh sounded false. "And—" I hesitated, feeling a sudden longing. "I suppose there's something in there that reminds me a bit of my mum. She wore a perfume I could never quite place but I think that's it in there."

"Hold on to those memories for as long as you can," Henry hissed. "Because soon you'll forget them and all you'll be left with is *her*, and you'll think it's *her* who makes you feel so warm and loved, but it's not. It's just how she gets you." His voice lowered further. "She'll never let you leave."

"I don't want to leave, I'm her boyfriend." I could feel the hairs on my neck rising in the cold.

"Really? And where is your *girlfriend* now?"

"She's away at the hotel awards ceremony."

Henry smirked unpleasantly and shook his head.

"How can a hotel that never has any guests win an award?"

"It's remote," I snapped. "Guests can't access it in winter."

"For Christ's sake, Eric, it's *always* winter." Henry propped the spade against his shoulder and crunched past me – still keeping a wide berth – to return to the hotel. "You know, I tried to help you back when you first left the hotel. When she was demanding to know where you had gone, I kept my mouth shut and hoped that I bought enough time for you to get away – you *could* have left. Maybe you still can. But let me assure you of one thing, Eric. Things are going to get worse for you." He said this without looking back. "And by then, you won't even realise it's happening."

"If you hate it here so much, why don't you just leave?" I shouted after him.

Henry paused to glance back, and we stood still, allowing the snow to swirl around our bodies, shivering in our thin, matching shirts.

"You try leaving and tell me how it goes for you."

As he turned, I hurried to catch up with him, my brogues soaked through to my socks.

"Well, what does it smell like for you?" I asked, ensuring to keep my distance. "The perfume?"

"Strawberries." He stared steadfastly ahead. "It's what my children smelled of."

As I followed him back towards the hotel, I glanced to one of the windows and was certain I had seen Delia and Edward standing side by side, looking out at us. That couldn't be right. Just as quickly, the white glare of the sun caught the glass and they vanished, leaving me staring at my own distant reflection.

# CHAPTER 20

A bit light-headed from the boozy afternoon tea, I stumbled up the stairs, where I intended to spend the remainder of the day, in bed. I knew it would put me out of sync for the following day, but there was nothing I needed to be up early for.

As I stepped onto my floor, I was surprised to find that the jute rug had been covered by a long strip of white canvas, the kind used by painters and decorators. There was a strong chemical scent that caused my eyes to sting as I walked unsteadily in the direction of my room. The normally cream walls were a patchy white and glistened as though they had only recently been painted. My bedroom door was open, with the floor covered in the same white canvas, and all my furniture was pushed up against the walls, protected by dustcovers, as Collin and Neil from maintenance stooped over the skirting boards, sanding furiously, the air filled with a million tiny particles.

"What the hell?" I felt the alcohol ignite my outrage. My cheeks burned furiously, and I stormed over to my bedside table and pulled open the drawer with more force than was necessary. My minimal belongings were still in place.

Collin and Neil glanced uncertainly at each other.

"Um, did you not see the noticeboard?" Collin rose to his feet and dusted off his overalls. His mouth was concealed by a bushy black beard, but I could tell he was concerned from his furrowed brow. Collin was the kind of man who looked like he had always worked in maintenance.

"No, I didn't see the *staff* noticeboard," I replied pointedly, clutching my manuscript to my chest, as though I was frightened one of them might snatch it off me. I turned to my bed in the corner, wanting nothing more than to pull off the dust cover and crawl inside. Despite my outrage, my eyelids were beginning to droop heavily.

"Delia put out instructions for this floor to be touched up. Wants to keep it fresh for guests and the like," Collin said gently. From the way his nostrils twitched I knew he could smell the alcohol and was pandering to me. "The notice has been up four weeks now – just assumed you'd know. I'm sorry you didn't. But it'll look all the better once it's done." He gestured to the skirting boards and seamlessly changed the direction of the conversation. "Stripping off these layers of paint is a nightmare. Teach us for just putting on a fresh coat every time we were asked, aye Neil?"

"Aye."

"Well, where am I supposed to go?" For a moment I was clenched by the awful prospect of being sent away. I wondered if Delia had seen how lazy I had become and grown tired of me as I languished at her expense, the ever-aspiring author. "Is this Delia's way of saying she wants me gone?"

Both Collin and Neil laughed heartily.

"Don't be daft." Collin shook his head, smiling beneath his facial hair. Rummaging in the pocket of his overalls, he pulled out a folded piece of paper and scanned it briefly. "Room twenty-four," he said eventually. "That's where you'll be staying while the work's done. It's the same floor as my room. It's unlocked, key's in the door and housekeeping have done the rounds, so it should all be nice and ready for you. That alright?"

"If you're not happy, you could speak to Delia about it when she's back from those hotel awards?" Neil added, trying to be helpful. "We're just doing our job."

I frowned at him.

"I think I saw her earlier today – through the window."

"Not due back until Christmas, I'm afraid." Collin was beginning to look a little embarrassed for me. "Christ, that's tomorrow, isn't it? Time flies in this place."

Room twenty-four was located at the other end of the building. I had to walk up a winding flight of stairs and was mortified to find myself perspiring by the time I reached the top. The maze-like nature of the hotel never failed to take me by surprise. I reached a door on the landing which led into a surprisingly narrow and windowless corridor. The floor was carpeted with a faded green-and-red tartan, and I paused to consider stroppily that this floor was far more in need of a touch-up than my one. There were six doors, five with numbers on them and one with a toilet symbol. I grimaced at the door to the toilet, hoping it wasn't shared.

As advised, number twenty-four was unlocked, and the heavy wooden door creaked open into a space that, to my relief, was only slightly smaller than my room. However, all the proportions seemed off, as though nothing had been properly thought out when it was being decorated. The narrow window was up against a dividing wall, as though it had once been one large window in one large room and the wall had been built to split the space in two. None of the furniture matched; it was all antique wardrobes and chests in proportions and varnishing that didn't go together. A grand four-poster bed swamped the room, though it had been neatly made with scratchy tartan throws that matched the carpet both here and in the corridor. It had been bleached in a long line where the sun shone through the window and stripped the room of any former vibrance. Huffing irritably, I sat down on the edge of the hard mattress, next to a bedside table holding an electric kettle and a tray of instant coffee sachets and tea packets. It wouldn't be as nice as the coffee I had brought up to me from the machine, but I supposed it would do, and, at the very least, I reckoned I would be grateful for instant access to caffeine the following morning when I eventually woke up. Despite its dated and frayed appearance, the room was clean and filled with the scent of polish and the air freshener housekeeping used, that pleasantly spicy gingerbread scent. Just like Christmas.

Stripping off my clothes, I crawled beneath the sheets, which had the uncomfortable cold feeling of a bed that had been made a long time ago and never slept in, almost damp, but not quite.

# CHAPTER 21

My father had always been a big drinker, but in the best kind of way. He was the sort of drinker who became increasingly jolly and was considered the life and soul of any Friday and Saturday night down the local pub. His friends would orbit his warm glow and smile at the pleasant boom of his voice, regardless of what he was saying. When he came home smelling strongly of his night out, waking me up with his clumsy entrance and a cheeriness that deflected the frowns of my mother, he would drown me in warm, beer-fumed hugs.

My mother didn't drink very much in my early childhood. She'd been the kind of woman who enjoyed a small gin and tonic at the end of the day to wind down. Even at neighbourhood parties she would nurse her drink for the best part of the evening. She told me when she was older that she didn't feel comfortable being drunk around me when she was the only responsible one around, which was often. Back then, I thought what she meant was when my father was at work, when really she meant all the time. It wasn't until I was older, perhaps in my early teens, that I noticed her drinking habits change. Unlike my father, she didn't drink because she was happy or sociable. She drank quietly and sadly, and the following day she would bear the tell-tale signs, the glistening grey sheen of a hangover, which only caused her to drink earlier each day to mask it. She didn't want me to know about it, and she would claim that the bottles were for cooking, although I didn't recall alcohol being used for fry-ups, sandwiches or stir-fries. Her mild manner became more abrupt, and sometimes she would say things at neighbourhood events that made people look uncomfortable and caused whispers to ripple through the suburban gaggles. My father would be mortified and apologise to our family friends. They would tell him that it wasn't his fault, and sometimes they would feign concern for my mother's wellbeing, but they never looked deeper than the fact that she was drinking too much. Nobody ever asked her why she didn't smile or laugh anymore. My father only confronted her about it when standards in the house began to slip and he would come home to a pile of dishes in the sink or a basketful of dirty laundry. He told her he was working all day and he didn't have the time to take care of the housework as well. For a while, that had seemed like a reasonable statement, and I had made it clear that I agreed with my father. I still recalled the look in her eye when I confirmed my allegiance and it made me want to take it back at once, but of course it was too late. Besides, my father was proud of me for standing by him. Years after she passed, when I asked my father why he treated her that way, he patted my back and told me solemnly that although she had been a good mother, she wasn't a particularly good wife.

I woke up on Christmas morning with the bitter taste of the night before coating my tongue and teeth in an unpleasant, gritty film. I had inherited my mother's predisposition for debilitating hangovers. My hand travelled up to my throbbing temples and I groaned audibly. Unlike my father, I wasn't able to get going with my day after heavy drinking. He had always sprung out of bed and any residual symptoms were cured by a hearty breakfast. Even the thought of food made my stomach lurch. He would have laughed heartily and mocked my weakness; "The stamina of a woman," I imagined him chuckling.

I wondered if my father had tried to call to wish me a Merry Christmas. He normally did, along with birthdays, and a small part of me hoped that he was worried about me.

There was no bathroom in the bedroom, but there was an old sink where I could splash my face with cold water and drink from the little glass that had been left for me on the porcelain. After three glasses, I made myself an instant coffee and threw on a clean dressing gown that had been left on a door hook. As I opened the door and peered out, the bedroom door opposite mine also opened and Henry stepped into frame with an infuriatingly smug expression. He was dressed immaculately in his pressed white shirt and grey trousers. His face lacked the wide-eyed hysteria of the previous day; he looked composed and refined, as though nothing had happened.

"Well, you were demoted pretty rapidly." He hesitated, mid-smirk. "Although saying that, I have no idea how long you've even been here. Time flies when you're having fun!" He lifted his own mug of coffee in a mocking cheers gesture. "Merry Christmas, by the way."

"Shut up," I snapped. "My floor's being refurbished. This is temporary." Reluctantly, I lifted my own mug to return the gesture. "Merry Christmas."

"Looking forward to the party?"

"Sure." I gestured to the bathroom door. "Is it a communal bathroom, by the way?"

"I'm afraid so. But don't worry, it's very clean." He pointed at the door at the other end of the corridor. "And we have our own communal living space. Everyone on this floor is relatively friendly, if you like that kind of company."

Before I could reply, another head popped through a door. Rob from housekeeping was grinning broadly and holding up a glass of what appeared to be Buck's Fizz. He looked enviably fresh.

"Delia's back!" He declared brightly.

I pulled on my clothes from the previous day and hurried down the stairs. Reaching the front of the building, I peered over the landing at the bustling men in grey and white, clinking glasses of orange juice and Champagne and hugging one another. In the midst of it all was a flash of red as Delia held up her own glass and wished everyone a Merry Christmas, smile glittering, her voice hovering above the buzz of excitement. As her gaze travelled and settled on me, her expression softened, and she gestured for me to join her.

I watched her for several moments before reacting. She seemed to move in slow motion before me, red silk shimmering as it skimmed her body. I wondered where she had been, why she would have been away in an outfit like that, but it didn't feel appropriate to ask.

"Oh, *Eric!*" she exclaimed, waving excitedly. "I've missed you. How have things been?"

"Yeah, good," I replied. "I've missed you too. I thought I saw you yesterday."

"You must really have been pining for me!" Laughing airily, she held out an arm to embrace me. As I approached, her nose wrinkled in distaste. "My God, Eric. Heavy night?"

I shrugged sheepishly.

"You smell horrendous." She rolled her eyes, although maintained her smile. "You'll need to get sorted out for the party tonight. Why don't you get showered and ask laundry to give you some fresh clothes? I think whatever you're wearing has seen better days."

I glanced down at the stretched buttons of my shirt and the faded jeans before nodding shamefully in agreement. Another flash of colour appeared behind Delia in the crowd of white and grey. A man I didn't recognise approached us. The door of the public bathroom swung shut behind him and he patted his wet hands on tight black jeans. He was younger than everyone else, with shaggy blonde hair that had quite clearly been meticulously styled to look that way. His oversized fluorescent jumper was decorated with cartoonish lightning bolts, frayed and faded so perfectly it suggested he'd paid extra for it to look like that. I watched his great, stomping boots leave wet marks on the slate floor and caught a number of staff glancing irritably at him.

"Alright, mate?" He nodded casually. I found myself surprised at how clipped his very London accent was, completely at odds with his appearance. I recognised men like him from my past, the cocky type with the self-assured swagger who resented the fact that they had never struggled for anything in life, because if they had then it might give them some depth of character. I realised that I was still staring. The young man cocked his brow in bemusement. A small silver stud in his eyebrow glimmered in the light of the chandelier above.

"Yeah, good thanks," I replied, just a fraction too late for it to sound genuine, extending my hand. "I'm Eric."

"Ollie," he replied briefly before turning back to Delia. "Dee, it's been a long night. Mind if I go grab us a coffee?"

*Dee*. I bristled. It seemed almost offensive.

"Of course not." Delia smiled brightly. "Help yourself."

Once Ollie had wandered away, I did my best to hide my frown.

"Who's that?"

"Ollie," she replied. "Nice, isn't he? Dresses awfully unusually!"

"Um, yeah."

"Anyway, please make him feel welcome. I have a million and one things to do before this party, so would you mind if I shoot off?" She planted a kiss on my cheek. "See you tonight!"

As she swept out of sight, I was left standing among the gaggle of uniformed men with my mouth hanging slightly open, poised to ask "And what the fuck is he doing here?"

# CHAPTER 22

"Well, don't you look dapper?"

I swivelled round to see Henry stepping away from his position against the wall, where he was nursing a small glass of Champagne. He had an unpleasant habit of appearing rather than approaching. The bar was still relatively quiet, as the party didn't properly start for another ten minutes. The decorations had changed from previous parties. The bushy pine tree dripped with what looked like glass and shards of silver, glimmering like icicles against the smattering of delicate, white fairy lights, and the walls were lined with deep-green holly that had been pinned securely over the cornicing and around the bay window, which looked out into the snow-storm. Each table in the bar boasted a large bouquet of frosted pinecones and leafy foliage within which were subtle flashes of crimson berries. Silver rather than gold this year. There was something claustrophobic about it, with the clutter of decorations and the way the storm swirled threateningly around us.

Acknowledging the fact that Henry wasn't complimenting me, I glanced down at the nicely fitting grey trousers and white shirt and shrugged. I felt considerably better after a hot shower and a few glasses of celebratory Champagne up in the communal living area on my new floor. Other than Henry, the men on the floor were friendly and had practically strong-armed me into joining them, which I was glad for. The living room was dated like the rest of our corridor, but pleasantly so. The worn leather furniture was comfortable, and the lamps gave the room a cosy glow that disguised most of the wear and tear. They had a proper coffee machine, their own record collection and I even spotted a couple of books tucked away in among some old, dusty ornaments. When I asked where the men had found the books, Collin told me that he had them in his rucksack when he came to the hotel. Apparently, he had been on a poorly planned mission of self-discovery when he met Delia in one of the nearby towns and she had offered him a job. All his belongings were now gathering dust in the communal room.

"New clothes?" Henry persisted, stepping closer towards me.

"Yeah, mine were dirty."

"I see." He nodded slowly, examining the room carefully, as though registering everyone's position. "You know, you look just like one of us now." He gestured at his own white shirt and grey trousers. "Like I say, you barely notice it until it's too late. Have you seen the new chap? Ollie?"

"I have." I gritted my teeth, keen to move away from him and join the small gathering who were ordering drinks at the bar and cheering noisily over the tinkling Christmas music.

"At first I thought he was very young, but then I realised that it's just because I've grown so much older. I think I was his age when I first came here."

"I guess he got a job here or something." I shrugged. "You always get young folk working in hotels."

Lowering his voice, Henry's eyes skittered from side to side.

"He's going to replace you, Eric, *can't you see that?*"

"Go away." I stepped back. Henry retreated with little encouragement, leaning back against the wall where he could survey the gradually increasing crowd. Marching away from him, I fixed my smile in place and wished everyone around me a Merry Christmas. One of the waiters hurried over to me to top up my glass before I had even taken my last mouthful.

Looking around at the identically dressed and well-groomed men, I couldn't help but wish that I stood out at least a little.

Although I had never taken any interest in fashion, I had always stood out among the crowd. I had been good-looking enough to wear jeans that were selected for comfort over appearance and twee woollen jumpers that would have looked ridiculous on most men. As I pictured one those jumpers in my head, I recalled a pleasant voice saying "You look like a model for Fair Isle jumpers." The voice had an irritating squeakiness to it, but it made me feel good about myself. "Perhaps I'll knit you another one." For a second, I saw a face, smattered with freckles and wisps of curly blonde hair, but as quickly as the image came to me it was gone again. For just a second I felt warm and secure, but I was left unsure why.

Touching my wrist, I realised that my watch was still in my old bedroom on the first floor. I figured that the tan leather strap and large blue face would complement the grey and white nicely, and perhaps allow me to stand out in the crowd, even just a little. I placed my glass on the bar and made my way to the first floor, excusing myself as I squeezed past the bustling party-goers who were swarming down towards the bar. I would need to be quick to catch Delia when she arrived, before everyone else tried to engage her in conversation. It was the downside to her being such an approachable employer.

On my floor, I was pleased to see that the skirting boards had been fully stripped and smoothed. The unpleasant smell of paint stripper had been replaced by the fresh paint smell that always made a space feel brand new. As I approached my bedroom door, I noticed that it was slightly ajar and I peered curiously inside, keen to see what work had been done. I was surprised to see that nothing had changed, and that the dustcovers had been removed from the furniture, which was no longer pressed up against the walls. Instead, it was positioned back in appropriate places, but not the spots I recalled. The bed was pressed against the wall on the other side of the room, and my armchairs and coffee table had been turned around to create an intimate cluster around the window.

Sat in my armchair, Ollie gazed contentedly out the window. His large boots were propped up on my coffee table, a gesture that seemed so obnoxious to me that I couldn't help letting out a displeased gasp. Becoming aware of my presence, he turned round and raised his pierced brow.

"Oh, hey mate. Can I help you with something?"

Unable to reply, I stumbled back from the door and out into the landing. As more of the staff bustled by me, I became caught up in the flow of grey and white traffic until I found myself back in the bar. Suddenly, everything looked unpleasant to me; the diamond glimmer dazed me and the sharp glass icicles on the tree looked menacing rather than elegant. The Christmas music that had seemed to tinkle so delicately before was now ricocheting in my ears, making me disorientated. The mild claustrophobia that I had felt earlier became suffocating as the cluttered room and the rumble of the storm began to close in on me, leaving me breathless and flustered. Lurching forward, I reached for my glass where I had left it and tossed the contents into my mouth. I waited less than a minute before the dutiful waiter noticed and refilled it. Nearby, Henry watched me closely.

# CHAPTER 23

When the call for dinner was made, I found myself jostled along with the excitable crowd that filtered through the dining room door like cattle. At the head, Delia oozed red silk across the floor, and Ollie, who had arrived late for drinks, walked by her side, still wearing his absurdly tight trousers and frayed jumper. There was a rush to get the best seats – in other words, the seats surrounding Delia's place at the head of the table. The staff bustled, not quite running as they pretended they weren't competing, but when they did get a prime seat, they lit up triumphantly and staked their claim by planting themselves firmly in place. I found myself near the end of the table, feeling very much apart from the excitement that buzzed noisily around me.

Although the food was undeniably delicious, each mouthful lodged in my throat, and when I eventually managed to swallow, it sat heavy and uncomfortable in my stomach. Instead, I drank. When I tried to join in the conversation at my end of the table, gesturing as I spoke, I ended up knocking over a glass and spraying red wine over the tablecloth, some of it splattering over white shirts. Everyone was nice about it, but they made biting comments, including "Well, Christmas is a time to enjoy yourself," and "Perhaps Eric is enjoying himself a little too much," followed by a hearty laugh to mask their disapproval. I flushed with embarrassment and stopped speaking altogether. I sat in silence, scowling in my party hat.

I watched Ollie closely as he sat next to Delia at the head of the table. His voice carried all the way to my end, a confident bass that made me hate him even more. When Delia excused herself from the table to check on the kitchen, I watched him wipe away his thin layer of civility as he addressed the men around him.

"Oh yeah, the city's great," he said, poorly concealing the fact that he was bragging to us. "I switch up my time between Edinburgh and London – it's exhausting though. No time for relationships or anything like that, but that's the great thing about the nightlife." He winked. "You don't need one when the options are limitless."

There was nervous laughter as the men agreed uncertainly, not entirely sure what response was appropriate. One of them asked why he had come so far north, in an attempt to change the subject, but his response was just as inappropriate.

"Delia gave me a great opportunity. Also, between you and me, got myself in a spot of bother with a girl." He lowered his voice as though he was sharing a secret with us, all like-minded men. "I'm just letting the dust settle for now." Sighing wearily, he shrugged his shoulders. "People have these expectations of you even when you make it crystal clear that you're only after a bit of fun, you know?"

"What happened?" one of the men asked, his eyes twinkling with intrigue.

Ollie paused to assess the table, his knowing smirk toying with us, as though gauging whether we were worthy of his trust and gossip. I hated the way we all leaned in eagerly, enthralled.

"Sophie Stein." He sighed, as though the sound of the name itself displeased him. "I knew her vaguely from nights out and such. She was one of these 'cool' girls, you know the type? Makes out like everything is just a bit of fun, very trendy – hung out in a group of clones, the kind you find in clubs that vet their clientele. Pretty tacky if you ask me."

I got the feeling that Ollie was completely unaware of the irony of his criticism.

"So, we hook up casually a few times, and as far as I'm concerned that's the end of it. And then I start a thing with a couple of her friends – a few of them maybe, you know how it is. All very casual, I should remind you." His eyes rolled. "Anyway, how was I supposed to know that she was a big client of the company I worked for? I'd only just started as well, so the whole thing was pretty awkward. You know you can't have it both ways – you can't pretend to be all cool and casual and then get upset about not being 'respected.' Genuinely, I don't even know what she meant by that." Shrugging, he emptied his glass. "Anyway, just as things were getting heated, Delia shows up at one of these conferences and we get talking. She made me the kind of offer that guys at my stage can only dream of, so it all worked out just fine."

Later, as we moved through to the living room, I could see Delia smiling and twirling excitedly as she pointed at various features of the hotel. Ollie stood by her side, nodding and feigning interest in the building's history. Hoping he would notice, I narrowed my eyes furiously in his direction, wondering if he considered her to be one of his "limitless options."

As Delia approached the fireplace, she began to tell Ollie about our storytelling tradition. He smiled mockingly before realising she wasn't kidding.

The coffees and gingerbread men were brought out as we settled into our chairs, winding down for the evening. I managed to push past one of the men to get the seat closest to Delia and Ollie. Delia was talking about music I had never heard of before, and Ollie was nodding along, making a strange "Yah, yah" sound in his deep, baritone voice, which didn't match his appearance. Without looking, he reached over the coffee table to the saucers sitting side by side and picked up my gingerbread man, not his. As he went to lift it to his lips, I intercepted him and snatched it from his hand. It snapped in my grip.

"That's mine!"

Ollie glanced at the two saucers on the table, realising his mistake, but instead of apologising he laughed at me in a way that made me feel small and insignificant.

"Alright." As he shrugged, I felt myself prickle with rage.

"No, it's *not* alright." I caught Delia frowning uncertainly at me and I turned my attention to her. "Why are you doing this, Delia?" I demanded, my voice cracking and coming out an octave too high.

"What do you mean, Eric?" Her voice oozed in comparison with mine, filled with a silky calm that made me sound louder and more erratic.

"You leave for ages and don't get in touch, then you come back, and you've barely spoken to me – and you've got him in tow! Why is he even here?" I swung round furiously to face Ollie again. "You took my room, you little prick."

"Woah, woah, *woah*." Ollie raised his hands in a surrendering gesture. "Mate, I don't know exactly what you think is going on here, but—"

"No, Ollie." Delia silenced him by placing a hand on his arm and looking at me with an expression I found impossible to read. "Eric." Her voice took on a familiar lull. I felt suddenly aware of all the eyes in the room upon me, and I shrank back, mortified. "Ollie's an interior designer. While I was away at the awards, I met with some representatives from the council to secure funding for a revamp of the hotel. There's a big push to improve tourism in this area, so they've been offering grants to local businesses." Her smile was pitying, and I hated her for making me feel so small. "Ollie has experience with hotel refurbishments in the city. He's leaving his old company and trying to set up his own business, so I decided to take a chance on him. He spent the day measuring up the rooms – the first floor is the first part of the project, since they're the most expensive rooms."

I opened my mouth but found no retort.

"Look, mate," Ollie smiled uneasily, "I finished measuring up your room today. We could always just leave it until last, or get it done first. Whatever suits you, just to get you back in there as soon as possible, if that's okay with Delia?"

I burned with humiliation, feeling like a monstrous toddler, my gaze falling to the floor.

"No, no," I shook my head. "I'm sorry, I don't know what got into me. I drank too much, Ollie. I'm sorry." My eyes travelled uncertainly up to face Delia, where I felt the real apology was due. "Delia, I'm so sorry."

She stared at me, expressionless for several seconds, which made me wonder if she was about to unleash her temper on me, but instead she smiled serenely.

"No harm done." Leaning forward, she touched my shoulder gently and lowered her voice just enough so that everyone could still hear us. "Maybe lay off the drink tonight, alright?"

I lowered my head again, mortified as I withered in my chair. Nearby, Henry was staring at me intently, with wide eyes and a clenched jaw. I glared at him hatefully for planting doubts in my mind.

"Alright, everyone, enough of these sombre faces!" Delia clapped her hands as though breaking a spell. Everyone visibly relaxed, and the low, familiar buzz of the party began to stir. "It's Christmas!"

A cheer erupted.

"How's about a story?" Tucking herself into her armchair, she surveyed the room. "Any volunteers?"

To my surprise, Henry thrust his hand into the air, his pale forehead glistening with nervous perspiration.

"Henry!" Delia looked mildly surprised, but clapped her hands and gestured for him to take his position. Henry approached, beckoned closer by the lick of the flames that danced in the hearth. Lifting his tumbler, he took a swig of thick, honey-coloured liquid before clunking it down next to his untouched coffee and gingerbread man. He appeared to swill the liquid around his mouth as he approached the beckoning fire. His gaze met Delia's, and although she was still smiling broadly, I could have sworn that I saw her eyes narrow.

"This will be your first story, won't it, Henry?"

Without replying, he took his place, and glanced briefly at me, before inhaling a deep, trembling breath. As he exhaled, his jaw loosened, and all trace of nervous energy drifted away in a long, calming breath. Instead of the hunched and evasive man who scuttled around like he had something to hide, I saw Henry for what he was. Henry the former lawyer was a tall man, entirely at ease with his own presence. His self-assured voice filled the room and commanded attention. The men swivelled their bodies round to face him, immediately drawn in, as we watched the transformation. The narrow features that had made him appear sly and untrustworthy were now refined and intelligent.

As his arms extended and his spine straightened, he looked at me directly, and, with the slightest hint of sarcasm, he said, "Once upon a time there was a prison surrounded by snow..."

I held my breath and glanced from side to side, as though awaiting an ambush. Whatever it was, it was no bedtime story that he was about to tell.

# CHAPTER 24:

## THE WITCH'S CAGE

Once upon a time there was a prison surrounded by snow. One night, inside the walls of this prison, four men sat in a pool of pale, silver light, the moon shining in through the window and illuminating the polished bar. The four men planned to escape that night.

At first glance, it didn't appear like a prison. It was nothing like the prisons you know from stories, or on the television. The only bars in this prison were lined with drinks and packets of salted nuts. The prison boasted a grand dining room and luxurious bedrooms, with every physical need of the prisoners meticulously catered to. The prisoners were offered a full menu each night, from which they could choose meals cooked by professional chefs, and during the day the dining room was lined with cakes and biscuits, which the prisoners could help themselves to whenever they liked. Parties and events were commonplace, and the prisoners were almost always smiling. You could be forgiven for thinking that the prisoners had everything they could ever want. But it was all a lie. Secretly, the prisoners were all desperately unhappy, even if they didn't really know it yet.

That night, the four men were silent, looking out the window at the fast-moving snow clouds. The clouds moved with the force of the violent gale, causing the moonlight to flicker, as though the building was surrounded by hundreds of emergency vehicles with flashing lights. Of course, the roads were inaccessible, and it was far too quiet for there to be any kind of commotion outside.

There were four empty glasses on the bar. It was supposed to have been a toast to wish them luck, but really it was to give them courage.

The barman sighed and looked pensively at the glasses which, up until that point, nobody had wanted to acknowledge were empty. The small group shared a lasting look and nodded their heads. Gathering their jackets and bags, they moved quietly towards the glass-panelled side door, which was largely unused. One of the men, quivering in fear, stepped forward and slipped a key from his pocket. They had agreed that it would be unwise to use any of the main doors, including those at the front and back of the building, since the warden was prone to wandering the prison at night. The side door creaked open on rusted hinges, its old panels rattling, unused to movement. Outside, a heavy snowfall masked the landscape, and thick snow clouds muffled the sky, silencing even the winter gale. The weather had become worse in the years the men had been imprisoned.

The frightened man hesitated, pulling back from the door and shaking his head. He looked to his friends and told them that something was wrong, yet when they pressed him he couldn't say why. One of his friends, the one with the shock of bright-red hair, gripped his shoulders and told him not to give into his fear. Maintaining his grip, he guided the frightened man out of the glass doors.

The frightened man shook his head, pulling away from his friend and stepping back inside the building. The key quivered in his extended hand.

"I'm telling you, *something is wrong*," he whispered. "I can feel it."

Ushering the other two outside, the red-haired man approached his trembling friend.

"Can you *see* something wrong? *Hear* it? *Smell* it?" he hissed, snatching his friend's lapel. "The weather is just going to get worse. This is our last chance." Taking a deep breath, he said, "Don't give up now – not when we're so close. Don't be a coward."

"Leave him be." One of the other men hurriedly tried to reason with him. "If he doesn't want to come, that's fine. We're not forcing anyone to do this. Let's get moving."

The man continued to grasp his friend's lapel for several seconds, looking at him pleadingly, before releasing his hold on him.

"Fine." He waved his hand. "You stay then."

Marching into the darkness, the red-haired man took one final glance back, nodding his head in what he hoped was not their final goodbye.

The frightened man stood by the door, watching his friends become smaller and smaller as they walked through the snow into the distance. He hesitated. A small voice inside him begged for him to run after them all, desperately trying to convince him that it really was just cowardice holding him back. However, he couldn't shake the prickling sensation that something was very wrong, and he paused to consider what was causing him to feel so ill at ease. Peering into the darkness, it dawned on him. They were being watched.

Throwing his rucksack to the ground, he fumbled with his torch and took a step outside, ready to signal to his friends to come back.

"Help me."

A small, feminine voice caught his attention from the direction of the woodshed. He moved towards the voice before hearing it giggle, a nasty little laugh that indicated no requirement for help; if anything, it betrayed a trap. Retreating, he realised that whatever lingered by the woodshed would bring him only harm. Up ahead, he caught a glimpse of movement in the darkness, something flashing across one of the distant beams from the torchlight. It wasn't the movement of his friends but a slight, dark shadow that flitted across his line of sight and vanished as quickly as he had spotted it. His friends continued moving forward, unaware of what was happening around them. There was more than one shadowy figure, and they began flitting around the group of three, increasing in number and approaching carefully so as not to be noticed. Too frightened to make a sound, he carefully closed the door, twisting the key and locking it from the inside. He sank to the floor, back pressed against the door, and turned away, clenching his eyes shut, unable to look at what was happening outside.

They later said that all three men had succumbed to the cold, having taken an ill-advised walking trip. They had crumpled into the snow with expressions so peacefully frozen in place that, when they were eventually found, no one would ever suspect that they had been fleeing in terror.

# CHAPTER 25

Henry drained the remainder of his tumbler and stepped away from the fire. It took us several moments to realise that he had finished his story, and we continued to stare at him, no applause or reaction of any sort. Without another word, Henry snatched a decanter from the shelf and refilled his glass before striding out of the room, his head held high. We continued to sit in uncomfortable silence, hoping that it was all part of the performance and that Henry would return for the grand finale. Eventually, as we realised he was gone, Delia spoke.

"Well, that was disappointing." She sighed and turned to Ollie. "Normally the stories are much better. That one had no structure, no plot, nothing. A real pity, actually. I expected better from Henry."

Thankfully, our uneasiness was short lived; none of us seemed able to articulate why the story had made us so uncomfortable, and we quickly settled back into the party spirit. I was quietly relieved that the attention had turned to Henry; it seemed as though my drunken outburst had been forgotten. The record player began to play music I didn't recognise and everyone brightened, some men getting to their feet and swaying to the rhythm, merry smiles on their flushed faces. I watched as Delia fixed her gaze on the door through which Henry had left only minutes prior, her brow furrowed in displeasure, as though she was deep in thought. When she caught me looking, her expression switched to a bright smile. Her hand reached over to

Ollie's untouched gingerbread man. She slipped it between her lips and bit off the head, maintaining her smile the entire time.

# CHAPTER 26

As I settled down to sleep that night – my bed thankfully no longer felt damp, an electric heater having been left on all day to pump out a dry heat – I tried to reassure myself that the refurbishment could only be a good thing. It seemed absurd that I felt anxious about it, since it would serve to bring in guests and more money for us. Strangely, I found myself saddened by the prospect of change; although my new bedroom would inevitably be grander and more luxurious, I liked it just the way it was. As I debated raising this with Delia, I reminded myself that, as I didn't technically own the hotel, I shouldn't comment.

I began to wonder, if I were to marry Delia, would the business become half mine? I wasn't entirely sure what the law of matrimony was. Maybe I'd ask Henry. If so, perhaps I could have more of a say over what was going on and I wouldn't find myself relegated to the staff quarters. As her husband, I would never have to sit at the end of the table; I would have my place beside her at every dinner party and event, while the staff observed us enviously. We could leave Edward in charge of the hotel and do whatever we wanted. We could travel to hot countries and eat fresh seafood in restaurants overlooking the ocean, glowing from the heat of the sun, our hands intertwined over the table, our voices becoming lost in the crashing waves.

As I drifted into a pleasant dream, I found myself abruptly awoken by a soft knocking outside my bedroom door. Convinced it was Henry skulking about, I swung out of bed and strode to the door, preparing myself for a confrontation. Realising that it wasn't my door that was being knocked, I opened it a crack and peered out to see Delia, her curled fist rapping on Henry's door. She had changed into her long, peach dressing gown, and her dark hair had been unpinned so that it tumbled down her back.

"Delia?"

Jumping in fright, she pressed her palm against her exposed chest and let out a small laugh.

"Oh, Eric! What a fright you gave me. What are you doing here?"

"This is my room while the first floor is being refurbished."

"Of course, of course." She nodded absentmindedly, turning back to Henry's door and knocking again.

"What are you doing?"

"Checking on Henry." She rapped on the door one final time before giving up and huffing noisily. "I'm worried about him. He seemed off this evening."

"I wouldn't worry. He's always off." I rolled my eyes, catching Delia frowning.

"Don't be cruel. I'm being serious." She pushed past me and strode into my bedroom, sitting down at the foot of my bed and kicking off her slippers. "Henry hasn't been himself lately."

"Skulking about, obnoxious, anti-social. Seems pretty in character to me," I said, shrugging, and sat down beside Delia. Edging closer, I placed my hand on her lower back and recalled my dreams of hot beaches and dips in the cool sea. The thought of the water, crisp against my skin and sparkling against a blindingly bright horizon, made me long for the sunshine. Inhaling her, I smelled all the wonder of Christmas and forgot about the dreams of beaches and tropical holidays – suddenly none of it seemed important.

"I'm really quite worried about him," she continued obliviously. "He has bad spells, gets these strange ideas in his head and thinks everyone's out to get him. I thought he was getting better, but I'm worried it's happening again. I just want to help him."

"Oh." I found myself unsure how best to respond. I supposed it made sense that Henry was unstable, going by his erratic behaviour. Why else would anyone leave such a fruitful life behind?

"You know, he left his entire family to come and work here, left behind a career in law. He was working all hours and, between you and me, I think he had some kind of unofficial prescription habit going on, just to keep him going. I suspect that's what made him snap in the end."

"Edward mentioned," I said. "You think he's having a breakdown?"

"I don't know. I'm hearing things from the staff." She leaned back and propped herself up on her elbows. "He's babbling about witches and being trapped – he does this. It's worrying though. I think he genuinely believes it."

"Yeah." I nodded.

"He's spoken to you?"

"Kind of. I didn't really pay any attention though. It was more rambling than anything else."

Delia groaned and rubbed her temples.

"I don't think he's sleeping in his room. He's avoiding me. I keep trying to talk to him, but I can hardly start chasing him about when he's this way, can I?"

I shrugged.

"Want me to try talking to him?"

"No, just leave it to me. I've dealt with him before. He's not a danger to anyone other than himself."

"Do you think we should call someone? A family member, or a doctor maybe?"

"No, definitely not. I think that would just make him more paranoid. If you don't mind, Eric, can you please be discreet about it? The last thing I'd want is for rumours to start spreading among the staff. That's the last thing Henry needs and, for the most part, he's happy here."

"Of course." Although I wasn't entirely convinced of Henry's happiness in the hotel, it certainly wasn't my place to question it. We sat in silence for several minutes as Delia looked around her, taking in the room's strange proportions.

"I like it in here," she said eventually. "It's kind of quirky, full of character. Between you and me, I always found the first floor to be a bit boring. I made the mistake of letting someone completely lacking in vision design it a few years back, and it ended up looking like one of those chain hotels."

"You think Ollie will do a better job?"

"Oh, definitely. He has such vision. I'm so glad I snapped him up. We've gone over some of the plans already and I love it. He wants to give it a hunting lodge appeal. Rich colours and comfort – a bit like in here!"

I laughed despite myself.

"What?" She looked at me quizzically. "Is there something wrong with this room?"

"No, of course not," I lied. "Like you say, it has much more character than the first-floor rooms."

Her smile relaxed. It pleased me that my happiness made her smile, so I would continue to pretend to like the room.

"While we're on the subject of the refurbishment, I have a little surprise for you."

"Oh?" I raised a brow.

"If we can sort out all the plumbing and the right space, we're going to install a swimming pool! I know how much you'd love a pool or a gym here." She prodded my soft middle playfully.

"Seriously?" My eyes widened, ignoring the urge to be offended by the way she poked my stomach like it was dough. I pictured myself again in crisp, cool water, my body suspended, muscles warm from movement. Any discomfort surrounding the refurbishment dissipated. "That'll be amazing. I've really missed exercise."

Delia appeared satisfied as she shuffled backwards, sliding

herself beneath the duvet and gesturing for me to join her. The tie on her silk gown came loose and my hands held her warm body against mine, skin to skin. Our faces were so close that the tips of our noses touched.

"Tell me," she said, ignoring my wandering hands, "how's your book coming along?"

I hesitated, my hands stilling.

"Slowly," I mumbled. My lumbering, evasive tone made me think of a distant memory, presumably from a long time ago, of sitting at a dinner table, the plain-faced blonde woman with freckles holding my hand beneath the table as the others, people who bore a resemblance to her, asked me about my blossoming writing career. They pressed me into admitting I had made little to no progress and, although they didn't say it, the discomfort in their shared glances betrayed their concern, not for me but for the blonde woman by my side. She squeezed my hand comfortingly the entire time, as they silently debated my ineptitude.

"But I'll finish it soon," I resolved, determined not to give Delia that same impression. Her body shifted over mine, one slender leg wrapping around my lower body as her hands slid up my chest. Glancing down, I could see her youthful fingers running through the hair of my torso, which had become surprisingly grey, and I wondered for a moment how old I was, realising that I couldn't actually recall my last birthday.

As she loomed above me, her hair and spiced scent tumbled over my face, our tangled bodies connecting. My questions and concerns seemed to drift away in the steam of our hot breath, which created a strange mist in the bedroom, where pockets of damp cold fought against the dry blast from the electric heater.

"And I'll dedicate it to you," I breathed into her. "I'll do anything for you."

# CHAPTER 27

With Henry neglecting his doorman duties, Delia found herself struggling to find someone agreeable to do the evening shift. I queried the purpose of a doorman, given that there were no guests, but she looked mildly offended and pointed out that they received evening deliveries and some tradespeople worked late, so it was important to have a presence at the front desk. Eventually, after everyone on the team had declined the position, I offered to stand in while she was looking for a new recruit. As it happened, it worked perfectly. Since there was no actual work to be done at the front desk, and the nights were long and uninterrupted, I found I was able to find the time to work on my novel without any disturbance. I had stopped frequenting the conservatory in the mornings – it had become too cold of late – and the snow had blanketed the glass almost entirely, leaving the space gloomy and unworkable. My stack of notebooks and loose paper had grown so high and jumbled that sometimes I forgot where in the story I was exactly, and other times I wrote without really knowing how or where it would slot in. That didn't matter though; that was something to be dealt with once I was finished. Just as long as I kept going.

Before the kitchen closed for the night, one of the chefs, Alistair, would bring me a plate of cakes and biscuits, freshly baked that evening, ready for morning breaks the following day. The treats sat on my desk, a small clutch of cupcakes and a gingerbread man – Alistair's specialty. The gingerbread man had been iced to make it look like he was wearing a white shirt and grey trousers. "Run, run, as fast as you can!" Alistair had said in a little singsong voice as he presented me with the plate, laughing so heartily that his belly quivered. When I looked at him quizzically, he added, "You can't catch me – I'm the gingerbread man?" His breath had the sharp tang of wine from earlier in the evening; baking club, I assumed. When I continued to stare blankly, he sighed and asked if I knew the story. I shook my head. "It's about a little gingerbread man who thinks he can run from everything," Alistair had explained, looking disappointed that I hadn't laughed at his uniform icing. "He gets cocky though and is eaten by a fox in the end."

Alistair aside, the nights provided me with the peace I needed, but there was an eeriness to it that I couldn't quite place. Sometimes the wind outside howled, creeping through cracks in the old building and wailing down the twists and turns of the corridors. I was glad there were no windows in the entrance, as they would only have looked out onto an inky black. I avoided looking through the door's glass panels. With the hotel entrance illuminated by the orange glow from the lamps, it made me uncomfortably aware that, for anyone lurking in the shadows outside, I was visible beneath a spotlight. Once everyone had filtered off to bed, I made sure to turn off all the additional lamps and leave on only the one at the desk.

One evening, I opened the door to let the cold wind in, allowing it to whip my skin to a ruddy pink, sharpening my senses from the comfortable warmth inside. When I stepped outside, my leg disappeared to the knee in the snow. The weather was worse than I had thought, with snow falling heavier and the winds so vicious they nearly knocked me over. Already shivering, I retreated inside and shut the door, pushing it against the resistance from the gale. Despite the door being closed not long after it was opened, the cold had completely infiltrated the entrance, and a ghostly frozen fog drifted eerily down the corridor. The chill prickled my skin. Unable to warm myself, I picked up my things and moved into the living room, gathering what little kindling was left from the evening. Placing the chaotic pile of papers from my novel on the nearby coffee table, I formed a small cage of wood and scrap paper. Using the matches on the mantelpiece, I lit the fire and waited for the kindling to take. The living room was close to the entrance, so I figured it wouldn't do any harm if I spent the evening by the fire where I could warm up. Surely Delia wouldn't begrudge me that.

I dragged the heavy leather armchair close to the growing warmth of the hearth, but before I had the chance to settle down, a rattling sound from the front door caught my attention. I wondered if it was the wind, but as I listened more closely, it creaked open and clicked gently shut again. There was someone in the building.

Hovering by the living room door, fearful of stepping out into the entrance corridor, I wondered if any of the bedrooms were close enough that their inhabitants would awake if I shouted – or screamed. My hands fumbled for the light switch as I peered around the doorframe. The corridor was submerged in shadows which seemed to flourish and crowd around the dim glow of the lamp at the front desk. I began to wish I hadn't turned the others off. To my relief I found the switch, and the corridor burst into bright, white light, causing me to squint at the figure standing by the door.

"Can I help you?" I said.

Letting my eyes adjust, I gradually saw a young woman, in a worn pair of loose jeans and a thick woollen jumper, who was brightening into a smile as she shrugged off a heavy coat, revealing a minuscule frame. She dropped a heavy box at her side and waved.

"Hello!" she chirped.

She appeared to be impossibly beautiful, with button features and comically large green eyes, her heart-shaped face framed by tumbling red hair flecked with snow. However, as I approached, there was something unnerving about her, almost as though her natural features had been manipulated, like a cartoon character's, into an exaggeration of stereotypical beauty: her lips slightly too plump, her nose so narrow that the ridge appeared almost blade-like before the sharp upturn of the tip. She was oddly familiar, but I couldn't figure out where from.

"Hi?" she said.

I stopped several feet away, observing her curiously, realising that she was the first woman other than Delia I had seen in a long time. It made me wonder if she really did look strange, or if I was just so unused to seeing women.

"Hi," she repeated, lips curling into a grin at my awkwardness.

"Can I help you?" I said eventually, realising that was what a doorman ought to say.

"I'm the plumber." She gestured to her toolbox.

"Oh!" I brightened instantly. "Are you here about the swimming pool?"

The plumber shook her head slowly before taking a small step towards me, watching me carefully, as though she thought I might run away if her movements were too fast.

"No, boiler maintenance." She paused. "I haven't heard anything about a swimming pool." Smiling a strange smile again. "But it sounds lovely."

My heart sank. I shrugged my shoulders and tried to pretend it didn't bother me. I had spent each day since last Christmas eagerly awaiting the swimming pool project to commence, but little progress had been made on anything. Nothing had changed. The hotel entrance was still lemon-yellow with worn slate flooring, and the large, garish taxidermy birds still gathered dust on their antique perches. Ollie had visions of panelled walls, antler chandeliers and landscape paintings to replace the portraits – "hunting lodge chic," he called it – but none of it had come to fruition. I often watched Ollie, with a hint of irritation, as he lazed about, joking with Delia and enjoying the perks of the hotel when really he should have been getting on with his job. Sometimes I cringed at the things he said to her, bragging about his escapades from the past and speaking to the staff as though they worked for him. I could tell he looked down on them, considering them to be basic and unworldly – unlike him.

"Are you the doorman?" she asked, moving slowly closer, her eyes drifting curiously over the length of my body.

"Oh, no, I don't work here." I laughed lightly, gesturing at my uniform. "Although I can see how you might think that. No, I'm Delia's…" I hesitated. "Boyfriend" sounded too young and silly, and "significant other" just sounded ridiculous. "Partner," I said. "But I'm covering doorman duties for the time being. So, yes, I suppose technically I'm the doorman."

"Ah." She took a step closer, her delicate white hands drifting towards me. The heavy sleeve of her jumper rolled down to her elbow as she reached up, revealing curled fingers that paused centimetres from my chest. "Well, that's handy."

Unnerved, I felt myself take a step back.

"So, how do you know Delia?"

"We've been friends for a very long time." She continued to move closer to me, either unaware or uncaring of my discomfort. "You know, she never told me she had a *partner*." Her lips moved around the word "partner" as though she was mocking me, and her body continued to sidle closer. Her large green eyes were speckled with blues and greys that swirled unnervingly, like an aerial view of Earth. Her hand slipped into mine, fingers intertwined and gripping tightly, her warm palm connecting with mine. She pressed her body firmly against me, dominating my space, her breath hot against my cheek. I tried to back away, surprised by the strength of her and dismayed by the sudden and unexpected physical contact. Unable to create distance, I felt my body slacken and start to slide down towards the cold slate floor, but her hands tugged open the front of my shirt, gliding up my chest to grip the sides of my face and force me to remain upright. My body refused to react, inexplicably weak in her grasp.

"Got you now," she whispered, contorting her expression into something I couldn't place. Her eyes widened even more unnaturally, taking up a startling proportion of her face, and I felt my mouth freeze into a small "o". For a moment I was motionless in panic, tensed, my limbs rigid, fingers extended and inflexible. I was paralysed. But swiftly following the panic came a heavy submission, and I felt my limbs collapse and my fingers slacken, giving in to it all, my sight blurring until all I could see were the wide planets of her eyes floating in a blackening void.

"Izzy."

I tried to turn my head at the sound of Delia's voice, but found myself numb and tingling, only able to blink. My lips tried to form words but only a faint breath in the form of a small cloud of condensation escaped my mouth. The two women's voices fuzzed like static around me; I was barely able to make out their words.

"Delia!" The plumber bounced to her feet, skipping from my line of sight, which was gradually returning in clusters of colour.

"What the hell are you doing?"

"I caught him!" she declared excitedly. "He was at the front door! I thought you'd promised me a chase."

"That's the wrong one!" she snapped back, her voice a low hiss.

"You said the doorman?"

"*He's* not the doorman."

"Oh."

"You should have waited for me. Trust you to be so reckless."

"Don't be grumpy! No harm done."

They moved towards me, blurring in my vision.

"Give him a few minutes and he'll be fine," the plumber continued. "I doubt he'll even remember. It'll be little more than a bad dream."

The plumber bent down, pinching my drooping cheek and tugging it lightly before pushing me to the side, my body flopping to the floor. I let out a small moan, feeling my voice slowly return. "Shall we have a drink before we go hunting?"

I watched Delia hesitate, glancing back at me.

"Oh, don't fret about him, Delia." The plumber patted my cheek, looming close so I could see her fine features clearly. "I put on my finest face tonight – I think he liked it," she grinned. "Didn't you, sonny boy?"

There was a flicker of recognition as I recalled that voice from another time and place, but it slipped away as soon as it came. I sensed Delia bristle.

"I don't like what you've done with your face," she snapped after the plumber, who was already walking in the direction of the bar. "It's unconvincing."

"It's not you I'm needing to convince." The plumber winked. "Now, come on, have a drink with me."

"Just a moment." Delia stared at me for several seconds as I lay before her, her eyes moving from my lower body to the torn buttons on my shirt and the dribble oozing from the corner of my mouth.

"Is she right?" she asked quietly. "Did you like how she looked?" Her fingers brushed against my exposed chest as she came to her own conclusions. "That's disappointing. I feel… betrayed." Frowning, she rose and moved out of sight.

As my body regained some of its function, I found myself able to turn my head and watch her disappear into the living room, which seemed to pulsate from the glow of the fire. Emerging several seconds later, she turned off the lights in the corridor and followed her friend, leaving me submerged in darkness on the floor.

Gradually, my hands began to twitch, my fingers brushing against crumbs on the floor, and I found that I could roll my ankles again, the small movements starting to awaken the rest of my body. Soon I was on all fours, crawling across the floor until I was steady enough to rise to my feet. Wobbling, I found myself leaning against the wall to keep myself upright, and as I reached the living room, now warm from the rumbling fire, I let myself tumble inside, moving clumsily towards the flames in the hope that my body might warm and regain its function faster. The blurred blaze licked furiously at something among the kindling and the wood, blackening the edges and causing the pages to curl. I moved closer and squinted. My book.

Reaching out, I attempted to snatch the remnants of my novel, scooping what I could into my hands, and watched in despair as the pages burned into little black flakes around me, my hands turning an angry red. Crying out in pain, I dropped the papers to the floor. One of the pages, still partially intact, drifted slowly in front of me, turning in its flight so the writing became visible.

*For Delia.*

Unable to make the angry roar I wanted to, my mouth simply fell open impotently, and I stared at the work that had taken me – I stopped to think – *months.* But surely that couldn't be right. I could gauge time by Christmas parties, but then I couldn't remember how many Christmas parties there'd been here; it all seemed one long blur of metallic decorations, laughter, Champagne and the intoxicating spiced scent, which seemed strongest on Christmas Day. *Years.* Years of work burned to nothing in the fire. I wondered if I could rewrite it, but when I tried to think back on it, I could barely recall the plot of my story. My brain ached from the exertion.

I staggered back up the stairs, neglecting my duties at the front desk, my limbs creaking back into their full range of movement. Forgetting that I had been relegated to the staff quarters, I stumbled onto the bright corridor of the first floor, desperate for familiar comforts. As I stepped onto the jute rug and peered down the length of it, Ollie was standing several metres from me. His body was motionless except for the movement of one hand, which held a roller that he ran up and down the wall in strangely hypnotic movements. A tray of cream paint sat on the floor by his side.

"Ollie?" I asked uncertainly. "Are you alright?"

He turned to face me, a strange, empty smile tugging at the corners of his lips. His youthful face was speckled with cream, the splatters striking his white shirt and grey trousers. Dipping his roller into the tray, he ran it back and forth until it dripped heavily with paint. The roller slapped against plaster and made unpleasant slopping noises as he began his slow movements again, maintaining his smile while staring vacantly at me.

"Fine, thank you."

"Why are you painting the corridor the same colour as before?"

"Oh," he turned, looking dreamily around him. "Delia and I decided that what was here before was best, so we're just touching it up rather than changing anything. Can't improve on perfection."

I felt my stomach clench, unnerved by the absence of Ollie's infuriatingly superior smile.

"And the swimming pool?"

His head fell lazily to the side, arm still moving up and down with the roller.

"What swimming pool?"

"Ollie." I approached him, my breath trembling. "There's something going on. There's a strange woman in the hotel. I think she drugged me – I don't feel well!"

"Surely not." Ollie smiled faintly again, turning back to the wall as he painted. "I often feel like I'm in a bit of a daze too," he murmured. "Sometimes I feel sad. I have these irrational thoughts that she uses and then discards me like I don't matter, but she says I'm being silly." His smile returned. "She's right, I think. Perhaps it's the country air."

I resisted the urge to shake him furiously and instead slid carefully past him, ensuring there was a wide gap between us. There was something about his vacant stare and empty words that made me frightened of him, like I might catch it. When I glanced back, I noticed that his eyes had followed me to the end of the corridor.

I broke into a run, confused by the hotel's maze-like structure, which seemed beyond logical proportions. I tugged desperately on unfamiliar locked doors, filled with the urge to hide myself in a dark corner, curling up as small as I could possibly manage where nobody would see me. Hurtling up a small, dark staircase, I found myself back on the staff quarters' landing, and I raced towards my room, relieved to find the door unlocked. Flinging myself inside, I slammed it behind me and pressed my weight against it, panting loudly and holding my hand to my hammering heart.

I began to settle, my panting lessened, and I realised that, beneath my own ragged breath, there was someone else breathing steadily. Long, deep inhalations. Someone was in my room.

# CHAPTER 28

M y shaking fingers found the switch and my body instinctively braced itself. I narrowed my eyes in the explosion of light.

Curled up in the corner of the room was Henry, barely recognisable, with gaunt features and clumsily cut hair. A shadow of stubble darkened his chin. My room had been turned upside down, with bedsheets sprawled across the floor and furniture dragged to the open window. We stared at each other in silence, nothing but our mismatched breath over the sound of the gale outside.

"She found my hiding spot," said Henry, breathing heavily. "She found it a couple of days ago – I haven't been able to sleep in two days. Is Isobel here?"

I nodded dumbly, assuming Isobel was Delia's friend.

"Oh no." Henry sunk his nails into the papery skin of his face. "They're going to find me again. Please, Eric. You have to help me."

I shut the bedroom door behind me and twisted the heavy key in the lock. My heart's steady thump slowed to a normal rhythm, the initial shock wearing off. "Where the hell have you been? And what are you doing in my room?"

Scrabbling to his feet, Henry approached me, his jerky movements causing me to take an instinctive step back. His hand slammed against the wall beside me, turning off the light and submerging us in darkness again. I let my eyes adjust, eventually making out shapes and then the room again, as if through a black-and-white filter. Henry snatched my arm and tugged me towards the open window, where, for a moment, as his hand pressed against my back, I wondered if he was going to try to push me out. Instead, he leaned out beside me, taking in long, grateful gulps of the night air. I breathed out in relief, my fingers relaxing their grip on the windowsill. I noticed that my hands were pressed against a powdery mould which had gathered at the edges of the sill, and the small black lumps of long-dead insects, their brittle bodies wound in webs. I recoiled in disgust, withdrawing my hands and shaking them clean. It was clear to me that housekeeping didn't bother with this room; we were forgotten.

"Your room smells of her." He wrapped his hands around the ledge, not far from where mine had been, his fingers obliviously crushing the dry insects, and he peered down at the ground below. "We need to get rid of all trace of her if you're going to see her for what she really is."

I reached over to the nearby lamp on the table, but Henry's hand swiped it to the floor. It landed dully against the worn rug.

"No!" He shook his head and indicated out the window. "They're all looking for me. They come out at night, and if they see I'm in here then they'll come for both of us. Delia will let them in."

The fresh air was sharpening my senses, reminiscent of stepping out of a pub on a cold night and coming to the grim realisation of how much you've had to drink. The other windows reflected the sky above, the clouds like giant sacks of flour emptying around us. It was like a winter scene from a theatre set. For a second, it looked almost absurd. A growing unease twisted my stomach, churning my intestines, and I felt a little sick.

"So, you met Isobel?" He nodded slowly. "I watched her from your window, creeping up to the front door."

My mind began to filter a jumble of memories until I identified the red-haired woman, her unnervingly perfect facial proportions and her eyes that swirled like planets. I was submerged in darkness again, with her eyes floating above me, two horrifying orbs. I could feel her touch, my body buckling beneath her. I felt vulnerable and afraid. My skin started to crawl at the memory and I instinctively wrapped my arms around myself, though I wasn't entirely sure what had happened.

"Yes." Nodding, I leaned further out the window, welcoming the untarnished memories brought by the cold air. "The plumber."

Henry snorted.

"She's no plumber." His voice lowered, as though he had heard something over the ledge and he paused for a moment, surveying the dark horizon before quietly reassuring himself. "She's one of *them*. They're all around us, all the time. I've never made it far enough from the hotel to see where they live or what they really are, but it's nothing good. It's not human."

"Your story," I turned to face him. "The one about the group who tried to escape?"

"It was true." Henry nodded. "It happened a long time ago; it's the closest I've ever come to actually getting out. I can't tell you how many times she's managed to draw me back in and make me think this is where I'm supposed to be." He grimaced. "I don't know why I told the stupid story; I always end up doing something like that, always just when I think I might be able to get away. Every time I start to realise what's actually happening, I'll do something to let her know that I know, something to wind her up – no, something to get her attention. Isn't that perverse? I told myself I wouldn't do it this time, that I'd find my own way out, but she has this effect on you – you *want* her to notice you."

"She burned my book," I said eventually, recalling the blackened, curling pages disintegrating in front of me. "The one I was writing."

"I'm sorry to hear that. Although I'll bet you stopped writing a long time ago. We all give up on our dreams here, even if we don't realise it at first. Now that you've got nothing else to focus on, you'll languish about this hotel knowing that the only thing that makes you feel better is her. You'll wait for her each day, you'll crave her love and, as she gives you less and less, you'll only become more desperate for it. She likes that."

I thought back, recalling myself sitting at desks, scribbling on paper, and realised I couldn't remember what I was actually writing. I furrowed my brow. Why couldn't I remember?

"I used to love chess. She gifted me a beautiful board when I first arrived," Henry continued. "I would play against all the staff and I even considered starting a chess club – that was back when I thought I was different from them. Of course, my board vanished. Probably turned into kindling, just like your book. I guess I loved it just a little bit too much."

"So, when you came here, you weren't here for work?"

Henry's laugh was unpleasantly smug.

"I was a successful lawyer with a family, living in a half-a-million-pounds townhouse. You think I'd give that up to work for free as a doorman in a rundown hotel?"

"Well, why are you working here now? Why would you take on a job that doesn't pay?"

"Why would *you*?" he asked dryly. "You seem to be wearing the uniform and covering doorman duties of late."

"It's a favour," I snapped defensively.

"Alright."

"She said you had a breakdown."

"Of course she did."

"Edward said so too."

"Edward is obsessed with her. He doesn't even need to be under her spell anymore. Maybe that's what happens after you've been here long enough." His eyes darkened. "That's the worst part of it for me. Edward can see her for what she really is, and he *still* wants her. How does that even happen?"

"You're not making any sense, Henry." With a tentative motion, I touched his arm. "Maybe we should go downstairs, let Delia know you're okay?"

Whipping away from my grasp, Henry shook his head.

"*No*," he hissed. "You don't understand what's happening here."

I held up my hands, moving slowly and carefully to avoid startling him.

"Well, maybe you could try explaining to me?"

# CHAPTER 29

Henry Randell used to have it all. He spoke of his past like he was reading from a story, with emphasis in just the right places and long pauses that left you waiting for more. At times his language became less conversational and more like carefully crafted prose.

"You see," said Henry, leaning back on the bare mattress of the bed, staring up at the ceiling. "There's this thing that happens when you come from a family like mine. A look that you can spot a mile off. Wealthy banker father, not so blessed in the looks department – short, weak-featured and ruddy-faced from a few too many jollies after office hours. The mother, a former model or actress with the kind of glossiness you'd think only exists in magazines until you glimpse it in passing and can't help but stop and stare, though you know you shouldn't. Anyway, they produce these kind of hybrid children – once you know about them, you'll start seeing them everywhere. They're beautiful from a distance, tending to inherit that height, or that glowing skin, or that thick glossy hair. On the face of it, they're perfectly proportioned. Then you get closer, and you see that the features aren't quite what you thought; perhaps a weak jaw, perhaps a little snub nose, perhaps beady eyes just a bit too close together. They'll never make it onto the big screen or into the magazines, but what they have is the twinkle of confidence – some call it entitlement, but I don't think that's quite it. All they've ever seen around them is success, whether through looks, brains or sheer tenacity. It's all they know." Henry raised a brow and smiled at me. "You're not one of them, that's obvious. I can see you hit the genetic jackpot, but that's about it. Your parents were either aesthetically flawless or their flaws complemented each other perfectly. Unfortunately, you're completely lacking in any motivation whatsoever. I could see that from the moment I met you."

Before I could open my mouth to disagree with his sweeping presumptions, Henry's uninterrupted speech lulled me straight back into his story, like I was child at bedtime.

Henry described how he had breezed through law school, landing himself a much-coveted position while his classmates continued to struggle through the application process.

"They just don't sell themselves as well."

The longer I looked at Henry, the more I started to see it. The smooth skin beneath the neglected facial hair; the stubble growing in fully, no patchiness or discolouration. When he moved his hands to emphasise his points, the first thing that came to my mind was that they were the hands of a pianist, long and elegant yet strong and sculpted. It was as though he knew exactly which parts of himself were selling points and, when he became comfortable, he naturally sold himself. As I looked closer, beyond the hands and the self-assured smile, I saw ears that were too small for the head, eyes crudely narrow and flanking an equally narrow, long nose. I shook my head, wondering if I was simply being taken in by his story and overthinking things.

"I loved my job; it gave me a real thrill. I worked in one of those indistinguishable glass towers, packed with floors of people breathlessly trying to keep on top of things. It wears some people down. But I thrived on it. I'd probably have worked every day if I could. I remember rolling my eyes when the HR department tried to make my team take our holiday entitlement. I live to work, not work to live. That was the attitude I expected."

"You sound like a dream to work for," I interrupted.

"But anyway," Henry continued, pointedly ignoring my jibe. "I did take holidays sometimes. Once a year, to be precise.

My family had this holiday home up north – I think it's close to here. I've been thinking about it, trying to map it out in my head. It was at this fantastic spot near the shore, where the surrounding hills were bruised with tufty heather and the cockles on the beach crunched like eggshells beneath your feet. And you braced yourself for the sea."

I could see it perfectly. I could even hear the waves crashing against the shore and rumbling in the distance, and feel the sharpness under the soles of my feet, not quite breaking the skin. The imagined colours around me caused me to inhale sharply. I had nearly forgotten that colour existed outside the hotel. Then there was the shock of the cold, white froth, the churning water lapping my toes. In my memory there was a family, exuding warmth, laughing, and there was a woman calling my name, beckoning me into the water. Although it wasn't Henry's family I was remembering. I blinked and the memory vanished as quickly as it had come to me. Where did those happy memories come from? Why wasn't Delia in them?

"It's one of those holidays you think you'll hate but you always leave with the best memories. Besides, my mother would have been devastated if I didn't go." A small smile traced a line across his face. "And that was where I met my wife. Claire."

He paused again, a natural storyteller, taking a moment to let the name linger in the air.

"It's funny, because Claire isn't the kind of woman you'd look at and immediately think that she's beautiful. She doesn't have that allure. Not like Delia. But she has certain things about her. A smile that spreads too wide. A bluntness that never fails to make you laugh. You know what it was like? It was like she was the first honest person I'd ever met. Not sanctimoniously so, just authentic. She didn't have the glossy façade of the people I was used to back home. And there was something nice about that.

"It took years, but I met up with her each summer. I suppose we were kind of like pen pals; through the rest of the year we'd send each other letters and little gifts, like a book or a small drawing. She was really good at ink sketches. Sometimes she'd send me those awful things people hang on their walls — you know, the ones that say "Home Is Where Your Story Begins" or something equally naff? Because she knew how much contempt I had for them. I kept them though. They made me laugh. I would come home from a long day at the office and I would see it on the coffee table and I would smile."

I nodded, smiling despite myself. I remembered those signs in my own home. I could visualise one in particular pinned against a white wall in a narrow corridor, a plank of wood on string with loopy white text that read "Happily Ever After." I wondered why I had it, given it definitely wasn't to my taste. I wondered if it had been there when I moved in. Or perhaps there was someone else who lived with me.

"We both dated other people. It wasn't actually even romantic between us for a long time. But it was that way where, whenever I was on a date with someone else, I'd constantly compare them to Claire, and I'd want to laugh with them about the same things I laughed with Claire about, and they just never matched up. As it turned out, she felt the same way. It was tough for her moving away from home and coming to the city. We had this big lavish wedding with all my friends and family there. I could tell she was uncomfortable, but it was just the way my family did weddings, and besides, it was my parents who footed the bill." He shrugged. "But I suppose that was part of the problem. I thought too much about what my family did and less about anything else. You know what it's like, especially with an over-bearing family — they just want to be involved and make sure that things are going okay for you."

I smiled, not wanting to say that I didn't know what that was like.

"I suppose we ran into difficulty over the kids issue. That was the first real problem. Claire had made it quite clear that she didn't want to have children, and I had always been in agreement with that, but that always raises certain questions."

"Like what?"

"Oh, you know, questions from other people. The way other people do. They find it strange when a woman doesn't want to have children, like they must be inherently flawed in some way. It's alright for men not to want them. People understand that." He grimaced, as though slightly ashamed. "My family and colleagues certainly had their opinions on the matter. And in the end, for me at least, it seemed easier to start a family than not, just in case we regretted it once it was too late. Too late for Claire more than me – as they kept reminding us." Henry rubbed his stubble with his long, sculpted fingers, making a loud scratching noise that filled the silence while he paused. "Not that we ever regretted having children. We loved them dearly. And Claire was a great mother. But something shifted in her. It was like she lost her sparkle, or her drive. I'm not entirely sure what it was. She loved Claudia and Alice – that's our girls, named after my grandmothers. But it was like she loved them too much to get on with her own life. I criticised her for that. I even started to find her boring. Although, when I think back on it now, I was never really around, so I don't know what choice she had, really." Catching my expression, he stiffened. "I was a good father. I just wanted to provide for my family."

I nodded.

"I think maybe that, because Claire was so preoccupied, I used that as an excuse for what happened with Jenna."

"Who's Jenna?"

"Oh, it's all embarrassingly clichéd." Henry visibly cringed. "She worked at the firm – a smart girl for sure, which for some reason I felt justified it. Isn't that strange? As though if I was only with her for the way she looked then that would have been a worse way to cheat on my wife? I guess you find any reason to excuse bad behaviour. The crazy thing is, nothing actually ever happened with Jenna. Which made the whole thing even more thrilling, if that makes any sense at all. It made me want her all the more. We shared flirtatious exchanges, and we went for drinks and dinner together, both knowing exactly what the other wanted. I would go out with her instead of going home to Claire at night. I told myself that because nothing actually happened, I was doing nothing wrong. I told myself that Jenna and I were just friends.

"I could see the raised brows at work, but I knew the whispers would be more about Jenna. They always are. So I didn't care.

"My 'friendship' with Jenna started shortly after Alice was born. Claire and I had discussed shared paternity leave, but I don't think I'd ever really taken it that seriously, assuming that after she had the baby she would want to stay at home. It wasn't the case. I didn't hold up my end of the deal and I went back to work. Things were busy. It really should have been a happy time, but Claire was resentful about being stuck at home with a newborn and a toddler, and there wasn't all that much I could say that would please her. She started accusing me of being unfaithful and of course I denied it, feeling entirely justified in doing so, since in the strictest sense I wasn't."

"And what happened?"

"It was the strangest thing, actually. One afternoon I'd booked a hotel for me and Jenna. It was a nice little place where we'd drink some wine in the bar and take an absurd pleasure in the knowledge that there was a room upstairs if we decided we wanted it. Though I knew I would never let it go quite that far. It was fairly out of the way, far from my usual stomping ground, which meant I never had any real concerns about getting caught. So, we're sat there at the bar, and, if I'm being honest, things were beginning to get a little strained. Jenna had started hinting that I ought to leave my wife. She seemed displeased, and I was starting to get paranoid that she was going to tell Claire lies about what was actually going on between us. And that's when I see Delia. She was sat there at a table by herself, at one of the windows, and I remember it so clearly. She was holding a flute of something sparkling, and she was wearing a very simple silk peach dress. Peach is my favourite colour. If I remember it right, even her hair was tied back in a peach ribbon. Her scent was fruity, like strawberries, sweet but not overbearingly so. It was as though she was set up to be the perfect trap – like one of those plants that catches insects, with flesh-like colouring and the sweet smell of meat to lure in the flies. I stopped speaking, and I looked at her for what felt like a long time, completely entranced. Jenna looked more confused than outraged, which struck me as odd given I was quite clearly gawping at a beautiful woman right in front of her. I got to my feet and walked over to Delia. She had this small smile, like she'd known the entire time I was going to come over. She didn't say anything. Instead, she put her glass down on the table and linked her arm in mine, walking me through the foyer and out the hotel door." He paused thoughtfully. "Little did I know, with all the late nights and unexplained absences, Claire had become suspicious and she'd managed to track me down to that very hotel. I'd become careless, stopped covering my tracks as well as I used to. I must have paid at the bar with the card for our joint account, or something equally sloppy. When I saw her standing outside, face clenched in a combination of devastation and fury, I froze. I very nearly made a run for it. But this beautiful woman, Delia, was still standing by my side, keeping me very firmly in place. I was horrified. I knew immediately what my wife would think when she saw her. Claire spotted me from across the road, staring at me furiously – and then, bizarrely, she broke into an embarrassed smile and waved over. I waved unsurely back, unable to even bring myself to smile. My heart thudded furiously in my chest as she crossed the road and walked right up to us. There was strange a expression on her face, which was more relief than the rage I had expected. For a moment, I wondered if her realisation had finally given her the closure she needed and she was about to demand a divorce. But that's not what happened."

I found myself leaning in, eager to hear the rest.

"Instead, she laughs this strange nervous laugh and says, 'Oh, fancy bumping into you here!' We both knew that she was lying, and that she had followed me, but I hardly felt I could criticise her for that. Instead, I glanced anxiously at Delia, who was practically sparkling in the sunlight. Claire looked at her and became a little flustered, flapping her hands in a gesture she obviously intended to be casual. 'I'm so sorry, you're obviously in a client meeting. I'll leave you be. The kids are with Mrs Wingfield at the moment, so I should probably go and pick them up before we lose our goodwill for the babysitting.' And then she let out a small, embarrassed laugh, kissed me on the cheek and walked away. Delia said nothing, instead tugging gently on my arm, so we walked down the street together to her car." Henry's eyes became glassy and he tilted his head up, stiffening his lips to control the slight quiver in the corner. For a moment he was so still that, as he sat in the dark room, it was as though he was carved in marble. He took in a deep, shuddering breath and relaxed his body. "And that was the last time I ever saw my wife."

I was suddenly able to picture my own version of this same story: a bustling Christmas market. The ground slippery with slush. The aisles twinkling with fairy lights and a mishmash of Christmas music from each stall, a garbled cacophony of tinkling bells. In among it all, she somehow stood apart from the crowd, and the noise and the bustle seemed to slow and quieten around her. She was beautiful. And monstrous. She gestured for me to approach. For a second, I turned my head to glance at a smiling woman beside me, ruddy-cheeked in the cold. She exuded a warmth that made me want to fall into her, a kind of comfort that I had forgotten ever existed. And then I walked away.

"Eleanor," I whispered eventually, causing Henry to raise a brow curiously. "Her name was Eleanor."

# CHAPTER 30

The memory of Eleanor lingered with me that night, as I lay uncomfortably next to Henry on the bare mattress. He had thrown away all the sheets, declaring that Delia had left her scent on them. I clung desperately to the image of Eleanor, aware of how precariously it teetered at the edge of my mind, threatening to vanish completely. It didn't seem appropriate to take my clothes off with Henry so close to me, so I slept in my shirt and trousers, grimacing every time my shirt rode up and my skin was exposed to the unpleasant, scratchy mattress, which was clean at least, but had greyed and sunk a little with age. By the following morning, I could picture her features more clearly, pale wisps of curly hair framing a plump face and the clumsy smattering of freckles over flushed cheeks. Sometimes I could even hear her voice, although I wondered if the reason it sounded so high-pitched was because I had become so accustomed to Delia's low drawl.

It was difficult to tell whether I had ever loved Eleanor. She wasn't beautiful to me, but there was a comfort to her that I missed. I missed her clammy hands, warm and firm in their grasp around mine, and the way she became excited at my plans and ideas for the future. I was unsure whether she could tell that they were just unrealistic dreams, but entertained them nevertheless to keep me happy.

I had a memory of her that stuck in my mind clearer than the rest. She was baking a cake for one of her friend's birthdays and, not being a keen baker, she had no idea what she was doing. As she littered ingredients across the worksurfaces, clouds of flour puffed around her before falling to ice the table-tops. She laughed, and I remembered being annoyed, wondering why she was wasting her time with something she was no good at. She was just making a mess. She gestured for me to come and help, but I shook my head and went back to what I was doing. Strangely, perhaps in a dream, I began to picture Delia carrying out the same task. She was slow and meticulous in her movements, carefully returning each ingredient to the cupboard after use, and mixing so slowly that my eyes followed the wooden spoon around the bowl; it was almost hypnotic. It took me a moment to realise that she was staring at me the entire time, a blank expression disguising a smirk. There was something monstrous about it and I wanted nothing more than to have Eleanor back, making a mess and giggling each time she sneezed in the clouds of flour.

I woke up cold. My breath had formed a white cloud that almost hovered above me, rising gently. It was the kind of unpleasant cold that made everything feel damp, with moisture and condensation sticking to walls and fabrics and starting to freeze. I was struck by the sting of bleach. The unpleasant chill and scent of abrasive cleaning products made me think of my mother's insistence on early Saturday morning housework, when she would tear open the windows, fire up the hoover and begin scrubbing, even though my father and I complained bitterly about wanting to sleep in. Inevitably, we would grumble and vacate the house, only returning when we knew the cushions would be pleasantly plumped and the smell of polish had overcome the smell of bleach. By that time, the windows would be shut and the heating would be on and we would be grateful for the tidiness.

When my eyes had adjusted, I sat up and looked blearily down at Henry, who was on his hands and knees rolling up the carpet. Around me, my room had been stripped bare, all fabric furnishings by the window, covers removed and airing.

"How long have you been awake for?" I asked, stifling a yawn.

"A few hours." He propped the carpet up against the armchair, clapping the dust from his hands. "I don't sleep too well at night anymore."

"Where did you get that?" I pointed at the three yellow bottles of bleach lined up by the wall.

"I slipped out and got them from the housekeeping trolley just as they were starting for the day. That lot don't notice all that much. Not anymore."

"Okay." Looking around me, I couldn't deny that there was a strange thrill in Henry's conspiracy theories. It was like being a child again and playing along with a game, just up to the point of being frightened. "Bleach is bad for the woodwork though."

Henry raised a brow, and I laughed despite myself.

"That's something my mother would say. Would have said." I waved my hand, pretending I had meant it as a joke. "Whatever. Do as you please."

"We're going to bury that tonight." Henry pointed to a box by the window.

I rose to my feet and padded barefoot towards it, noting the soaps and the delicate glass bottle of cologne. I could very nearly smell it, despite Henry's efforts, the spices a reminder of everything I loved. I saw flickering images of the grand spread at Christmas dinner, the twinkling lights and the rich pines decorated in red and gold. Then I pictured her, Delia, standing alone in the Christmas market, the crowd blurred around her. Her lips moved ever so slightly, and her hand extended towards me, glove peeled away and white fingers, smooth as stone and beckoning me to come to her.

"We'll bury it in my spot by the woodshed," Henry continued obliviously. "Delia's friends don't usually come that close to the hotel, so it's only Delia we need to keep an eye out for."

# CHAPTER 31

That evening in the restaurant, nothing felt quite as it should. It was as though a veil had been lifted or a spell partially broken. Normally at dinner time, the restaurant buzzed with chatter, and the doors of the kitchen could be heard clattering over the muffled instructions of the chef to frantic waiting staff. When those doors opened, the smell of food would waft between the tables and fill the room, the laughter and merriment pausing for just a moment as everyone inhaled appreciatively.

However, the restaurant was quiet despite being full. The dust drifted eerily in the dim light, swirling around the staff who slowly dragged themselves to their tables, slouching in their chairs and waiting in silence. The walls, still red from the last Christmas party, seemed oppressive rather than festive, and in the absence of the fairy lights and the flash of green from the pine tree they appeared almost sinister – bloody, even.

The staff sat around me with subdued smiles on their otherwise blank faces, waiting patiently for their meals. The room had the feel of a primary school dining hall after all the pupils had been shushed by a teacher, nobody daring to be the first to speak. Eventually, I broke the silence. I turned to Callum from the breakfast kitchen team; he looked back at me, glassy-eyed and content.

"What's that smell?" I asked, wrinkling my nose at an unpleasantness that was becoming increasingly potent.

Callum smiled and pointed at the menu folded between

us, printed on ivory card. Snatching it, I narrowed my eyes, surprised to see that there was no starter and that the main read "*Roast fillet of halibut with a lobster bisque risotto.*" On paper it sounded exquisite, but the smell from the kitchen was rancid, like leaning over the wall of a polluted harbour and breathing in the stench of the seaweed and decaying matter ejected from the sea. I clasped my hand over my mouth and nose as the plates were placed in front of us, the tranquil men in white shirts unwincing despite the burning heat of the crockery in their hands leaving angry read marks.

The fish lay, steaming and white, over a creamy bed of risotto, and I found myself pushing back my chair in disgust, looking around to check if anyone else had noticed the stench. Nobody reacted. Instead, once all the meals had been served, they moved in unison, selecting their cutlery and slicing into the rancid fish. There was something stomach-churning about the way their heads sank down and they wordlessly shovelled the food into their mouths without a hint of emotion.

I got to my feet, intending to go to the kitchen and complain to the chef. I was convinced Alistair would take one look at it and insist on recalling every meal. It baffled me that it had slipped through despite his usually impeccable standards.

"Is something the matter?"

I turned to the table near the window, where Delia sat with Ollie holding her cutlery in her hands before her untouched meal. Ollie's head was lowered, and he didn't look up, continuing instead to chew dutifully on his fish.

It surprised me that I hadn't noticed her before. Ordinarily I would gravitate to her presence, drawn in by her glossy appeal in the centre of any commotion. Instead, she sat quietly on the sidelines, observing everyone around her with a small, satisfied smile.

"It's the fish," I began. "It's not—"

"Not to your liking?" she asked, surprised. "Alistair will be very upset to hear that. It's halibut; not cheap. Would you say that his standards are… slipping?" A sharp, dark eyebrow arched almost viciously. "Because I pride my hotel for its exceptional cuisine. I do need to know if things aren't satisfactory."

As I opened my mouth to reply, I glimpsed Edward at a table by himself. There was no meal in front of him, but he sat ready for dinner nevertheless. His pale eyes met mine and, very slowly, very carefully, he shook his head so subtly that for a moment I wondered if he had even actually moved. Was he warning me?

"No," I replied eventually, finding the wooden back of my chair with clammy hands and sitting down. Delia continued to watch me carefully, her scrutinising gaze magnified in the room of blank stares and quiet compliance. I glimpsed Edward again, his shoulders relaxing a little, relieved. "No," I repeated. "It's lovely."

"Excellent." She smiled, satisfied. "I'll pass your compliments to Alistair."

Turning back to my meal, I churned up the risotto with my fork and breathed through my mouth to try and block out the smell. I stabbed and picked at the meal, without taking a single bite, until it barely resembled its original form. Scooping up forkfuls of the fishy mulch, I brought it as close to my lips as I could stomach. I didn't dare look up, aware that that I was being watched the entire time.

150

# CHAPTER 32

I began to hate the hotel, particularly at night, when Henry
insisted it was safer to wander. It felt like the walls were
curving inwards, and the silence in the corridors was heavy
and somehow threatening. Now the saying "The silence was
deafening" made sense to me. I had used that phrase a lot in my
writing – cheating my way out of actually describing the atmo-
sphere – but now I could feel the corridors coming together,
offering themselves to me, finding meaning in the old cliché.
The chill that couldn't be explained by the cold, the prickling
sensation against my skin and the tentative steps forward, at
odds with the thumping of my heart. I wanted to pick up my
pen and write it all down.

There was something strangely thrilling about it all as I
followed Henry's footsteps. He seemed to know exactly where
to step to avoid the creaking floorboards, nimble and practiced.
It was like being young again and playing games of the imagination, being pursued by monsters and going on epic adventures.
Undoubtedly things had become strange; there was no questioning that. I told myself Henry was a fantasist and, although it
was amusing to play along, I should be wary not to become too
sucked in. It would all be fun until it something went wrong.

"Henry," I whispered, as we approached the turn in the corridor for the kitchen. He turned sharply, eyes wide. I pointed.
"Want to stop at the kitchen first? I'm starving. You could make
yourself a sandwich or something?"

"No." He shook his head, content with the small plate of

biscuits I had brought up for him after dinner. "She starves them out. She knows it's where they're most likely to go – she'd catch us for certain."

"Them?"

"The men who try to hide." He continued tiptoeing down the corridor. "There've been plenty."

I followed him, passing the kitchen reluctantly, distinctly aware of my unhappily rumbling stomach. I half expected Henry to turn round and snap at me to shut up.

In the bar, the moonlight through the window cast a lattice across the floor; long, silver rectangles. As the glass doors rattled against the wind, I could picture Henry's story, the five frightened men standing by that very door, preparing to make a run for it into the darkness. I had to remind myself firmly that it wasn't true.

Henry approached the door and turned the rusted key in its lock. It clicked, and the door loosened on its hinges.

"A prison with no bars," he murmured to himself.

The doors were flung open by the force of the gale, but he managed to catch them just before they shattered against the walls. The loud sigh of the wind filled the room, a hundred mouths breathing against me, raising the fine hairs on my arms and neck. Henry gestured for me to come closer.

"Hold the doors," he whispered. "If she comes in, pretend you're just getting fresh air, shut the doors and leave me outside. Don't make her suspicious and don't let her touch you or even come close. Do you understand?"

I took the doors wordlessly, which he seemed to interpret as agreement. It seemed absurd to think of Delia as being any kind of danger, especially when I thought of the many nights we had spent, naked and vulnerable, wound around each other's limbs as we drifted to sleep. I paused at the thought, wondering how many nights we had actually spent like that. The fleeting memories suggested that we spent most nights together and yet, when I actually thought about it, tried to pin those memories down,

I could recall only a handful of occasions. My head began to ache from the effort. I wondered if Henry's paranoia was starting to infect me, corrupting my memories and my image of Delia. It dismayed me that, when I thought of the woman I loved moving down that dark corridor in our direction, I was terrified. The image I cherished of us unclothed and tangled in bedsheets flickered to a memory of her standing over me as I lay paralysed in the corridor, examining me like an ornament she had accidentally dropped, a cursory once-over for breakages, frowning at me like damaged goods before becoming satisfied and walking away. Her indifference was chilling as I lay there, exposed and struggling to move, my lips unable to beg her for help.

I turned my attention to Henry, who was barely visible in the darkness. His faint, silvery outline was like a soft charcoal sketch as he struggled through the snow with practiced determination. For a moment he hesitated at his spot by the woodshed, before reaching for the spade, still propped against the side, and began digging his hole. Hurriedly, he tipped the entire box inside, and began shovelling back the snow, patting it down with his bare hands. Satisfied, he straightened up and turned to head back to the hotel. Then he stopped, ears pricking, his body stiffening like an animal approached by a predator. I hesitated, leaning slightly out the glass doors into the darkness and, for a brief moment, I thought I heard it too. Voices travelling on the wind, suddenly shrill and close to us, filling the air like a jangling warning. It passed as quickly as it came, but Henry dropped his spade as he hurried back, trudging breathlessly through the snow, and snatched the doors from me. He resisted slamming them shut, instead slowly and gently clicking them in place before turning the key. Brushing himself off, he rubbed his trembling hands together, and I could see where his skin was shrivelled and blue-tinged from the cold, his facial hair glittering like frost.

"Jesus," I whispered, incredulous. "You were only out there a minute. How cold can it be?"

"They're out there," he said, ignoring my comment and pushing past me, leaving clouds of his hot breath to freeze in the air behind him. "I think they knew I was there. We need to hide – *now*."

We darted from the bar into the hotel entrance, glancing back at the doors as they disappeared from view. I found myself grateful for the slate floor which was silent beneath our feet, allowing us to move quietly if not particularly quickly. Around me the stuffed birds strained their long necks, following me with their suspicious glass eyes. I moved as swiftly as I could back to the foot of the stairs, which I could ascend and return to the safety of my bedroom. Looking up, I saw something I'd never seen before.

"*Henry!*" I hissed, grabbing his arm and pointing at the landing. "*Look!*"

The door to Delia's office was ajar, casting a long beam of pale yellow light across the darkness. In all the time I'd lived in the hotel, I'd never seen Delia's office unlocked. Despite the urgency of the moment I felt a bubbling of excitement at the base of my stomach, eager to explore the mysterious room, thrilled by the thought of nosing through Delia's private affairs: her letters, her photographs, perhaps even a diary. I imagined her smell permeating the paper of her letters and lingering on the furniture. A surge of warmth coursed through me at the thought of finding anything that could bring me closer to her, that could allow me to better understand her. It seemed strange that I had ever been afraid of her. I placed my foot on the first step.

"*Come on!*" I urged.

Henry shook his head, stepping away from me.

"Something's not right."

"Oh come on, Henry. Maybe it'll be good for you." I was imagining us finding old invoices and booking records that would prove to Henry that Delia did in fact run a perfectly legitimate establishment. Perhaps then he would return to work or, even better, resign his position and go back to his family. I paused and wondered for a moment if they even existed or if they were another figment of his imagination.

"She *never* leaves that door open," he hissed.

"Exactly!" I grinned. "Now's our chance!"

"You don't get it." He pulled further away from me. "She's left it open on purpose. It's a trap."

Before I could accuse him of being paranoid, he scuttled away from the stairs, darting through the shadows with the nimbleness of a rat. I frowned, wondering where he would go, given that the living room didn't lead anywhere else. I'd have to investigate alone.

I pushed open the door to the office. It wasn't anything like I expected it to be. I'd anticipated vintage grandeur. An old-world appeal. Perhaps long wooden desks with green lamps, and walls adorned with oil portraits. Instead, a bare bulb swung from the ceiling, filling the room with an unpleasantly stark light. It was a small, oddly proportioned space, with no windows, and its walls had been hastily decorated with simple, dimpled, greying wallpaper that might once have been magnolia. It was torn in places to reveal pink floral wallpaper underneath and, beneath that, where the pink paper had been damaged too, exposed brick. It all clashed horribly with the worn, mint-green carpet, which was almost colourless in patches and stained in others. A cheap plywood desk was pressed up against a wall, and a modern office chair had been rolled back from it, adrift in the otherwise empty room.

My nostrils twitched at the odd smell that filled the space. It was nothing like Delia's scent; more like decay, or something beyond decay, when the sweet scent of rot is fading to inoffensive mustiness. My skin prickled and something niggled at me to leave the room, something that was growing urgent and pleading. Deciding to get out, I noticed the landline telephone on the desk, an old cream-coloured device with a curly cable connecting the receiver. I found myself staring at it, bewildered by the opportunity to communicate with someone outside the hotel.

After this long, the idea was almost alien. Shakily, I approached the telephone and plucked the receiver from its stand, slowly pressing it to my ear, half expecting to hear the long beep of a disconnected telephone or simply silence. Instead, I could hear the dial tone. I reached for the buttons, dialling one of the only telephone numbers I knew from memory.

My heart thundered in my chest. The tone became a ringing. I waited for the click and the sound of a familiar voicemail message. Instead, a cough and a spluttered greeting.

"*Hello*?" The voice had the tone reserved for answering a call after socially acceptable hours, an edge of annoyance concealing slight worry.

"Hi, Dad." The words sounded foreign on my tongue and were followed by several seconds of silence. I felt the blood pumping through my neck and ears as I waited for his response.

"Eric," he said eventually.

"How are you?" I felt my voice crack a little. My father sounded hoarser than I remembered, weaker.

"Surprised," he replied. "Actually, no," his tone became sharp. "I'm not surprised at all. Disappointingly unsurprised."

"Dad, I—"

"You vanish without a word – nothing. No happy birthdays, no Merry Christmases – nothing. Poor Lily and Gemma kept asking about you."

I pictured my half-sisters, plump and rosy-cheeked children.

"And the next thing I know," he continued, "is some poor lassie's calling me telling me you walked out on her – turns out you're engaged. And I had no idea! Name was Ella, Ellie, or—"

"Eleanor."

"Aye, that's the one. The girl tells me you didn't even bother collecting your stuff. She was worried about you, seemed to think it wasn't something you'd be capable of. But don't worry, I set her straight. I said it was the exactly the kind of thing you'd do. When life doesn't fulfil your little fantasy you'll drop it all in search of something better. I told that girl you'd happily walk out on friends and family if the grass looked greener on the other side. The thing is, Eric, you've never understood the meaning of loyalty and commitment."

I felt my stomach clench and an involuntary, guttural snort escaped me.

"Seriously?" My voice rose an octave. "You can hardly lecture me on loyalty or commitment after how you treated Mum! You didn't even have the decency to actually leave her." I paused, before adding maliciously, "How's Annie, by the way?"

I heard my father huff defensively, and I could picture him puffing out his chest like an animal trying to assert dominance. I knew his face would have pinkened and his hairs risen. My father had never needed to fight; he simply inflated until the other side backed down. I wished someone had called his bluff before now, even just once.

"Don't you lecture me on something you don't understand. At the end of the day, your mother didn't want any help – there was nothing I could do. You have no idea what I went through."

"Christ almighty, Dad." I forced an unpleasant laugh. "What *you* went through? You broke her heart!"

"Same as you broke that Eleanor lassie's heart?" I sensed him lower his voice, regain control. "Only difference between us is the fact you didn't bother to hang around. Maybe you inadvertently did the most selfless thing you've ever managed to do." He snorted disparagingly.

As I opened my mouth to retort, I was interrupted by a muffled voice at the other end of the line.

"Who is it, Allan? Are Lily and Gemma alright? Is it the grandkids? What's going on?"

I tensed at the sound of her voice, still sickly sweet even when laced with concern. I could see her clearly, probably in her rollers, wrapped in a fluffy dressing gown and smelling of cheap cherry perfume from the local pharmacy. I frowned. *Grandkids?*

"Kids are fine, Annie. Don't you worry." My father's voice was gentle and soothing. It was the kind of tone he had never used with my mother. His attention turned back to me. "Right, it's one in the morning. You don't call people at this time. You've gone and upset Annie now. Goodnight, Eric."

The telephone slammed down at his end and left me listening furiously to the conclusive beep, my mouth hanging open ready to hurl insults and accusations back at him. I held the receiver there several seconds longer, the conversation still swirling in my head, barely coherent. I wondered again to myself: had I really heard Annie say grandkids? Lily and Gemma were just little girls. I shook my head, telling myself I must have misheard her. She must have just said "kids."

I wanted to redial, furious, partly just to reignite my father's rage. However, before I could, the lightbulb flickered out. For several seconds I was plunged into darkness. And, before it flickered back on, my eyes caught a sliver of pale light from the back wall. Illuminated again, I dropped the receiver and approached the wall, looking for where the light had been. A brick was fitted unevenly and sat slightly out of place. I pushed my fingers gently between the gaps and sidled it out. The musty smell rushed from the space behind it, nauseating; I gagged, stepping back. Allowing myself a moment to recover, I braced myself for the smell and stepped forward again, cupping my hands around my face and pressing my eyes towards the gap to get a better view inside. To my surprise, there was an entire room hidden behind the wall. A room without a door. It was floral and girly pink, like the wallpaper beneath the drab grey in the office space. The pink was decorated with beautifully painted old-fashioned flowers. Small cross-stitch patterns hung side by side in oval frames. There was a large window with great, draping curtains, almost entirely drawn, save a gap of several inches. I recognised it as the window I'd seen from outside – the one with curtains never open. The room was filled with antique furniture, and carefully chosen vases and artefacts lined the cabinets and dressers. The shelves along the walls held an assortment of teddy bears and beautifully dressed dolls, pale beneath a layer of dust.

An ornate single bed occupied the centre of the room, veiled by a white canopy that fell from the ceiling and draped over the sheets. Where once it would have tumbled down delicately to the floor in folds of white lace, it now hung limply to the side, some of the hooks partially torn from the ceiling, exposing some of the rumpled bedsheets within. As my eyes adjusted further, I saw clearly the source of the unpleasant smell.

The body sprawled across the bed was fully decomposed, nothing more than a skeleton, long, ivory bones where strong limbs and plump flesh ought to have been. A toothless skull smiled at me and beneath it fabric framed the outline of ribs, sinking down into a jumble of vertebrae. For just a moment there was a calm familiarity to the grey layer of dust resting upon it, as though it could be an old piece of furniture, the dust muting any colour that may have been left and making it appear strangely peaceful, something untouched. It was only after several seconds of wordless staring that I staggered back in horror, clamping my hand over my mouth to stifle a scream. At first because of the room's décor, I assumed it to be the remains of a child, but I could see the stiff collared shirt of a man among the crumpled clothes, and a long pair of trousers, and at the feet were a large pair of boots lying as loose as the bones.

Resisting the overwhelming urge to run, I took the brick and pushed it back into the gap in the wall, a vain attempt to separate myself from the body. I wanted to seal it away, the body that lay still and silent, to brick it off both in that room and in my mind. I felt my already uneasy stomach flip, churning up what little contents remained and threatening to expel them. The smell of the corpse seemed to summon with it the stench of the rancid fish earlier that evening, and I felt myself stumble unsteadily against the desk, my body threatening to collapse.

Grappling for the telephone, I felt the receiver fall through my shaking fingers and clatter against the desk as I readied myself to call the only other number I knew off by heart. 999. My chest felt tight and my hands trembled over the digits.

Before the receiver reached my ear, I stopped at the sound of creaking outside the office door. The bulb above me flickered again, and I took a step away from the desk, my body pressed up against the cold, grey wall.

I watched her appear silently in the doorframe, both beautiful and monstrous, her face forming something resembling a smile.

"Eric." She toyed with my name on her lips. "What are you doing?"

# CHAPTER 33

T he faint buzz of the dial tone was the only sound between us as the receiver hung limply in my hand. The bulb had stopped flickering and I squinted in the harsh light. Delia remained in the shadows by the door, her body draped in a red silk evening gown, which was strange as I didn't recall there being any events or parties that evening. She remained firmly on the other side of the door; her presence wouldn't have seemed appropriate in the dirty, dated little space.

"I'm…" I looked down at the phone and then back at Delia. I desperately wanted to move towards her, to be out of the horrible room, away from the smell of rot and instead enveloped in her scent with my hands pressed against the soft silk of her body. "I was calling my dad," I said eventually, recalling some sage advice that to lie convincingly you ought to stick as close to the truth as possible. I sensed my voice crack, riddled with fear. "But he slammed down the phone on me."

Delia narrowed her eyes at me and took a glance around the room before holding her breath and stepping inside. I dropped the telephone and took a step away from her.

Her small hand picked up the receiver and pressed it to her ear, she peered down at the numbers as she tapped in 1-4-7-1. I remembered that from my childhood; with mobile phones nobody used the redial code anymore. We waited for the ring.

"Hello?" my father's voice barked. "Eric, if this is you again, I swear to God I'll—"

Delia carefully placed the phone down, satisfied.

"Gosh," she murmured. "He's unpleasant, isn't he?"

"I'm sorry, Delia. I couldn't sleep and the door was open. When I saw the phone, I just thought—"

She shushed me, touching her lips lightly with a long, white finger.

"No need to apologise," she replied silkily, gesturing for me to follow her. "I couldn't sleep either."

I found myself relieved to be out of the room and back in the body of the hotel.

"Why are you all dressed up?"

"Oh, I was out. I've only been back a couple of hours." She wrapped her arms around herself, shivering against the cold. Instinctively, I made to reach out to hold her, but Henry's warning echoed in the back of my mind.

*Don't let her touch you. Don't let her come close.*

"Fun?" I asked, pretending to admire the shadow-cast portraits on the walls.

"Yes, very much so." We descended the stairs and she paused by the living room door. "I'm cold. Shall we light a fire and have a little catch up? It feels like ages since I've managed to spend any quality time with you. Things have been so busy, as you can imagine, with all the renovations and such."

"Of course."

Inside the living room the shadows made everything look somehow longer, as though the furniture had been stretched to absurd proportions, and the chandelier cast a long, claw-like shape across the wall.

"Stack the kindling, will you, please?" Delia indicated the basket of sticks and paper by the vast fireplace. "I don't know about you, but it seems particularly cold tonight."

Nodding silently, I approached the fireplace and began building a small wooden cage stuffed with paper, just as I had been taught by housekeeping.

"You know, I'm going to throw my own party," Delia announced, pacing around me, her fingers trailing surfaces and chair backs as though inspecting for dust. "My friends, they always throw these fabulous parties, and it's been so long since I've done one." She laughed airily. "I'm almost frightened they'll stop inviting me if I don't step up soon!"

I sensed her watching me and returned my attention to the fireplace, wondering why I had never been invited to one of these fabulous parties.

"It's going to be wonderful. I've already got the kitchen onto it and maintenance are going to decorate the place. It'll be even grander than the Christmas party! Imagine that."

"Which friends are coming?" I asked carefully, as it occurred to me that I knew nothing of Delia's social life.

"Oh, you haven't met most of them. They live around here, fellow business owners." She paused. I sensed her watching me more intently, radiating like a heat against my back. "Isobel, she'll be coming. You've met her?"

I was careful in my response, keeping my head turned.

"Oh yes, the plumber." I steadied the stammer in my voice. "So, when is this party?"

"Next week. I sent out the invitations a while ago. I'm surprised you haven't heard about it already."

"We haven't spoken properly in while." I hesitated before adding, "Because you've been busy."

"Yes, I have been."

Leaning forward, I placed the final piece of wood on top of the precarious structure and, as I moved to step back, a disturbance of black dust fluttered from above. Blinking away the soot, I peered up to see a dirty hand reaching down and waving frantically at me. It was too dark to make out anything else other than the hand, eerily white against the black of the chimney flue. Someone was hiding in the chimney. Henry. Stumbling back, I turned to Delia, who was approaching the fireplace with a small box of matches. She hummed a soft tune on the edge of her breath, a sad melody I recognised as one of Edward's songs from his choir. It was tuneless until you listened closely, and then the assortment of flats and minors wound together to create something beautiful.

There was a sharp scratch, then a small burst of orange light that illuminated Delia's face as she drew in her wrist, ready to toss the match into my cage of kindling. For a second I stood frozen in place, my options spinning through my head, but my body reacted before I had landed on a decision and I swiped out, knocking the match from Delia's hand. It landed on the cold stone hearth and flickered out in a short gasp of grey.

"Eric?" She looked at me, puzzled.

"I've missed you," I lied, planting my hands on her cool cheeks and leaning in. There was a moment where she felt like marble, hard and cold against my lips before softening and warming, her body melting into my embrace.

Suddenly it wasn't a lie anymore and I wanted her desperately. Burying my head into her hair, I inhaled her, my arms tightening around her waist, and I pulled her in as close as I could.

"God, I really have missed you," I repeated, desperate for her to mirror my sentiment. She said nothing, instead letting her body react with mine, curling into my embrace and breathing softly into my ear.

"Let's go upstairs," she whispered.

We stumbled almost frantically out of the room, still tangled together and grasping desperately at one another. At the first landing, a soft light came from her office. I snatched a moment to peer inside.

It was just as I expected: rich cobalt blue walls and expensive mahogany furniture. Oil portraits lining the walls, illuminated by a green desk lamp. The kind of grandeur I had imagined. I couldn't identify why exactly it confused me so much. Delia caught me staring and smiled.

"Oops, forgot to lock up." Releasing her grip of me, she pulled the door sharply shut and twisted a key that had appeared from nowhere. "Now, where were we?"

# CHAPTER 34

"Wait."

I paused, staring at the door of her office. "There was something…" I struggled to find the words on the tip of my tongue.

"What is it?" Her breath brushed my neck, raising soft hairs, and her hands tried to guide me upstairs away from the landing. "Is something the matter?"

"There was something wrong," I murmured, feeling her hands trail around the belt of my trousers, untucking my shirt, finding their way around my sides and roving lower. I cringed at the thought of my pale podginess, remembering the once fine ripple of muscle, now an unpleasant doughiness gathering around me, clumping like porridge around my buttocks and outer thighs. I used to think that that strange, fleshy, oat-like consistency was something only women got when they stopped looking after themselves. At this thought, I was struck by a fleeting memory of a woman with dimpled arms and legs standing before me, her skin lined with unexpected silver stripes. I knew she had noticed the disappointment flash across my face, and she had pulled the covers over herself. Memories of the way she positioned herself to hide her flaws from my sight. *Eleanor*. I sought desperately to hold onto her name in my memory, her face, her comforting lavender scent.

"What was wrong?"

Delia asked this in her way, barely a question, still edging me away from the office door. I stood firmly, unwilling to move until I had remembered and said what I wanted to say. I looked again at the office door, saw in a brief flash the image of a body concealed behind a brick wall, an eerily preserved child's bedroom. But I was certain that couldn't be what was bothering me. It was an old building, after all, and I was sure that lots of people would have died in it; perhaps it was simply easier to brick them up here in a tomb of sorts, rather than go through the official channels which may have raised lots of questions and unnecessary hassle. Perhaps there were lots of bodies entombed in rooms throughout the hotel. It didn't seem as important as it had before.

"Swimming pool," I said eventually. That was it. "When are we getting a swimming pool?"

A small, satisfied smile formed on her lips.

"Soon," she reassured me. "These things take time. You need planning permission for listed buildings, you know." She paused. "And besides, why are you so impatient? We have all the time in the world."

"Sorry." I shook my head before returning the smile. "I'm just really looking forward to it. I knew I shouldn't have listened to Henry saying we would never actually get one – he's always so negative."

Her body stiffened, fingers becoming taut on my chest as though she might plunge them, knife-like, into my ribcage and snatch one of my bones.

"Henry." She kept her voice even. "You've seen him?"

"Yes." I nodded, keen to be of assistance. "He's hiding in the chimney in the living room – you nearly set him on fire!"

Retracting her hands from my body, she left me standing ruffled and indecently aroused. I shuffled in discomfort.

"That was good of you to tell me," she continued. "What else has he said to you?"

"Oh, silly things. He was talking about monsters in the snow. He says we're trapped here."

Her laugh trickled across the landing.

"Oh dear. Poor man." She glanced down the stairs. "You know it's all fantasy. You're welcome to leave whenever you want." She paused knowingly. "Do you want to leave, Eric?"

"No!" I shook my head emphatically, reaching forward to snatch her hand. "Never."

"I'm glad to hear it." Unclasping my hands, she descended the flight of stairs.

"Will you come see me later?" I asked after her, trying to hide the anguish in my voice, wondering if my desperation had put her off. I began to suspect she found my ageing, fattened body repulsive. Without turning back, I saw her shoulders shrug.

"If I have time."

Her silhouette vanished into the shadows of the corridor.

"Eric." A small voice hissed just a moment later. Peering over the banister, I was surprised to see the downstairs toilet door edge open and Henry peer out suspiciously before creeping up the stairs towards me. I frowned.

"You're in the chimney?"

Puzzled, he shook his head.

"No, I hid under one of the floorboards and then slipped out when you did and hid in the loos. Why would I hide in the chimney and risk being burned to death?"

"Then who was in the chimney?"

"I don't know." Henry glimpsed fearfully back over the banister. "Probably one of the men in hiding. There are a few from a long time ago. This place is far bigger than it seems. I've tried speaking to them before, but they're too far gone. Even if they get out, they'll always be hiding. That's what we want to avoid becoming. That's why we need to get out of here."

"This makes no sense." I rubbed my temples, trying to clear my head of the strange fug. "There was something I wanted to say, and I don't think it was about swimming pools."

"What are you on about?"

Turning back to Delia's office door, I held my breath, concentrating hard.

"Body." I pictured it again, sprawled unceremoniously across the rumpled bedsheets, grey with dust. Suddenly the sensations of horror and disgust washed over me again, clearing my hazy mind. "She has a body bricked up behind a wall in her office. A corpse. A man."

"What?" Henry's eyes widened. "*Who*?"

"I don't know." I glanced over my shoulder, lowering my voice. My senses seemed to sharpen, and I felt myself trying to brush the scent of Delia from my clothes, disgusted with myself.

Something horrible occurred to me, and my body stiffened with a newfound fear. "Christ, Henry. What if that's where the ones who retire go? Do you think she *murders*—"

But before I could finish my sentence, we were interrupted by a piercing shriek and the sound of clattering from the living room. The man in the fireplace.

***

"Move!" Henry barked, pushing me up the next flight of stairs and into the long corridor. We raced through the doors, ignoring them clanging noisily behind us, and up the spiral staircase back to our narrow hall of bedrooms.

"She said she might come back *tonight!*" I hissed, as we slammed the door behind us and turned the key. Henry shook his head.

"She won't," he reassured me, propping a chair against the door nevertheless.

I sat on the bare mattress of the cold room, breathless. There was a hollow feeling at the base of my belly and, as I let myself fall onto my back, I wondered with a pang of shame if it was disappointment I was feeling.

# CHAPTER 35

Henry formed a plan that we pored over like excited schoolboys for several days. He said that Delia's party with who he called "the witches" was the perfect opportunity for us to make our escape. The witches would be distracted and drunk; that way there would be nobody to stop us in the hills as we travelled back to civilisation, and from there we would make it to Henry's family holiday home, which he assured me must be close by. When I queried how he knew this when he couldn't even pinpoint our location, he replied, "It's hardly as if we're in the Canadian wilderness, it's Scotland – it can't be that far."

I couldn't help but think of my father's older brother, my uncle, who had worked in mountain rescue in his youth. He was a grizzly creature, like a padded-out version of my father, more weathered and wizened. My father used to shrink in his presence, visibly irked at the notion that there was someone more manly than him. When they were together, he would drink more whisky than usual and shout louder to compensate for what he felt were his shortcomings, but it simply made him seem smaller. My uncle used to complain bitterly about the "city types" who were so comfortably complacent in their metropolitan existence that it never occurred to them that, in the absence of heating, telephones and immediate access to food, the great outdoors could be a dangerous place. "They get out there into the hills wearing the bare minimum of new designer gear," he would grumble, "and they wonder why they're so cold and hungry, because they never thought to wear thermals or take supplies. The panic soon subsides though, gives way to a weariness that slows them down and they get so cold that they're tricked into thinking they're comfortable, and then they just stop."

I didn't say anything to Henry. Every time I started to doubt our plan or have second thoughts, I would see that small window in the brickwork and remember peering through into the antiquated bedroom, the moon cast over the corpse like a spotlight. In my mind's eye, the light was flickering like an old projected film, an old black-and-white horror film – comical, if it wasn't so horrifying. I desperately wanted out, but I knew I couldn't do it alone.

We were all tired in the run-up to the party. Delia had us working overtime to ensure that everything was up to standard for her guests. We cleaned furiously, and the kitchen was thick with steam as the chefs cooked and marinated in advance of the big day. I had been asked to help in the kitchen on top of my doorman duties but had quickly been relegated to dishes when they realised how inept I was with food. When I spoke, they glanced uncomfortably at one another, as though wishing I would just keep quiet. They didn't approve of a man who couldn't cook and made it abundantly clear that I was there to clean dishes and nothing more. I would never really be one of them. It was a lonely few days.

After work one evening I decided to take a brief nap in the living room, exhausted after a day of domestic drudgery in the kitchen. I didn't much like being in the hotel at night by myself, frightened that Delia might suddenly appear without notice, but Henry had reassured me that as long as I acted normally then no harm would come to me. I made an effort to smile at her when she passed me. She would smile briefly back, a sting of rejection. My eyes followed her as I wondered what had happened to the man in the fireplace.

One of the challenges Henry and I had faced was the lack of practical gear available in the hotel – all the clothes were the sort that would become heavy and waterlogged. No Gore-Tex, not even tweeds. A distinct lack of boots and jackets. I had discovered an assortment of odd bits in the basement, dusty and dressed in cobwebs. A rucksack with a broken zipper and a couple of flimsy waterproof jackets had been plucked from the pile. There were some wallets and books, scabby trainers and even a few nice pieces – an expensive watch with a luxurious leather strap. I was tempted to pocket it but reminded myself that I needed essentials only. From deeper in the pile I had pulled out an old woollen jumper that stank of damp and was full of holes either from moths or mice. A faint hint of lavender rose from the sleeves, and I examined the pattern more closely with a glimmer of recognition. It was Eleanor's. Or, rather, it was the jumper Eleanor had made for me a long time ago. When I pulled it over my head it seemed to have shrunk, and it smelled so strongly of damp that I didn't imagine it could ever be truly cleaned. Reluctantly, I returned it to the pile. Instead, I found a couple of newer jumpers that were a better fit, one of them strangely decorated with fluorescent cartoon lightning bolts like something Ollie used to wear.

As I sat in the sunken leather chair at the far corner of the living room, mentally ticking off all the items I had gathered as the bones of the frame dug into my rear, my concentration was broken by two voices from the corridor. I glanced beside me at my gingerbread man, looking sadly back up at me, cold against the porcelain saucer and probably stale after being left sitting out for so long. The small, spiced body had warped a little so that that icing had spread, causing its expression to droop miserably. Henry told me not to eat them since even they were infused with her scent. I twisted my head further to identify where the voices were coming from.

"Oh, for goodness sake, where is Eric? He's meant to be on door duty." It was Delia, clipped and stroppy as she marched across the stone floor with a gentle pitter patter of bare feet. Carefully, I peered over the back of my chair to see her standing with Edward in the corridor. I opened my mouth to announce that I was still here but was interrupted by Edward.

"The men are working hard at the moment to make sure everything's perfect for your special day," he said. "Maybe he's just gone to bed early." Edward moved in closer and placed a hand on her cheek. Instead of pulling away as I had expected, she placed her own hand over it and relaxed into his touch.

"I know, it's just that after Henry, I'm anxious that one of them might ruin it for me. I just want everything to be perfect. The things he's been saying, I just don't know what the other men might think. I should have gotten rid of him a long time ago when he started becoming a problem, but it's hard, you know?"

"I know, my love, I know." Edward pulled her in closer to his chest, soothing her with soft noises and pressing a kiss onto her forehead. "But I'm there; I'll make sure it's perfect for you. Don't I always?" For a moment she looked small in his arms, her head tilted up, and she kissed him on his lips, her free hand stroking the grey of his beard.

"You do," she cooed. "You always do."

I thought I might have felt furious with envy, exploding with the kind of rage that causes words to tumble out of your mouth before you've even had the chance to consider them. But I didn't. Instead, I felt immensely sad.

Where I ought to have been disgusted at the sight of Delia's youthful form in Edward's weathered embrace, that wasn't what I saw at all. Instead, I saw a tangible fondness between them as they slotted comfortably into each other's arms, familiar and safe. I distantly recalled the sensation of gentle kisses and soft strokes against my own body, those little touches of affection that made you feel appreciated and loved, far more so than the sweaty thrusts and clawings of lust. I realised that I had never made that distinction between sex and love before.

I continued to watch them, strangely fixated on the movement of their hands and lips. In another time and place it would have felt wrong to observe, but there was no voyeurism to it. Rather, I realised it was a longing. Not a longing for Delia, but a longing for what they had between them. I wanted it desperately.

Hand in hand, they quietly retired upstairs, unaware of me peering at them from the shadows. I imagined that they would sleep side-by-side with their hands clasped and soft smiles on their faces. As I pictured it, I realised I had been quietly weeping. Hot, salty tears rolled down my cheeks and into my mouth. I acknowledged despairingly that, in this grand building, never short of company and a beautiful woman who provided me with all the things I thought I wanted, I was the loneliest I had ever been.

# CHAPTER 36

Throughout my life I had attended many parties. One of the perks of being so outwardly attractive was that I didn't need many friends to be invited to occasions. People thought that I was mysterious when really I was just not interested in them. I liked that they took pleasure in my acceptance of their invitation. It made me feel powerful.

I had never thrown any parties myself. Party planning had never really been my thing and, besides, my accommodation never lent itself to social gatherings. When people spoke to me, sometimes I glimpsed awe in their eyes, and I could tell that they thought my lifestyle must have matched the way I looked. I knew they thought that if only I invited them in then they could be a part of it. The fact that I never did made it seem all the more exclusive.

In my early twenties I went to the kinds of parties that didn't serve food. They were the sort of parties where you could feel the rumble of anticipation before you went inside, and you were greeted by an uncontrolled crowd, throbbing music, overflowing drinks and little plastic bags that promised to make the night even better. Nobody ever really spoke to anyone beneath the heavy beat of the music; instead they formed connections through grins and wide-eyed stares, their pupils shrinking to pinpricks. Sometimes those connections became physical, neither person having any expectations beyond what they would do with each other later. The next day, I would peer through puffy, bloodshot eyes and we would mumble our goodbyes, with vague promises of doing it again.

Eleanor had never been to parties like that; the sight of me in that condition would have horrified her. Eleanor was the kind of woman who didn't really believe that drugs existed; not in her world, anyway. She was the kind of woman who described herself as, "Too drunk" when she started to giggle a bit, whereas my "too drunk" bar was set at the point of partial facial paralysis. Thankfully by the time I met Eleanor, those parties had started to bore me. It turned out that instead of being spontaneous and unpredictable, they followed the same old pattern, and I never felt particularly good the next day. Instead, Eleanor favoured dinner parties. Her friends were the sorts who thought that rosé wine was a character trait and considered playing board games to be a good time. That's not to say I hated those things; not exactly. There was a comfort and a warmth to it that had an appeal of its own in the same way that the chaos of those former parties had. In my memory, as they laughed and gossiped, the room burned with a warm glow like a fire was rumbling in a hearth next to them. I wanted desperately to fit in; I didn't want to think that they were boring and unoriginal. If it meant that I could feel the same contentment as they did, sitting around the table and holding their breath as they tossed the dice, then I wanted to be boring and unoriginal too.

Delia's party was neither of those extremes and yet had the feeling of both. Every fire on the ground floor was alight and a comforting heat filled the rooms along with the warm glow. The scent of fresh canapés drifted from room to room, cooked with the finest ingredients and to Alistair's impeccable standards. Any trace of the rancid ingredients used over the past few days had gone; the faint smell that had lingered had been wiped away like it had never existed. A person could be forgiven for mistaking the evening as a gathering of old friends who planned to catch up over fine food and wine by the fire. However, if they stopped to listen to the screams of the gale outside rattling the windows, they might hear it warning us of what was to come in from the cold. They would look at the men who hovered about, perfectly preened and poised to welcome guests, and they would see them tremble with anxiety, eyes flicking from side to side to ensure that everything was perfect.

Delia appeared in a rose chiffon gown that swept the immaculate floors behind her. It concealed her neck, taut around her throat, and she held herself high, her dark hair slicked back into an elegant knot. Conservative, yet suggestive. She touched her chest with a delicate hand in a gesture that we interpreted as gratitude, signifying what a wonderful job we had done and how marvellous we all looked. I watched as the men visibly relaxed, lapping up her implied compliments and flushing in delight.

Glancing at one of the kitchen assistants, I was surprised to see his vacant, appreciative smile as he hovered by the table of cold canapés. Earlier that day, while I was helping to clean the dishes, I saw him carefully remove a baking tray of delicate meringues from the oven. They had been left in a touch too long and a couple of the meringues at the back had a soft caramel tinge to them. As though she had sensed from afar that something had gone awry, Delia burst through the kitchen doors, hair wild in freshly washed curls and her hands gnarled in a strange, claw-like fashion, which I later realised was because she had just applied her nail polish. Her eyes scanned the kitchen looking for fault, and everyone froze. Her gaze settled on the tray of meringues and she stormed towards the bewildered man, snatching them from his mitted hands despite his warnings. I had gasped as she held the hot tray in bare hands, seemingly oblivious to the heat against her skin. After staring at the offending meringues for several seconds, she let out a furious roar and hurled the hot tray in the direction of the young man. He shut his eyes to await the blow but the tray missed him by several inches and the meringues exploded against walls and surfaces. Delia demanded that they be remade and slammed the door behind her. When the man began to tremble and look around him for support, nobody reacted, other than to sigh wearily and begin to clear up the meringues. Nobody was sure why he was so upset. The tray had missed him, after all.

I remained at my post by the door, keeping myself to myself for the best part of the early evening. Delia had inspected the entrance and nodded in satisfaction. My instructions were simple. I would greet and smile obligingly, taking coats and offering appropriate compliments. I would guide the guests into the drawing room, where they would be greeted with Champagne and canapés. Then I would make my way upstairs, where Henry would be waiting for me, with our rucksack and additional layers. We would get changed and slip out the front entrance while everyone was distracted in the drawing room, and we would disappear into the darkness together.

I first realised that they were coming when the wind stopped screaming. The windows stopped rattling, and everything went still and quiet. Looking out the glass panel of the front door, I watched dark figures approach just beyond the security lights. There were no cars or appropriate clothing; I saw the vague outline of dresses and fashionable coats, the depth of the snow not hindering the figures as they moved steadily towards the hotel, their movements slow and purposeful. I felt sick with fear, a hot thump of blood swelling in my ears like the beat of party music. Suddenly the warmth around me from the fire and the fine food seemed obscene, a calculated front to the horror that approached. It had the distastefulness of a luxurious last meal before execution. How could anyone be expected to enjoy that? I wondered what that must be like; would the smell make you nauseated regardless of how pleasant it was? I wondered if, acting on autopilot, you would thank those serving the food, those assisting in the end to your existence. That was something more horrifying than what followed; the pleasant meal before certain death, torturously drawing out the process under the guise of kindness. There was a disturbing absurdity to it all.

# CHAPTER 37

They stepped beneath the light of the entrance, eyes glimmering in the orange glow. I found myself opening the door obligingly, a professional smile plastered across my face, and welcoming them inside. "Look nice," Delia had commanded us.

An assortment of colours swept by me. Blood-red silks, purple satin and shimmering cobalt blues. Extravagant jewels caught the light of the chandelier and refracted rainbows across the floor and walls, illuminating the stuffed birds' glass eyes. The women shrieked in delight as they entered, as though they had broken through some invisible barrier. They sounded wild and dangerous.

Bowing my head subserviently, my eyes fixed on the stone floor, I allowed coats to be slung over my outstretched arms like a hanging rail. A heavy chestnut-coloured fur struck my face.

"Thank you." The red-haired woman, Isobel, dipped her head down to force eye contact with me, winking wickedly with her unnervingly smooth and pinched features. Before she could say any more, Delia appeared from the drawing room, clapping her hands in delight and releasing a shriek of her own. Isobel shrank away, smoothing her long ripples of hair and turning her back to me. I breathed a sigh of relief, realising that my hands were slick with nervous sweat under the weight of the coats. I watched Delia greet each of them individually, her eyes darting over their gowns, bolder in colour than her own and more revealing in cut. Self-doubt cast a shadow over her face for a moment, and she touched her stiff collar against her throat as if wondering if she ought to have been more daring.

"It's *so* wonderful to see you all," she declared, shrugging off the moment of insecurity and gesturing for everyone to follow her into the drawing room. Glancing over her shoulder, she waved her hand in my direction. "Get those coats hung up and come help with the drinks and canapés, please."

I hesitated, keen to get back upstairs and prepare for the escape. However, Henry had warned me to be careful, telling me not to leave too soon and draw attention to myself – that way nobody would notice when I eventually slipped away.

Edward sat by the piano as we filtered into the drawing room. Despite the way his fingers drifted nimbly across the keys, his eyes moved warily around the room, observing our guests. My hands were immediately taken up by a tray of Champagne flutes that Ollie thrust upon me. The fear of dropping them and drawing attention to myself only served to make me tremble more. I was relieved when they were all quickly plucked from the tray.

"Oh, Delia." A woman in a bright terracotta dress flung herself on an armchair and gestured around her. "What a wonderful job you've done with the place." Her eyes caught the garish oil portrait of Delia's aunt and she smirked. "I'm so glad to see you've finally made this place your own."

"Thank you." Delia eyed me cautiously as she took a glass from my tray and turned back to her guests. "It has been a challenge, but I think I'm finally there."

"And these men." Another gestured at the staff, nodding approvingly. "What a handsome bunch. You're a lucky woman, Delia."

They all cackled in unison, and the staff looked uncertain for a moment, aware that whatever the joke was they weren't in on it.

"I'm being serious, though," the woman continued, peering at the men with her startlingly narrow features. She was blonde and strikingly beautiful in an unpleasant way, with teeth slightly too large for her mouth and a long straight nose that by all accounts was perfectly aquiline but looked out of place. "How do you train up such a good team? Just look at them, so beautifully turned out – respectful!" Pausing, she pressed a liver pâté oatcake between her lips and sprinkled the crumbs from her fingertips onto the rug below. "Mmm, excellent cooks too. I really am envious. I've all but given up on my staff. I find many of them to be slovenly these days, turning up in creased uniforms, very little attention to detail – and the *attitude!* It frustrates me that there's such a lack of respect for a good old-fashioned work ethic and high standards these days. I know you shouldn't lose your temper at your staff, but honestly, I can't help it sometimes. There are certain expectations."

Murmurs of agreement through oatcake-filled mouths.

"Oh, absolutely." Draining her glass, Delia gestured for me to approach with a new one. I did so with my head bowed. "Although, if I'm being honest, I can't take all the credit. My team really are excellent. A lot of it is about mutual understanding – they know what I expect of them and they're aware that, in turn, I provide good working and living conditions." She shrugged. "It's a two-way street."

I frowned, recalling the scalding tray of meringues in the kitchen. To my surprise, the men around me, instead of frowning too, were smiling and nodding alongside Delia. I quickly caught myself, flipping my frown into a vacant smile, resenting every second of humiliation before I could relax my expression back into neutral. My cheeks ached from the effort.

"Well, bravo Delia." Isobel raised her glass in congratulations. "Although I do recall you having a little difficulty with one lately – the doorman, was it? Whatever happened with him?"

"Oh, hardly." Delia waved her hand flippantly, as though embarrassed. "You know what they can be like at times. I can only assume he's vanished into the woodwork, as they do in these sectors." Her eyes jumped to the walls and fireplace. "I've already replaced him." She gestured at me and smiled brightly. I cowered as their eyes settled on me.

"Oh, I was hoping for a younger model!" one shrieked in delight. The accompanying laughter made me burn with shame, but instead of blushing I smiled politely.

Once my tray was empty of drinks, I sat it down on a cabinet and edged towards my escape, but I was stopped at the doorway by Ollie juggling two new trays, one of which he handed to me, grateful. His cheeks were flushed from running back and forth to the kitchen and bar.

"Cheers, mate," he said breathlessly.

The women became rowdier as the evening continued, jostling, spilling drinks and trampling food into the rugs, which we dutifully cleaned up after them. At one point, one of the women slid next to Edward at the piano and began spoiling his piece, thumping high, discordant notes with her index finger. Edward smiled patiently and continued playing, waiting for her to get bored and wander away.

"What's this?" one of the women demanded, prodding a platter of canapés. Cocktail sticks pierced squares of cheese wrapped in crisp ham. I had eaten some of them in the kitchen earlier; they were good.

"Manchego cheese wrapped in Parma ham," Dennis replied, pronouncing Manchego as "manchengo". He was a shorter-than-average man with a constellation of moles around his thinning hairline. He shrank even more in the presence of the woman.

"Man*chengo*!" the woman parroted cruelly, catching Delia's attention. "How long has he been calling it that for? I hope he doesn't work in your kitchen."

Dennis pinkened in shame as Delia glowered.

"Not for much longer at this rate!" she replied with a slightly desperate grin, vying for their approval.

As their inhibitions diminished further, they showed more and more interest in Ollie. They started by including him casually in their conversations and asking his opinion, which he skirted around nervously, loathe to get the same treatment as Dennis. Eventually, they encouraged him to hand his tray to another staff member and sit with them on the sofa. I watched as they admired his youthful skin and thick hair, occasionally brushing him with the backs of their hands, timing it with their conversation so it appeared playful, appropriate. Ollie's grin wavered, as though he wasn't entirely sure if he was enjoying the attention or not. Some of the staff stared hatefully at him, aware that the special attention resulted from his youth and good looks. It only served to highlight their own age and physical shortcomings, amplifying disguised insecurities. When I looked closely, I was surprised to see that they were older than I recalled, plumper and greyer. Glancing down at myself, I wondered if I fell into the same category of fat old men who were of little interest to the women around us other than what we offered on our platters. My physique had lost its youthful definition, rounded in the centre with soft tissue that descended with gravity and time.

I burned red with a hot shame, unsure why it bothered me so much, given that I intended to leave. I hated to admit that there was a part of me that wished they would gesture for me to join them on the sofa, to turn their heads with interest when I spoke and touch me appreciatively. The thought of their touch made me feel both sickened and excited at the same time, an odd combination of sensations. There had been a time when I was appreciated in that way, but I had simply accepted it as part of my life, ignorant to the fact that one day it would be taken from me. In the restaurant where I used to work, where the staff were all beautiful, I would see the envious glances of clientele who were older or less genetically blessed. Most of them weren't even ugly, they were just invisible.

My thoughts were interrupted by Delia calling for attention over the sound of the record player. Her voice didn't hold the same spell that it used to; her low, magical lull sounded droll, and when she shrieked it was less charmingly girlish and more startling. I resisted the urge to wince, instead mimicking the entranced smiles of the men around me.

"Ollie's going to tell us a story!" She gestured at Ollie, who fumbled his hands nervously. A shy smile twitched at the corner of his mouth and he looked more pleasant than I recalled, more humble. Ollie hesitated, glancing at the expectant crowd around him who were nodding in fervent agreement. Before he could argue, he was jostled up from the sofa and directed towards the fire.

"It's his first," Delia continued, "so I wanted everyone to be nice to him, alright?"

As he stood by the fire, the shadow of his twiddling fingers like giant black spiders against the wall, I thought of the pale hand above the hearth, waving desperately at me, warning me not to light the fire.

"Evening, everyone." He gave a nervous wave. We responded with a friendly chuckle and an assortment of greetings. "Tonight, I would like to tell you a fairy tale. A fairy tale that begins with a young man, a self-proclaimed artist with an abundance of charisma and charm. A young man who lived his life the way he pleased, and savoured every moment of his indulgent existence, until, one day, he stumbled upon something monstrous."

I looked at Delia and the women, leaning forward in their chairs, eyes wide and hungry.

# CHAPTER 38:

## A FAIRY'S TALE

Everyone knew about the fairies that lived in the forest on the hill, just above the town. The fairies rarely ventured close to the town and, for the most part, the townsfolk stayed away from the forest. The older folk knew not to meddle in matters that didn't concern them and, although the younger men of the town would sometimes sneak into the forest to look, most of them would do just that, a look and nothing more before rushing back to town, breathless and dizzy with adrenaline. They would whisper excitedly to their friends about what they had seen, until someone more senior would hear and clout them over the head, calling them foolish and impulsive.

It was well known that the fairies were not particularly interested in the townsfolk. Each night they would form a circle in the clearing in the forest, illuminating the trees with twinkling lights, where they would sing and dance together. The few who had spoken to the townsfolk and come back to tell the tale had relayed their disdain of the town, of the men who dwindled away their days in dingy pubs, caged together like stinking animals, drunk but not merry. The fairies liked to be free, stripped of their clothing and able to dance among the trees and the animals, long hair flowing luxuriously down bare backs as they twirled in ecstasy. The townsfolk would occasionally grumble about the lack of decency, but secretly at night they would look longingly out their windows at the glow from the forest, and wish that they too could be free.

The young artist had lived in the town all his life. He painted portraits for the wealthier families who lived in the surrounding land: large, lifeless portraits of unsmiling people and children with startlingly stiff bodies, having been warned not to move. When the artist saw his portraits hanging he would wince, wondering how the families could take pleasure in such misery. He thought the townsfolk in general were boring, rigid in their ways.

The artist found himself fascinated by the stories of the fairies in the forest, those creatures who danced naked and free. He longed to be so happy and liberated. However, the artist knew of the stories and warnings that had been passed down through the generations. If a young man were to venture into the forest and stumble upon the fairy party, they would welcome him into their circle and let him choose a fairy to dance with. If the man danced with the fairy beyond midnight, the spell would be complete and the man would be doomed to dance with that fairy for all of eternity. Of course, if the man were to leave before the stroke of midnight, he would be free to return home. Many sons, brothers and husbands of the town had been lost to the fairy circle, after losing track of time.

However, the artist knew that so long as he was careful, he could enjoy that freedom each night if he pleased. So, he went to the watchmaker in the town square, and he spent what little money he had left on a beautiful golden pocket watch. Given his means he ought to have bought something far cheaper, but he was renowned for being a little extravagant when he could. He strutted like a peacock down the road home, the sun glinting on the gold in his breast pocket, preparing to preen himself for the evening.

That night the artist felt his polished shoes pressing into the waterlogged earth and mosses like sponges. His socks became cold and wet. He was beginning to regret his decision to venture into the forest. His visions of bare feet against warm ground and dancing in a spot-lit glade suddenly seemed romanticised. If it was cold and wet, he didn't want to dance. He would much rather be at the pub nursing a dram that was well outwith his budget.

Then he saw it, the flickering lights, and heard the sound of tinkling laughter over delicate music. He couldn't tell what instruments were playing, it was almost as though the natural sounds of the forest were singing, forming one beautiful song. The branches beat like gentle drums in the wind, which blew a song to a chorus of night animals. As he approached, carefully, he saw them in the centre of the clearing, moving so quickly and nimbly that he was unable to count them vanishing and reappearing behind trees. Their bodies were small and lithe, so delicate, he thought, that if he were to pick them up they would be no heavier than a sheet of parchment. They didn't care when he stepped tentatively out; they continued to dance merrily. Instead of questioning him, as the tales told, they simply beckoned him into their circle.

They clasped hands and danced around him, unashamedly naked, all smiling and wordlessly inviting him in. His eyes settled on a fair little creature with soft red ringlets, which wound over her body like an auburn shawl and which, as she held eye contact and swayed to one side, fell aside to expose her small breasts. The artist held out his hand and she took it gladly, welcoming his touch against her body and guiding him to move to the rhythm of the forest.

As the night went on, the artist paused and checked his watch regularly. And soon it was five minutes to midnight. With little effort, he released the fairy, letting her stumble back before, after a moment of confusion, she joined her fairy friends again, proceeding to dance like nothing had happened. The artist wiped his sweaty brow, slightly drunk somehow, despite having not touched a drop, and waved goodbye, returning to the town.

As the weeks went by, the artist returned most nights to the fairy circle. He would pick a different fairy each time, thrilled by the options available to him. They would dance until midnight was almost upon them, eyes locked as though their gaze would never break. Then, sure enough, the artist would check his watch and release the fairy. Each night he left with a warm belly, as though he had eaten a hearty meal or swigged generously from a bottle, and his mind was free of worry, savouring the memory of their bodies around him.

One evening, as he examined the fairies, it took him longer than usual to select one and hold out his hand. He had danced with so many of them now, and he relished the thrill of something new to excite him.

Leaping from the circle, the little red-haired fairy from his first night twirled into his line of sight, a familiar smile on her face, and extended her hand. The artist shook his head and looked beyond, indicating a fairy behind her, one with darker features and a shapelier body. This fairy stepped forward, taking the artist's hand. The red-haired fairy stopped her dance and stared at him, her smile faltering, blushing from the insult, her dancer's body curving uncertainly inwards. The other fairies lost their rhythm for just a moment – hesitating, stalling, some almost stumbling – before picking up their dance again. In the seconds in which they faltered, a knowing glance passed between them.

Ignoring this peculiar blip in the evening, the artist proceeded to dance with his latest fairy, curling his fingers into her thick black hair and pressing her against him as they moved. He enjoyed the nimbleness that the dancing so frequently brought to his body; he felt muscular and flexible, like his body was capable of all sorts of things he could never have imagined.

Unusually, the fairies began dancing around him, reaching out and touching him, curling into his movements. He was enjoying it for a while, until they started pecking at him curiously, like little hens. Then he noticed one of them playing with his pocket watch, the glimmer of gold catching on the lights in the trees. He snapped at the fairy playing with it and stuffed it back in his breast pocket, swiping her away. Unfazed, she continued to dance.

The evening went on as it always did, and the artist felt pleasantly sleepy from all the dancing, belly full and slightly drunk. He found himself more tired than usual and decided to end the evening slightly earlier. Checking his watch, it read quarter past eleven.

"That's enough," he said, smiling at the dark fairy and trying to loosen his grip on her, but he found himself unable to move his limbs of his own accord. His arms continued to twirl the fairy around and his legs danced beneath him to the forest's tune in perfect time. He saw the fairies around him grinning mischievously, and the one that had been playing with his watch giggled gleefully.

"You changed the time on my watch!" he cried, looking despairingly down at his feet. "You monster!"

The artist danced for what felt like hours; daylight didn't break over the canvas of the forest. Eventually, the dark-haired fairy released him from her grasp. But, before the artist could gasp a thank you, the little red-haired fairy took her place, smiling wickedly at him. She danced at double pace, and he was forced to follow.

"You belong to all of us now," she whispered.

As the days – perhaps weeks, maybe even months – passed, the artist wondered how long it would be before he died from exhaustion. He wished that death would come soon. The fairy spell meant that he never felt hungry or thirsty. Quite the opposite, in fact; his belly felt so full that it was increasingly unpleasant to dance. However, no matter how tired he was, his eyes would not close and his feet would not stop moving. His fine leather shoes had holes in their soles, and their tan colouring had turned a rich burgundy from the blood that seeped from the ragged blisters on his heels. The artist had grown used to the pain of his broken toes and torn skin. He waited to die, longing to escape the fairies who had once appeared beautiful to him, but who he now recognised as monsters in disguise.

One evening, during the party, the forest paused in its tune and the fairies fell still, ears pricking at the warning in the trees. The artist continued to dance regardless, moving in the quiet, his head hung in submission. He had no energy left to beg or cry anymore, so he had fallen into total silence.

Pushing through the foliage, a woman appeared. She was taller than the fairies, with long dark hair and cat-like eyes. She was fully clothed, which the artist found strangely refreshing, and her steps were slow and purposeful, a change from the fleet-footedness of the fairies.

"*It's the witch!*" one of the fairies whispered to the others. They bowed their heads in unison and greeted her respectfully, letting their hair tumble forward to cover them modestly.

"How may we serve you?" one of them asked, scuttling forward and crouching at the witch's feet. Wordlessly, the witch pointed at the artist, who continued to dance, his bloody trail marking out his steps on the grass. The fairies bristled for a moment, glancing at one another before resigning and skipping over to the artist.

Suddenly he wasn't dancing anymore. He couldn't feel his feet and would have crumpled to the ground if the witch had not caught him. She was surprisingly strong, smiling at him with the glint of a slightly uneven canine protruding from her otherwise perfect mouth. She propped him up.

"Poor thing," she whispered. "Don't worry, you're safe with me now."

The fairies giggled, beginning to dance again as the music resumed. Just as the witch turned away, the artist in her arms, the little red-haired fairy leaned in close to the artist's ear, her voice barely rising above the tune of the breeze.

"This will be far worse for you."

# CHAPTER 39

As the room exploded with applause I turned to Dennis, who was still shrinking in shame, and handed him my tray. He took it obediently, without asking anything. It was funny how if you handed someone something without saying anything they would just take it. I recalled hearing about a study that had been done on it; nobody questions it, they just obey and don't think about it until it's in their hands.

As I turned to leave, Dennis caught my shoulder with a chubby hand.

"You know," he whispered, "I used to be someone that people respected. Where I'm from, the men aren't treated this way."

I hesitated, glancing from side to side to make sure nobody was listening.

"Do you want to leave?" I asked.

"Oh no!" He laughed, slightly shocked. "No, no. Delia's just wonderful, isn't she?"

"Isn't she just," I replied flatly, turning and leaving. Dennis's eyes were back on Delia.

# CHAPTER 40

Will she forget me?

This thought occurred to me as I pulled on a second pair of trousers, a size larger so that they fit over the first. I secured them with a belt I'd stolen from one of the bedrooms down the hall. I wanted to escape her, and yet the idea of her forgetting me left me rattled. Whenever I had pictured her recently, I saw her smirking at me, or looking through me, or even one of her flashes of anger which frightened me. In those images there was something unnatural in her perfect features, something I couldn't quite place but knew wasn't right. Reptilian, perhaps? However, at the thought of leaving her, the image flashed back to that night at the Christmas market when she stood both within but apart from the crowd, a presence about her that was nothing less than irresistible. I thought of the pleasure it gave me to see her smile, the mischief in her eyes that separated us from everyone else. Then, of course, there was her scent.

There were smells I could summon with ease; pleasant smells that had been around as long as I could remember, like the smell of recently baked bread, or the cotton freshness of washing detergent. They meant something that went beyond the smell itself – the excitement of going to the bakery in the morning, knowing you'd get a pastry for breakfast, or the inviting joy of clean bedsheets. However, Delia's scent was more complex; it was as though it had been specifically manufactured to replicate everything that meant something to me. It was impossible to recreate in my mind, largely because it didn't really make sense to me. I wished that, just one more time, I could capture it and store it in my memory. The idea of losing that scent forever was devastating. I wanted to breathe her in, just once, before I left.

"Eric," Henry snapped impatiently. He looked ridiculously frumpy in his layers, the toggles of his waterproof pulled tight around his chin. We hadn't been able to find gloves, but the jumpers were long enough to stretch over our arms. "Stop thinking about her."

"I'm not."

"We all do."

Each step I took felt restricted by the impractical layers of work attire and mismatched items. I was relieved to hear that the excitable shrieks of the women were confined to the drawing room on the ground floor, but we remained alert, uncomfortably aware of the sound of our breath and the rustle of our clothes.

It seemed almost too easy as we reached the laundry room and opened the back door, which led out onto the courtyard where the bins were kept. For the first time I wondered who collected those bins. I had never seen any council lorries.

Henry took the first step into the blizzard, with the confidence of a man who had taken risks all his life. He briefly grimaced as his brogue disappeared into the snow.

"Wait," I said, touching his arm, my words trembling in my throat. "Maybe this is stupid. We're not prepared – people die in the hills in winter."

"It's not winter," Henry replied simply, brushing my hand off. "She just wants us to think it is."

"What if we wait until morning?"

"Won't work." He shook his head. "They'd catch us. For now they're all here, all distracted. I'm leaving."

He took another step into the darkness, eyeing a broken security light suspiciously.

I glanced behind me, back to the warmth where the laundry

room tumble dryers rumbled contentedly and pumped out a pleasant heat. I thought of the fire in the drawing room, of drinks and canapés and beautiful women. I thought of Delia, her smile, her smell. Warmth, comfort, routine. Sex. Lies, manipulation – the corpse in the bricked-off bedroom. I shuddered, disturbed by how easily that image slipped from my mind, as though I was only very loosely holding onto it, as though standing there in her office was already a memory from years ago. I thought of the skull, the bones of the fingers that might once have reached for help. I wondered if he had been like me. We were insects, wrapped up in her silken web, subdued by venom.

I stepped out into the cold with Henry, the door shutting behind me. I sensed his relief, though he didn't say anything, just trudged ahead. I noticed the glow from the drawing room windows, which were just around the corner of the building, casting a dim orange light across the snow. I couldn't resist slipping round and crouching by the window ledge, rising cautiously until my eyes were just above the stone. My hands were pressed firmly against the wall, bracing me in my fear of slipping and attracting attention. At least there was no danger of them hearing me over their shrieking and the music. Edward remained by the piano, but his choir now accompanied him, their lips keeping pace with the song.

The women were dancing but their movements didn't match the music; they were disjointed and chaotic, their mouths stretched into long, perfect-toothed smiles that spread symmetrically to both ears. Their ears were neatly pinned back, flat against their skulls. The serving staff slinked back up against the walls, heads bowed low as though ashamed of watching.

Snatching a glass bottle, one of the women jumped up onto a table, spinning around as she poured the yellow bubbles over her face, only catching some of them in her gaping, red-lipped mouth. The hem of her dress knocked glasses and ornaments from the table, sending them shattering to the floor. When she was done with it, the bottle followed, an explosion of glass against wood. When one of the men approached her, crunching over broken glass to pick up the debris, she snatched his hands and pulled him up onto the table to dance with her. The man glanced around him, self-conscious and unsure of what exactly was expected of him.

I watched Delia move towards the fireplace, the oozing trail of her rose gown dragging shards of glass with her. She paused by the fire to observe her party, lips curled at the corners as though satisfied.

"*Eric.*" A hand gripped my upper arm painfully. Henry's face was white with frost that had gathered over the hairs on his brows and chin. He looked old. "We need to move or we'll both freeze to death."

Turning one last time to look at her, with the intention of memorising every piece of her, I found that I didn't much like what I saw. It wasn't a face I wanted to remember. There was no mischief in her eyes anymore, nor any depth to her smile. She used to exude a playful affection, but now she seemed hardened and smooth like polished marble. Even draped in warm rose, with her face painted in pleasant pinks and blushes, everything about her seemed cold and cruel. The woman by the fire with the loveless smile and empty eyes, who dragged broken glass behind her, was not the woman I wanted to remember.

# CHAPTER 41

Time seemed to pass differently in the hills. The wind and the snow slowed us down, and there was only a few feet of visibility in the heavy snowfall. The world before us was a monotonous veil of drifting grey-white, time itself seeming to slow as we did. It was like waiting in anticipation for something in a room with a ticking clock. Nothing changing, and nothing to signify the passing of time but the gentle *tick, tick, tick* of the clock hand. Gradually, the ticks would slow and become louder, echoing, somehow grander. The space between each tick would stretch until, just for a moment, you would start to wonder if time had actually stopped. I thought of white hospital waiting rooms with waxy vinyl floors and grey plastic chairs. Stony faces. *Tick, tick, tick.* Time taunted us.

I wondered if I was sleepy, my eyes becoming more difficult to open, and realised that my eyelashes had begun to freeze and stick to one another. I rubbed them furiously, clearing my vision. We paused briefly to share some biscuits from the rucksack, both craving fast energy, clueless about how far we had walked in silence. We fought with the broken zipper and gratefully crammed several biscuits into our mouths, pausing so that the chocolate melted to the roof of our mouths, mimicking warmth. It seemed strange that I had once denied myself chocolate biscuits out of vanity. I wanted to eat them one after the other until the whole packet had vanished.

I moved my jaw to speak, feeling it creak uncomfortably as

though frozen. Trying again, I raised my voice to be heard over the wind.

"What will you do when you get back?" My teeth chattered noisily. "The first thing – what will it be?"

Henry looked up me, his outline only just visible in the darkness.

"I'll find my children," he replied simply, followed by a wheezing cough when he breathed in the frozen air. "I'll find them and I'll tell them how sorry I am. I'll make it up to them." He nodded, as though in agreement with his own plan. "I'll get my legal qualifications back up to scratch, catch up on everything I've missed so I can get another well-paid job, and then I'll take them on a holiday somewhere nice – somewhere really nice. Maybe the Mediterranean. Can you picture it? The heat of the sun, crystal blue sea, colour all around you?"

I looked around at the monotonous grey-white world. When I thought of colour, all I could picture were those stuffed birds in the hotel reception, once vibrant feathers dulled with age and natural bleaching, glass eyes still bright, alert and watching everything.

"Yeah," I lied. "Yeah, I can picture it."

"And what about you?" He tucked the biscuits back in his rucksack and gestured for us to continue moving, his pace quickening, as though energised by unrealistic visions of the future.

"I'll go back to Edinburgh," I replied. "I was engaged before I came here, did I tell you that?"

"You didn't."

"Well, I was, and technically I never broke it off, so I guess I'm still engaged, maybe? Her name was Eleanor. She's one of these types that worries a lot – a real natural worrier. I bet she's still looking for me."

"It's been a long time."

"I know that." I did my best trying not to sound defensive. "But Eleanor's loyal. We had this great future planned out together."

The future suddenly seemed brighter than ever, her beautiful Stockbridge flat with the high corniced ceilings and the big bay windows. Once all her tat had been cleared out, it had real potential. Eleanor was guilty of being a bit of a hoarder, Christmas decorations and artwork from her pupils scattered everywhere. She had promised me one of the rooms as my writing room, and I'd had it all planned out. I was going to strip back the floors to original wood and have them varnished, and paint the walls a simple off-white. Eleanor would eventually realise how much better things looked and agree to decorate the rest of the flat similarly. I pictured her baking in the kitchen, puffs of flour and icing sugar everywhere – but this time it didn't annoy me at all, in fact I would enjoy watching her, small and plump, with her smattering of freckles, as she bumbled about humming to herself. She exuded sunniness. Perhaps I would even agree to have children; the image of her smiling face with a baby hooked under her arm now seemed more appealing than it had before. A real family. Her grandparents had wanted to divide their considerable wealth among their grandchildren after they died, which meant it wouldn't be long before we came into a considerable amount of money. We would be able to enjoy an even more luxurious existence. I knew it was wrong to look forward to someone's death, but I had never particularly liked her grandparents anyway. They were the worst kind of snobs, turning their noses up through forced smiles while pretending to be interested in my background. Eleanor thought I was imagining it, but I had met enough people like them to know.

"Well, that's nice," Henry replied, sounding unconvinced. He had a look about him that I recognised: a pandering acknowledgement that at the same time made it very clear he thought I was wrong. Clear enough that I knew, but I couldn't raise it because he would just say, "What? I didn't say anything!" I felt myself bristle in irritation.

"I'm soaking," I complained instead, lifting my foot from the snow, leather and cotton saturated and squelching. "I don't recognise anything – it's like we've just been covering the same ground for hours."

"We should have reached a road by now." Henry squinted through the darkness. We both turned around to examine our limited surroundings before realising we had forgotten the direction we had been facing in the first place. Disorientated and cold, I felt my temper rise.

"*Fuck*, Henry." I curled my hands tighter into the fabric of my jumper. A flutter of panic was rising through my stomach and up into my throat, making me dizzy. I pictured my uncle, weathered and grizzly as he rubbed his thumb against his fingers, yellow-stained from tobacco. Even when he wasn't smoking, he made that rolling motion, it was a habit. I pictured him frowning at me through the night, weighed down in his Gore-Tex, wet on the outside and warm on the inside like an insulated bear. He shook his head, his dry lips mouthing "City fools."

"We just need to keep going," Henry insisted, his voice lacking the confidence it had held before. I noticed him fight a shiver.

"Going where?" I snapped. "This is insane – we could die out here!"

"My family holiday home. It can't be far." Suddenly he sounded whimsical, like he was living out a fantasy. I cursed myself for trusting him.

"Oh my God, you're a moron. I don't know why I listened to you. Look around! I don't see *anything*!" My lips wobbled as panic rose like bile. "We're going to die. We need to go back – they probably won't even have noticed that we're gone yet – we can slip back inside."

Swivelling around, I guessed the direction we had come in and pointed optimistically.

"You can go." Henry moved away from me, hoisting his rucksack more firmly into place. I reached out, snatching a strap out of fear of losing sight of him in the blizzard.

"We can hide," I insisted. "We've both seen them, the men who live in the walls. We can stay out of sight and make better plans – maybe they can help us."

Swiping me from his grasp, Henry took a step away from me.

"If we go back, we never leave," he said. "We end up like that man hiding in the fireplace. Stealing scraps and making cramped nests in the walls like rats. We'd decay there, going mad with the rest of them, always fearful of slipping up. Then, if we did get caught – who knows, maybe we'd end up like that body you said you found. You want to go back to that?"

"We'll be bodies out here at this rate!"

"Better out here than back there." Henry turned his back on me. "I'm taking my chances. You go back if you want. I won't stop you. I'm going to find a road and I'm going to get help."

He vanished into the blizzard, leaving me standing alone, clutching the sleeves of my jumper and shaking. The grey-white world spun around me, tugging at the flaps of my clothing as if teasing me. I felt hot tears forming in the corners of my eyes, too ashamed to let them roll down my cheeks.

Shutting my eyes tightly, I hoped the tears would freeze up and I could flick them away. I wanted warm arms around me. I wanted those fat arms that I recalled from my childhood, the arms that my mother hated but I had always loved. I loved the softness and the safety of them, the way they could squeeze until I was breathless, but never actually hurt me, no bony edges or sharpness to them. My mum's warm scent became fresh in my mind, making the hint of it that Delia had about her seem like a cheap replica. It was the scent of safety and of love. That was what I craved.

I thought back to a time when I had started to understand what was going on, astonished by my own naïvety. The more I understood, the more I noticed. I picked up on the way my father shuffled guiltily when he left in the evening, making murmurs about going to the pub, whereas if he was really going to the pub he would be loud and jolly. I associated the unpleasant cherry perfume with his return, and I noticed the way that the blonde woman who wore too much make-up and used to pinch my cheeks would avert her gaze when I passed on the street with my family, as though ashamed. It baffled me that my mother said nothing, maintaining her placid plod and a sadness that she never quite expressed. One evening, as my father shuffled out the door, I waited until he had closed it and then turned to my mother, who was dutifully cleaning the dishes after dinner.

"Why don't you just *leave?*" I had asked, exasperated and mortified that my friends at school might find out and poke fun at my mum's expense. They might call Annie a slag, but I didn't care about that – they could call her whatever they wanted; she deserved it. Meanwhile, my mum was easy to make fun of, with her quietly non-conforming nature, and it saddened me that they would taunt her for her most lovable trait. She didn't like the other mothers' groups, and her stint in the parent–teacher association had been short lived. She described them as wolves: there was the leader and then the rest of the pack. You always had to be careful not to break the pack rules, and even more careful not to question the authority of the pack leader, unless you were prepared to see it through and risk the pack tearing you apart. I laughed at the image of all those women with chunky highlights and over-applied blusher morphing into slavering wolves. In my mind's eye, the wolves' coats had blonde highlights too.

My mother didn't say anything at first; instead, she paused over the sink with a plate and scrubbing brush in her gloved hands. Then, very slowly, she placed them to the side and peeled the yellow Marigolds from her arms, leaving them inside out on the drying rack. She had a strange, resigned expression about her, one I would never forget, as she walked slowly towards me. She spread out her arms and held me tightly so that my face squashed into the softness of her shoulder. I wanted to struggle away and tell her that a hug wasn't going to help. Instead, I willed her to summon the rage, rage that I could only assume was simmering inside her, and march over to Annie's where she would kick down the door and shout for them to come and faced her. When Annie appeared in what I imagined was a suggestive silk dressing gown – which she would be clutching around her front, gasping as though she was the victim – I pictured my mum grabbing her limp yellow ponytail and telling her exactly what she thought of her. I wanted her to win, regardless of the means. Although, back then I wasn't sure what winning was. On one hand, I hoped that my father would have walked past Annie, seeing clearly for the first time in months and realising how much she disgusted him with her fake nails and her caked-on makeup. He would take my mother's hand and they would walk home together, triumphant and glowing with a rediscovered love for one another. On the other hand, I burned hot with rage at the humiliation my mother had suffered and, once she was done with Annie, I hoped she would look my father in the eye and tell him she was finished with him and that she was leaving. But then I would pause and wonder what life would be like without my mum and dad together, and that thought pained me. I loved them both.

My mother held me tightly for several seconds before answering me, her voice soft and resigned.

"Where would I go?" She lifted her hand to my hair and gently tucked it behind my ear. As I pulled back, it was her subdued smile that chilled me the most. "What would I do?"

I blinked back to the present, back to the reality of the bitter chill and the heavy snow flooding around me, threatening to freeze my eyes shut. I didn't want to be trapped like my mother.

"Henry!" I shouted after him, staggering clumsily in his direction. "Wait for me!"

# CHAPTER 42

What did I want out of life? I supposed everyone would have a very different answer to that question. Some people might say financial security, others adventure. For the lucky ones, the two might come hand in hand, but I imagine that usually isn't the case. Many people would like the finer things in life, but there are others who'd be happy in a billowing tent out in the wilderness, where the drudgery of ordinary daily living might not touch them.

It seemed like a question people ought to ask each other more often. When I thought of all the people I knew, I realised that I didn't actually know what it was they wanted out of life. This wasn't especially surprising, given that I didn't seem to know what I wanted either. Much like the financial security versus adventure dilemma, I wanted love and comfort, but I also wanted thrill and excitement. I wanted wealth and success, but I also wanted an easy life. I envied people who knew what they wanted, people who had the drive to get it. Eleanor had a friend, Thomas Wilson, who was an accountant. I knew him from back when he was finishing his training and studying for his exams. He was always so focused, and I never understood why anyone would invest so much effort just to stare at spreadsheets all day and tally up numbers for other people. However, he passed his exams and would gush about how much he enjoyed his job without ever actually offering me a convincing example of why he enjoyed it. I suppose there was the social side to it, one boring accountant mingling with other boring accountants over a glass of wine on a Friday at five-thirty. He met his wife, Samantha, another accountant, through work. They were the dullest couple I had ever met and I used to dread it when Eleanor invited them over for dinner, especially after they had their baby. I couldn't even remember its name. They would share "hilarious" anecdotes about their child that may or may not have been funny to someone who actually had children. Their humour was very sensible, and when they laughed it would catch me off guard; I'd think they must be laughing at something I'd inadvertently done, as what had just been said couldn't possibly be so hilarious. They were the kind of people who were neither attractive nor ugly. If you were walking down the street they would blend in with the crowd, invisible unless they made the effort to draw your attention. You would forget their faces as soon as they left your sight, remembering only a name and maybe the fact that Thomas's hair had started to thin even though he was only thirty. I used to think that they were both so unfortunate.

Oddly, as I pulled myself through the snow, timing my steps with Henry out of fear of losing him, I couldn't stop thinking about Thomas and Samantha. I used to think that they were two tedious, plain people who had settled for each other. However, the more I thought about it, the more they struck me as two people who shared exactly the same interests, enjoyed their jobs and delighted in the child they had brought into the world. Two people who would laugh at the same rubbish jokes, probably repeating them well into the week to elicit giggles from one another, and they always smiled. They had achieved what they wanted out of life; simply put, they had managed to find happiness. I winced at the fact that I found myself envious of Thomas and Samantha Wilson. Why couldn't I have that?

The snow had lessened slightly, allowing the sky to brighten into a heavy grey, disguising the sun in a colourless film. I found myself squinting, my eyes having adjusted in the night to the dim glow of the moon, which had been veiled by clouds.

Every part of my body ached as though it had been frozen then thawed to the point where I could move, but only just. Joints and muscles creaked warningly, threatening to give way and send me tumbling into the snow. Each breath that came out was a soft sugar icing cloud, yet ragged and laborious. Glancing at Henry, I could see that he felt the same, but neither of us wanted to admit it yet.

A moment later I was on my knees, without recollection of dropping to the ground. There was a blank in my memory. My bare hands were buried in the snow as I leaned forward on all fours. It didn't even feel cold anymore. Annoyingly, I still couldn't shake Thomas Wilson from my head. For the first time I could picture his face clearly, his permanent smile, which he probably wore to err on the side of caution lest anyone ever think he was unhappy. He had colourless eyes, or at least the kind of colour you could never actually pin down, sometimes green, sometimes a nondescript brown, sometimes something else. I could see him smiling at me, looking down from above, knowing that I was going to die, but refusing to give up his smile. He would say something like "Gosh" or "Bad luck, but you just never know what might be around the corner!"

"Fuck you, Thomas," I muttered. Squinting, I reached up to him. He looked warm and dry, and I wanted his soft cardigan and shoes, his lovely cashmere socks. The thought of pulling Thomas's socks on, still warm from his own feet, made me laugh a little. In another life, the thought of wearing Thomas Wilson's old socks would have made me recoil. I started to laugh. A strange laugh that sounded foreign on my tongue.

"Eric!" The figure bent down and gathered me under his arms. It was Henry, not Thomas Wilson. I shook my head.

"I thought you were Thomas," I murmured.

"Who?"

"I don't like him, but he seems happy."

"For Christ's sake, Eric." Shaking me aggressively, Henry began pointing. "Look! We're on a road. We made it!"

I rubbed my eyes, clearing the frost gluing my eyelashes together. My hand had become so numb it felt like someone else was touching me with lifeless fingers. The snow seemed to have lightened a little, falling in tiny powder-like flakes. In the distance I heard a rumbling, and both Henry and I sprung to attention at the sight of a large vehicle growing bigger and bigger as it approached. It juddered unsteadily over the lumpy snow, gasping exhaust fumes from its rear. Henry gripped my hand tightly in his.

"It's a bus, Eric!" he cried out in delight, flinging himself from the raised verge and stumbling out onto the road, waving his arms frantically. "Help!" he roared, his voice hoarse from the cold. "*Help!*"

I felt a glimmer of recognition. I knew the bus somehow, recalling the sound of the exhaust and the metallic clang as it trundled determinedly along. I had seen it before. My hand reached out, brushing Henry's arm, then nudging him with more force when he ignored me.

"*Henry*," I hissed. A sharp burst of adrenaline thawed my limbs further and I felt myself become more alert. "I think I've been here before. I think I've seen this bus!"

"So?" Henry continued waving and I watched as the bus began to slow.

"I just can't remember… I think I tried to catch it once," I insisted, twitching fearfully as though an electric current was running through me in warning. "I don't know why I didn't get onboard. I don't remember."

The bus juddered to a halt; the side windows were steamed up so we couldn't see inside. We waited in silence as the doors trembled open. I found myself gripping Henry tightly, leaning into him for support before realising that he had no strength left. We both tumbled into the compact snow on the road, landing more painfully than I had anticipated.

"Oh my!" I heard the bus driver exclaim, turning off the engine, the bus grumbling slowly into silence. I heard commotion further down the vehicle, hands rubbing the condensation from the inside for a clearer view. My cheek was pressed against ice, a stinging that spread to the rest of my face. I wondered what Thomas Wilson was doing at that moment. Probably still in bed with his wife, the baby wedged between them. Of course, it wouldn't be a baby anymore.

"Hello?" A flash of pale orange appeared above me, owl-like eyes looming over. I recognised her immediately. She was the elderly bus driver I had seen all those years ago. Leaning closer on creaking limbs, I heard her huff in pain as her hands supported her knees for the bend.

"Ladies!" she cried. "These gentlemen need help!"

There was an excitable bustling on the bus as it trembled from movement, and one by one the elderly women filtered out, gasping in surprise as we sprawled on the road before them.

"Please." Henry lifted his torso from the ground, straining from the exertion. "Can you help us?"

"Of course, of course!" The old woman nodded frantically and glanced behind at her passengers. "Can anyone give me their coat?"

Warm, dry hands were suddenly all over me, peeling me from the icy ground and wrapping something soft around me. Fur. I let my face fall forward into the thick chestnut, silky soft against my nose and lips. I could melt into it.

"Come on, up." The hands gripped me, too weak to do anything alone but together able to pull me to my feet.

"Careful, now." A white-haired woman with a long, narrow nose tensed beneath my weight. "I'm not as strong as I used to be!"

"Thank you." I felt my mouth form the words, but I was unsure if any sound had come out. Henry and I were ushered onto the bus, grateful for the dry, artificial heat filling the narrow space. The seats were small and rickety, with a thin blue layer of padding over the plastic, and there didn't appear to be any seatbelts. A proper old country bus. After being guided down the aisle, I found myself sitting on one of the hard chairs, although the coat's fur served as a cushion. Henry slumped next to me, letting his body fall into the fur, spreading a warmth I was grateful for.

"I think they need medical attention." One of the women placed her palm against my cheek, tilting my chin up and examining me carefully. "Mary, didn't you used to be a nurse?"

"Aye." A robust woman with steely hair bustled towards me, the other women jumping to the side. Mary did look like a retired nurse, I thought to myself. They never lost that officiousness about them. I found myself inclined to do exactly as she said.

"Can you call someone?" Henry asked hopefully, straightening his back but still squinting. Mary placed two fingers on the side of his throat, pausing to count before answering.

"Aye," she said again. "We don't have mobile phones, do we?"

A murmur of "no" rippled down the bus.

"Alright, we'll need to find a house or a phone box. This time of year can be tricky for the landlines, but we'll get you help." Her face became stern, matronly. "What were you two playing at anyway, out here wearing barely anything?" She looked at my hands, raw and bare, and tutted disapprovingly. "Keep these warm or your fingers are going to need chopped off at the hospital."

I nodded compliantly, sliding my hands back into the sleeves of my damp jumper.

"These men need warmed up!" Mary barked at the passengers behind her. "Has anyone got a thermal flask? Coffee? Tea? Soup?"

A gnarled hand dipped into a handbag and presented a steel container. Mary pressed it firmly into my hands; it was delightfully warm.

"Drink this, both of you," she insisted, moving into the seat beside us. "You need to warm up quickly. Izzy, get that heating back on!"

The driver nodded and shuffled back to the front. The engine rumbled, and gusts of hot air smothered us.

"We need to move." Henry's eyes searched for the driver, words slurring clumsily in his mouth. "Please, we need to get out of here *now*."

"Alright, sonny boy." The driver shut the doors and pulled the handbrake. "You just focus on warming up and we'll do the rest."

I fumbled with the flask, my hands now burning even though it couldn't have been that hot. A strange tingling sensation ran up my wrists, which had turned an angry pink. I imagined my entire body was bright pink and ruddy. I unscrewed the metal lid, it toppled into my lap, and I was greeted by the hot steam of what was undoubtedly mulled wine. I smiled in thanks at the woman who had given me it, uplifted by the thought of her having spent her day shopping in town, now merry from her hot wine. The thick, purple liquid filled my mouth, running down my throat and warming the base of my belly. I found myself breathless and tired when I pulled it from my lips, handing it to Henry.

"I think that might just have been the best thing I've ever drunk," I laughed lightly, letting my head loll to the side, watching the flashes of white as we drove along the road through immaculate hills. The landscape made me think of iced desserts, sweet and spiced like the wine. "I forgot how much I like mulled wine."

Henry pulled the flask from his lips, reattaching the lid and placing the bottle between his thighs. He sighed wearily and rested his weight against me.

"That was good," he murmured, his eyes beginning to close, his voice becoming softer. "I've never had strawberry juice before."

# CHAPTER 43

I thought that I'd tried to argue. Perhaps I had; I wasn't entirely sure. The initial look of panic on the faces of the elderly women had gone and they had returned to their seats, where they resumed reading their books or talking discreetly in words I couldn't make out. Henry snored gently next to me, intoxicatingly peaceful. When I tried to wake him up, he mumbled incoherently, and I found I didn't have the energy to persevere.

As we approached the hotel, a giant gingerbread mansion in the distance with a delightfully frosted roof, I opened my mouth, knowing that something was wrong, but I wasn't entirely sure how to say it. In the end, I didn't say anything at all.

"Don't worry, dear, you're going to be just fine," the driver said to me once she had pulled up by the front entrance. Her voice was crackled with age and reassuring. As she touched me with her arthritic claws, I thought how easily breakable they were and how I could have simply pushed her over and ran. I was at the front of the bus already. However, it all just seemed too hard. Henry stirred beside me, blinking sleepily and peering at the hotel, unsure how he ought to react.

"No," he said eventually, his lips turning downwards. "Not here, keep driving."

"We need to get you two out of these wet clothes and warmed up while we call for help," Mary reassured us. "This is the nearest place we can access a telephone."

The women ushered us to our feet and we stumbled along with the support of their small, stooped bodies. Flickers like sharp electric currents encouraged me to make a run for it, or even to hijack the bus, but those notions vanished as quickly as they came and left me limp and exhausted.

"There's a witch who lives here," I said quietly, my words heavy and clumsy in my mouth.

"Oh dear." Mary turned to the driver on my other side. "Confusion. It's a symptom of hypothermia. Get them inside, fast."

The black doors swung open and my feet met the slate floor, my socks squelching unpleasantly in my soaked shoes. Henry slapped alongside me; we were a pair of frogs out of water, clammy and clumsy. We glistened beneath the crystal chandelier. The birds on either side of us stared intently, their glass eyes twinkling.

"Oh my God!" Delia emerged from the drawing room door in a wave of rose chiffon. Tendrils of dark hair had tumbled from her formerly slick bun and spiralled chaotically over her shoulders. Behind her, the men looked exhausted as they filed out with bowed heads and sluggish movements. Their creased clothing indicated they hadn't been to bed yet either.

"No!" I turned to the driver, hoping to reason with her. Instead of the old woman with the spectacles like magnifying glasses and the pale strawberry blonde hair, Isobel was beside me, watching me with her planet-like eyes, her delicate hand gripping my upper arm with disproportionate strength. I found myself crying out in fright and stumbling back. The woman I thought was Mary on my other side caught me and held me upright. She was still stern-faced with a long narrow nose, but she was youthful and impossibly beautiful in the same unnerving way as Isobel.

"We found them outside," Isobel stated. "Drunk, I think."

"Very dangerous," the woman I had believed to be Mary added. "We'll need to get them warmed up to avoid hypothermia setting in."

Delia clamped her hands over her mouth to convey shock, but her eyes didn't move. The women were playing a little game with one another, wolfishly portraying their parts as they circled us in faux concern.

"How could you do this to me?" Delia's voice was delicate as fine glass, threatening to shatter. "I've been up all night sick with worry. You ruined my party."

"Delia," Mary said, the sternness in her voice mimicking the elderly woman on the bus. "I understand you're upset, but we do need to get them warmed up."

"Of course." Nodding, Delia straightened herself and dropped her pouting expression. A wickedness flashed across her marble face. "Well, get them out of these wet clothes, then."

It took me a moment to realise what she meant, and I stood dumbly as the women's hands scrabbled over me, grasping and tugging at my clothing to strip me bare. Opening my mouth, a strange squawk escaped my lips, and I could almost hear the stuffed birds around me cackling from their open beaks. One of the women laughed and clucked mockingly at me, and suddenly the birds and the women felt one and the same, cawing and cackling.

"That's enough." A voice from the gathering of subdued men rose above the commotion. The grappling hands paused, distracted by the interruption, and Edward stepped forward from the crowd, tall and grey. Soothed by the friendly face, I mouthed his name, which came out as a gasp of relief. He bent down to the floor and gathered up the fur coat, slinging it back over my shoulders to cover my bare chest.

"Delia." He turned to her. "They've been through enough. Just send them home and be done with it."

Delia remained still and stony, her eyes set on Edward, some-how looking down on him even although he was the taller of the two.

"Edward, darling," she said, with a tight smile playing on her lips. "I'm afraid this is none of your business."

"I think it is," he replied unexpectedly. I heard the sharp intake of breath from the women near me, excited as they craned forward to observe the unfolding drama. There was something ghoulish about it; I sensed their eyes widen without even having to look. "I do everything you ask me to," he continued, "and I do it because I love you. I have loved you since the moment we left that little island together, with you wrapped in my arms on that boat. You didn't even need to manipulate me with your silly tricks and spells, I was always yours, and I would have done whatever it took to help you." He took a breath. "But it's gone too far. Let them go."

Delia's smile didn't falter. Instead of replying to Edward, she strode carefully past him, with heels that clicked like a ticking clock against the slate, and approached Henry. Cupping his chin in her hand, she leaned in close to his face and placed her other hand on his cheek. I watched him melt into her warmth.

"Do you want to leave, Henry?" she asked gently. "It's alright if you do."

Looking up slowly, his eyes squinted, struggling to focus.

"No."

"See?" Dropping his chin, she let it bump off his chest and spun back around to face Edward. "They want to be here. They're happy here."

"That's not true." Edward shook his head and reached forward to grasp Delia's arms. "When will I be enough for you? How long will it take before you realise that none of this will ever make you better? You can't make it better this way." He paused, hesitating about what he was about to say. "You're just hiding, Delia. This isn't going to change anything for you."

Delia's eyes flashed briefly from Edward to the women surrounding me before she smoothly brushed Edward's hands from her.

"Don't touch me," she said simply. "You're fired, Edward. Pack your things. I'll arrange a taxi to pick you up this evening."

Audible gasps escaped the group of men as their eyes lifted

from the floor, suddenly alert. They shuffled uncomfortably, as though nervous of committing some misdemeanour that might carry the same penalty.

"Delia," Edward began.

"You're fired," she repeated firmly. "Get out of my sight."

"No. Please." His lined hands reached out for her, but she took a resolved step back. The men behind her bristled as though they had been activated to defend her. They stepped forward, forming a defensive line. Edward's eyes widened in dismay as his peers snarled at him.

"She said get lost," Isobel chimed in, a tinkling of glee in her otherwise smooth voice. The women shrieked in delight, the noise agitating the men, who seemed alert to danger but unsure exactly where it was coming from. I felt my gaze flicker fearfully from side to side. None of the reactions around me seemed appropriate; it was like all the social cues I was accustomed to belonged to another world. It was a room of wild animals, and I couldn't predict what they were about to do.

I caught Delia watching me, her head tilted to the side, observing my discomfort curiously. Then, slowly, she approached me and extended her hand. There was no room for me to back away, as the women clustered tightly, hands still gripping my body which was heavy from the weight of the wet layers.

"Come on." Her hand wrapped around mine. "Let's get you warmed up. You must be exhausted."

The women released me and allowed me to stumble forward into her so that our noses were millimetres apart. Her high cheekbones cut through her face, perched above the fine line of her jaw with the kind of elegance women tried to achieve with make-up and surgery. I imagined that when she was younger her features would have been too defined to meet the standards of prettiness, lacking the plump softness and snub noses that gave children their sweet appearance. Her nose suddenly pressed against mine, her warmth radiating through me, and I saw us as we had been, discussing jazz over a bottle of wine and skirting round the sexual tension that hovered delightfully between us. Neither of us were tethered by rules or mundane jobs that made us miserable during the day, jobs we took home with us and lamented having to go back to the following day, missing the weekends before they were even over. We were free. Together.

I thought of Thomas Wilson again. Bland Thomas with his benign wife and their boring jobs, trapped by the demands of a squawking infant. I thought of his sagging posture at his desk in his office, where they enforced a "clear desk policy" – but he snuck a photograph of his wife and baby on there anyway in what was the greatest act of rebellion Thomas had ever committed. I thought of the way he seemed to think that numbers were an interesting topic of conversation, and the way he panicked at the mention of a holiday to somewhere he hadn't been before, lest he be surprised in any way. I gripped Delia's hand more tightly in my own and let her guide me. I pitied poor Thomas Wilson because he would never be anything more than what he was now. I smiled to myself, grateful not to be like him, grateful to no longer be the waiter whose tips depended on his appearance and were influenced by the appearance of everyone else was on the floor that night, pitted against each other in a perverse beauty contest just to cover their bills. I was no longer the man who needed to date below his aesthetic grade to boost his own ego and edge himself into the lives of those whose lives I desired, lying both to and about myself. I didn't have to be that man with Delia. I was the luckiest man alive.

# CHAPTER 44

What happened the next day wasn't anyone's fault. Not really. Accidents happen.

I didn't really like to think too much about what had happened, since the night before had been so wonderful, perfect in every possible way. Delia was upset at what I had done, of course; she was probably even angry. But if she was, she did her best not to show it. I apologised for being so reckless. Thinking back on it, I couldn't even fathom what I was thinking, going wandering drunk into the snow. It was even more perplexing that I chose to do it with Henry, the person I liked least in the entire hotel.

We had reconnected that evening, Delia and I. She admitted that she had been absent for some time and blamed it on the stress of the renovation. She had wanted everything to be complete already, but Ollie was taking longer than she had hoped and was very slow in painting the guest bedrooms. I wondered fleetingly why an interior designer was doing the paintwork – I thought that was the job of a painter and decorator – but what did I know of that industry?

I felt guilty for spoiling her party, particularly given how much I knew she had been looking forward to it. It wasn't often that Delia got to spend time with her friends, and she had gone to such effort to try to make it perfect. A lump had formed in my throat as I watched her drop her rose gown to the floor and stare sadly at the crumpled heap of fabric that had held so much promise before she first put it on. I told her how sorry I was and I promised to make up for it, that I would do anything for her. She smiled appreciatively, but I knew what we were both thinking: "What, Eric? What can you do?"

Once she had checked on Henry, just to make sure he was alright, she ran a bath in one of the first-floor rooms – the large cream ones I recalled from when I first arrived at the hotel. Compared with the cramped shower in the communal bathroom on the top floor, everything felt outrageously luxurious. I ran my hands over spotless porcelain and marble shelves, breathing in the hot, scented steam that rose from the slipper tub. Our bodies slid in with ease, immediately slick with spiced oil. At first my skin burned where it had been pink from the cold, reacting to the heat of the water, but slowly all the discomfort from my misadventure escaped me, and my muscles let go. I allowed myself to sink.

I watched Delia dab her glistening forehead with a white facecloth, rubbing away the makeup from the night before that had been smudged by tears. Her hair flowed in silky tendrils on the surface of the water and her body shimmered, distorted by the rippling water. She told me she forgave me and I wept with gratitude.

That night, our meal was served to us in the bedroom; we had wrapped ourselves in white dressing gowns and she wound her damp hair tightly in a towel turban. We ate in bed, picking at truffle chips and toasted steak sandwiches, which was unlike the cuisine I had become accustomed to but, strangely, exactly what I wanted. We drank wine, even though Mary had advised me to be careful around alcohol after being in the cold for so long, but she'd also told me to avoid hot baths and I was fine. Delia winked as she poured me another glass. "Our little secret."

I was glad to hear that Delia's friends had left once they knew that Henry and I were alright. It seemed that Henry was in a worse condition than I was, delirious from the cold. I didn't see him again until much later that night, when Delia and I ventured down the stairs, hand in hand in our pyjamas.

The entire hotel seemed sleepy, strangely self-indulgent. Delia smiled at me, her face free of makeup and skin still flushed from the heat of the bath, all perfectly in tune with how I felt. In that moment, nothing could make the evening more perfect.

The men were gathered in the room and Alistair was handing out coffee and biscuits. The scratchy jazz from the record player was echoing from wall to wall, and Alistair muttered something about Delia hating jazz almost as much as he did, but I supposed he just didn't know her as well as I did.

"Alright, mate?" Ollie patted my shoulder as he passed me. "I'm glad you're okay."

I watched his attention turn to Delia, who was tucked under my arm, a flash of uncertainty crossing his face before he caught himself and looked back to me.

"Thanks, Ollie," I replied, too content to revel in his jealousy.

"A story would be nice," Delia murmured, drawing the attention of the room with barely a whisper. "Who would like to tell a story?"

We all peered at one another, nobody acknowledging Edward's absence. We had come to an unspoken agreement that we wouldn't talk about him again. He had upset Delia and now he was gone. We would do our best not to miss him.

"Henry?" Delia tilted her head, gesturing towards Henry who was quietly dozing on the sofa. His face was smooth, shaved of his patchy beard. Someone had neatly clipped his hair so it fell how I recalled, parted at the side in soft waves peppered with silvers and greys. I had a memory of a man who looked like him in my bedroom, frantic and quivering like a stray animal in the shadows. I thought of the men who hid behind plaster and beneath floorboards, clinging to the brick inside chimneys and praying that nobody would light them from below. There were corpses in hidden rooms, laid ceremoniously in antiquated beds, and witches who lived in the snow disguised as harmless old women. I wondered if those ideas came from a book I was writing. I had little interest in writing now.

"Gladly." Rising to his feet, Henry greeted the room. The only evidence of our escapade was the ruddiness of his nose and his chapped lips, which had been whipped raw by the wind; otherwise, he was calm and collected. He was happy.

Licking his lips, he let them stretch into a dreamy smile before he spoke.

"Good evening, everyone." His eyes met mine as he spoke, but there was no sign of the recognition of a co-conspirator. "First of all, I would like to apologise to those who I upset last night, and to thank you all for so graciously accepting me back." He bowed his head, and we accepted his apology with a hive mentality, nodding and releasing a low murmur of acknowledgement. "I hope that my story will go some way in lightening the mood for you all, and reassuring you that I am one of the team, regardless of what my previous actions may have suggested." The fire backlit him in orange as he extended his arms. "Let me tell you a story about a young man who worked in a glass tower deep in the city of birds, where the magpie people lived…"

# CHAPTER 45:

## THE MAGPIE PEOPLE

The young man was the son of a lord and heir to the family title. He lived a life of many privileges, raised between the exquisite grounds of the family estate and the city of the magpie people. Mortal men were rarely permitted in the city of magpies, apart from the lord and his friends who were welcomed with open wings. The magpie people were clever creatures, obsessed with wealth and status – or anything shiny – and they saw merit in friendships with men of certain means.

As with all his children, the lord was keen to have the young man work with the magpie people in one of their great glass towers. A job in the glass towers was a dream for young men, promising status and riches. Besides, the lord was keen to ensure that his son stayed on track for what was expected of him, particularly if he was to carry forth their family name. The young man had already proven himself to be difficult on occasion, rejecting every suitable match that the lord and his friends had arranged for him, beautiful women with names to be proud of. Instead, he had taken a wife for himself from the countryside, a common crofter's daughter. The lord couldn't fathom this and sent his son and daughter-in-law to the magpie city, where he hoped she would refine herself and be unable to cast any aspersions on the family's good name. He relaxed a little when she provided him with two grandchildren, despite the fact that they were girls. At least it meant that one day she ought to be able to provide his son with a true heir: a boy.

The young man did well in the glass tower, socialising with the magpie people and delighting in the glittering opulence of their parties, which seemed to burn on through the night every day of the week. The young man noticed that the magpie people never tired. They worked and they threw parties; their desire for gold and riches seemed to have replaced a need for sleep. Sleep, they said, was what made humans weak.

One day, when the young man was assisting with an audit of the magpie people's gold vault, he met a magpie woman. She liked to put aside time each day to wander the vaults and see the mountains of gold, her round black eyes glittering in the reflected light of heaped coins, her tail lifting and fanning into its full shape, a feathered diamond. When she turned to look at the young man, the glittering reflections of gold remained.

Magpie women were a rarity in the city, odd-looking creatures who made themselves up to look as human as possible. The magpie men wore their oily black feathers proudly, sharpening their beaks and squatting low, perching. When leaving the tower they hovered on the window ledge, overlooking the great descent, and spread their wings before swooping into the night sky. However, the magpie women stood tall like humans, forcing their four-clawed feet into expensive stilettos and smoothing their feathers to emphasise the humanoid aspects of their body shape as much as possible. They rarely flew.

She asked if the young man enjoyed looking at the gold and he shrugged, explaining that he was largely disinterested in the wealth of others owing to his own family wealth; it had never been something he thought about. The glitters of gold in her eyes flashed more brightly.

Looking at the gold was not enough for the magpie woman. She didn't want to look upon the wealth of others; she wanted it for herself. She began watching the young man, chattering with other magpie people about his family and prospects. The more she learned, the more she desperately desired him. It came as a surprise to her when she learned of his wife, a common creature who was only permitted entry to the city by virtue of her husband's status – and, worst of all the magpie woman discovered, she rejected all invitations to the magpie parties, preferring to keep to herself. She couldn't understand why the woman would do that; opportunities like that for people of her standing did not come around often.

The magpie woman began watching the couple at night, creeping into their garden and spying on them through the window. She watched the way the young man wrapped his arms around his wife and tenderly kissed her cheek. Although the magpie woman could not feel love – certainly not human love – she envied the status of such a high-profile husband. If she could have him, she would have his family gold and family name as well. She ruffled her feathers excitedly at the prospect, her breast and neck expanding with the thought of it. She pictured their wedding: Champagne fountains, glistening chandeliers, golden drapes dripping from the ceiling, their magpie guests mingling skilfully before flying back to the tower, seeking solace in the gold in the vaults which would never really be their own.

The magpie woman knew that she would never match the appearance of the young man's wife, not with her thick, oily feathers, her folded wings, her leathery feet and hard beak. So, one night, in a fit of wild frustration and razor-sharp ambition, she plucked out her feathers and rid herself of those features that made her more bird than human, – a terrible procedure that left her bald, red raw and hurt. But she wrapped her newly naked body in fine clothes, concealing some parts and accentuating others, and decorated herself with eye-catching jewels, hoping that the young man was as drawn to sparkling things as she was. Back in the tower, she made sure to bump into the young man, and when she did she reminded him of the time they met in the gold vault. He screwed up his face in concentration, struggling to place her, and nodded to avoid embarrassment, overcompensating for his perceived lack of manners by asking her to accompany him to one of the parties that evening. The magpie woman smiled with her painted-on lips. She turned his offer down.

One of the things that the magpie people were particularly good at was getting their own way, and they were aware that the things they wanted the most were the things that were denied to them. They knew that this wasn't exclusive to magpies.

The young man began to notice the magpie woman, baffled as to why she would have rejected him. Ordinarily, people swarmed around him, eager to be his friend. Where his wife offered him the warmth and affection that a childhood in boarding schools and holidays with stern nannies had denied him, the magpie woman offered him something different – the shock of rejection, and an intense desire to rectify it. He spent more time around her, taking opportunities to speak to her in the tower and approach her at parties. Finally, she relented and allowed him to have her.

The magpie woman was horrified to discover that once the young man knew he could have her, his ego returned intact and he ignored her. One day, down in the darkness of the vaults, she followed him as he was carrying out his audit, and she whispered in his ear:

"*I'll rip your wife's heart out with my claws and peck out the eyes of your children.*"

Knowing that a threat from a magpie person was as good as a promise, the young man resumed his relationship with her, doing his best to appease her for the sake of his wife and children. The magpie woman began demanding more and more of him, disgruntled even by his need to sleep, which took some of his precious time away from her.

Nothing was good enough for the magpie woman, not when she didn't truly have the young man as her own. The man became frightened that she would follow through on her threat to tear out the heart of his wife and peck out his children's eyes; it wasn't unknown for magpie people to act out in a violent rage when they didn't have the opportunity to pursue status and wealth. At heart, they were monstrous and violent creatures.

Realising that he would never be free and his wife never safe so long as he was with the magpie, the young man made his plans to escape. He planned to take his wife and children with him and flee the city of magpies. His family would never accept him back in the knowledge that he had betrayed the magpie people; their good name would be tarnished, and that was worth far more to them than he was. So, the young man waited until the magpies in the tower were at one of their nightly parties and he crept into the vault, packing as much gold into sacks as he was able to carry, enough to provide his family with a comfortable future.

Just as he was filling his third sack with gold, the door of the vault creaked open and his magpie lover appeared in the dim light, a dark shape in the subterranean candlelight. She hadn't realised that he would be down in the vault – she had simply come to look at her gold – and she was not prepared: her exposed flesh was an angry pink, dotted with holes where she had plucked out her feathers, and her face bare without makeup to disguise the self-mutilation. Her black eyes blazed with a raw fury.

"What are you doing?" she hissed from her lipless mouth. The young man stumbled back, causing one of the sacks to topple and spray gold across the stone floor. He mumbled an excuse, which the magpie woman instantly swatted away and stalked closer to him with her flapping arms peculiar without their feathers, too long, and bending in the wrong direction to be human. She kicked off a shoe to reveal a gnarled, four-clawed foot, which she drew up to strike at his chest.

Before she could touch him, the vault door flew open with such aggression that it smashed against the stone wall, sending up a cloud of powdered stone. One of the security guards glowered at them, her slender human physique framed by the vault's threshold, backlit by the tunnel beyond. Her hand gripped the long blades carried by the night guards, tense at her hip. The magpies had found human night guards more trustworthy around the vaults.

"What's going on here?" she asked, taking a step forward so that she loomed over the little magpie woman.

"She was trying to steal the gold," the young man said quickly, scrabbling further back so that the magpie woman was left standing in the midst of a scattering of coins. "I tried to stop her but she attacked me."

Without another word, the guard swept forward and pushed her blade between the ribs of the magpie woman. The magpie didn't scream or cry out in pain; magpies rarely did. She died a dignified death, eyes fluttering and bald wings slumping limply to her side as she crumpled to the ground. The punishment for theft in the city of magpies was death.

"Magpies," the guard spat. "Greedy creatures. We've to let them look, but sometimes they get a little too excited around the treasure."

The young man scrambled to his feet, breathless and trembling, and looked down at his magpie lover, her disfigured body a small mound on the floor.

"Thank you," he breathed, reaching forward to the guard. "How can I thank you? Please, let me take you out tonight."

The guard smiled, revealing a snaggled canine slipping over one lip, as she slid her bloodied knife back into its sheath.

"Thank you, but no," she replied mischievously, walking him out of the vault and taking position by the door, gesturing for him to continue along the tunnel.

The young man, surprised and intrigued by her rejection, continued down the tunnel compliantly, looking back over his shoulder as he went, hoping not to lose sight of her in the subterranean light.

# CHAPTER 46

The following morning we were woken by screaming.

I had learned to differentiate between types of screams. There were differences between a scream of pain and the scream of a sudden shock, or screams of delight. Then there were screams of horror – an entirely different sound altogether. People instinctively reacted to those kinds of screams, like mothers responding to the cries of their babies. I wondered if it was animalistic, a warning to the rest of the pack so that they had a chance to run. They were the kind of noises that were dragged up from the base of the belly, a pitch that ricocheted through the ears and brain, spiking adrenaline and ringing a warning siren.

The warmth that lingered in the base of my belly from the night before vanished and my still-aching limbs forgot their fatigue, springing into action as I leapt from the bed. I was disorientated for a moment, looking around at the luxury of the first-floor bedroom, forgetting that I had not returned to my usual quarters. I knew there was no one else sleeping on the first floor, so I stumbled into the empty corridor, hesitating like a trapped animal, the white walls seeming to close in on me. I tried to push a long-repressed memory from my mind.

The screams of my father from across the magnolia hall of our home. I was fifteen. The way he screamed, it could have been either a man or a woman. He screamed in horror; all his notions of masculinity and how men should behave were stripped away. He stopped me at his and my mother's bedroom door just before I could rush inside, gripping my shoulders with his strong hands and pressing my face into his pounding chest, telling me not to go in. When the ambulance came, he made me go to the neighbour's house and sit in their kitchen, where they offered me warm drinks and empty assurances that everything would be okay. I could tell that they were being careful not to reassure me that my mum was alright. They all knew already.

Staggering out from the hotel corridor onto the stairwell, I was relieved to find the other men thundering down the stairs in the direction of the screams. They were still in their dressing gowns, reminding me of the snowball fight all those years ago, sweeping excitedly through the building like a gaggle of white geese. I joined the flock, a swell of white descending to the entrance of the hotel.

The slate floor was painfully cold against the soles of our feet, and a sharp gust of wind created a tunnel effect beyond the reception desk, forcing us to hold down our dressing gowns to protect our modesty. The front doors were wide open, letting gusts of snowflakes billow in, pumping in the rhythm of a heart. They melted against the slate, turning quickly to slush and leaving a glistening pool in the uneven dips.

At the front step, Delia was crouched in the snow, her hair flecked with white and her hands jangling frantically around her. Her screams continued, ragged, as though her throat had been torn to pieces from the inside. The crowd of men pressed around me, more like a protective cluster than the result of a bottleneck.

We wiped our eyes against the falling snow, squinting to see what had happened and forming a semi-circle behind Delia. The gasps rippled through us one by one as we saw the source of her horror. Splayed across the ground, stiff fingers grasping claw-like in the direction of the front door, was Edward, dead and frozen. It looked as though he had been trying to crawl back towards the entrance. His once friendly face was blue, and tilted to the side so that I could make out his expression, a gathering of frost around his eyes and lips, where tears and saliva had formed a sparkling mask of ice. Each strand of grey hair appeared to have frozen individually, protruding from his head like stalactites and stalagmites.

"Edward." I formed the words with my lips, not making a sound, and yet his name seemed to form on the breeze, hovering for a moment before shattering amid Delia's screams. We clustered around her, trying to touch her with shaking hands, some of us covering our eyes and shaking our heads as though willing it not to be true.

Her fingers touched Edward's face, trying to turn his head, which remained stubbornly in place as though his blood had frozen solid inside him.

"No. Please, no," she moaned, scrabbling forward and tugging at his clothes, unable to properly grasp the stiff fabric, which cracked unpleasantly at her touch. She placed her hands over his face, rubbing desperately as though trying to warm him. "Come on, my love," I heard her whisper to him, her voice void of its usual seductive drawl. "Wake up."

"Call an ambulance!" Ollie cried from behind me.

I saw myself as a fifteen-year-old boy, my father roaring at me to call an ambulance, now that he had stopped screaming. I went downstairs and stood by our landline, the receiver pressed against my ear. Somehow it seemed impossible for my trembling fingers to hit the three buttons. Nine, nine, nine. I could see my hand hovering above the number, unable to press down. Whenever I returned to that memory, I wondered how that one simple action had seemed so hard. Nine, nine, nine. I still had dreams about it, nightmares about calling the emergency services when something awful had happened. Sometimes I was too afraid to hit the buttons. Sometimes the number nine was missing from the telephone. Sometimes even when I did get through, I was greeted by a belligerent operator who wouldn't listen to me.

I turned away from the body just as Delia's screams turned to hopeless wailing, her face twisting in a way that made all her features move in the wrong direction – lips, eyes and nose all out of place like she had been taken apart and clumsily put back together again.

I became aware of the hot tears rolling down my cheeks as I stumbled towards the stairs. By the banister, Henry stood motionless, fully dressed for work in his pressed white shirt and grey trousers. I reached to him, shaking, in search of comfort, encouraged by the presence of the man who had held me upright in the snow and given me dry socks when I couldn't walk any further.

"Do you think they killed him?" I asked breathlessly, keeping my voice low. "The witches – do you think they killed Edward?"

Henry stared blankly at me, ignoring my outstretched arms and shrugging.

"I wouldn't know," he replied breezily, moving past me through the gaggle of men in white dressing gowns, and returning to the reception desk, ready to begin his day.

Ascending the stairs, I felt my breath ragged in the back of my throat. Delia's office door was open again, I imagined in panic or carelessness, revealing the luxurious office space. When I blinked, I saw peeling wallpaper and cheap, sparse furniture before it flickered back to luxury again. Blaming this on my confusion and panic, I grasped the doorframe for support and tumbled in to grasp the telephone on the desk. The cool plastic pressed against my ear, my trembling fingers hovering above the numbers.

"Hello, you're through to an operator. Which service can I direct you to?"

"Help." My voice was broken by sobs. "Please help us!"

# CHAPTER 47

I told them that he was dead. I spluttered out the words "dead" and "body" and I wasn't sure what else I managed to say before Delia swept in and took the phone from me. She kept me calm, stroking my head as I lay crumpled on the floor, weeping, and she spoke very matter-of-factly on the telephone, a glaring contrast to her hysteria downstairs.

At first the flashing lights didn't register, harsh in the dimming afternoon as the police car and ambulance parked outside the front entrance. Henry welcomed the uniformed men inside politely, offering them tea or coffee, which they politely declined with sombre expressions. They didn't arrive with sirens blaring, and we all knew what that meant. There had been a small flicker of hope in all of us that somehow, against all odds, Edward might still be alive. I thought of those animals found in ice that had slowly come back to life after being carefully thawed – whether those stories were true or not, I wasn't entirely sure. I couldn't imagine how the paramedics would even begin to do that anyway; a part of me wanted to ask if it was a possibility, even just to know, but I thought better of it. If they thought they ought to thaw out Edward then they would do it. Instead, his stiff body was zipped up and wheeled into the ambulance on a silver stretcher. The wheels rattled on the ramp like a supermarket trolley and I felt sick, thinking of packaged meat.

The police and paramedics were well versed in how to behave, maintaining their grave faces and sympathetic bowing gestures until they had assessed the situation, at which point they relaxed their expressions and lightened their tone. Delia played her part perfectly, composed to just the right degree. She led me from her office and firmly shoved me away from the door, which she locked behind her before racing up the stairs in a swirl of silk. By the time she returned she was dressed in a suit, wearing a strained smile that was appropriate for the circumstances, eyes a little bloodshot. Her voice was broken just enough as she apologised for her appearance, saying that it was "all just such a terrible shock."

The police constables sat down with her in the bar, holding their small black notebooks. The youngest of the two maintained a professional frown as his colleague spoke. I imagined it was a face he practiced, working his muscles into that position until one day, like his more experienced colleague, it became habit. They remained undistracted by her obvious beauty, barely registering anything other than her answers. When they returned their gazes to their notebooks, Delia observed them carefully, assessing them.

"He must have been a hillwalker," she said, shaking her head and pressing her palm against her pale cheek. "You do come across them sometimes, underprepared and underdressed – we've taken a few in in the past, actually. Gamekeepers sometimes pick them up – they get so angry – sorry! I'm babbling."

I clenched my jaw, recalling how she had asked us to change his frozen body out of his uniform and into the moth-eaten clothes from the basement storage. She said it was to preserve his dignity, that he wouldn't have wanted to die in his uniform. Now, I realised, there was nothing tying us to him. He was just a lone hillwalker.

I couldn't bear it. Turning from them, I stalked outside to the carpark, where the police car and the ambulance sat gathering a roof of snow. I tried to ignore the cold and the ache that had returned to my tired limbs.

"You doing alright?" One of the paramedics leaned against

a wall, inhaling from an e-cigarette that was partially concealed in his fist. He was dressed in green and I couldn't help but stare, wondering how long it had been since I had seen the colour green outside. It seemed almost obscene against the snow. I blinked and nodded.

"It's a real shock." He offered a soft smile, genuine rather than practiced. "Finding a body."

I shuffled towards him, endeared by the warmth in his stubbly face. He had the look of a man who wouldn't take any nonsense, heavy-browed and features furrowed, but kind beneath it all.

"Is this the first?" he asked.

I stared silently at him.

"First time you've seen a body?" he clarified.

I hesitated, recalling my face burrowed in my father's chest, feeling him hold me tightly against him. He hadn't allowed me to look inside, and I didn't have the courage. Then I thought of the loose brick in the wall, the bed that had greyed with layers of dust and the body so carefully laid out with its loose finger bones and the unhinged jaw. Glancing up at the hotel, I could see the window with the closed curtains, a slight gap between the fabric allowing the sun to shine a narrow ray across the bed, a spotlight on the corpse. He was still in there.

"No." I shook my head. "Not the first time."

"Ah." The paramedic sucked his e-cigarette and released a puff of unscented vapour. I breathed it in gratefully. Catching me inhaling, he reached into his breast pocket and pulled out a small packet: an e-cigarette cased in plastic.

"Here, take one. They're disposable." He edged it into my hand. "They're not great for you – I should know. My missus has me giving up. I promised this would be my last pack, so I guess this'll help speed up the process, you having the last one. Take it." He gestured emphatically. "Bite the bullet, as they say."

"Thank you." Easing it gently out of the packet, I studied it curiously. "I've never had one before. They were just new back when…" I paused thoughtfully. "Back… I don't know."

The paramedic furrowed his brow at me.

"You sure you're alright?"

"Mhmm." I pressed the plastic between my lips, sucking in and letting the warm vapour slide down my throat. Then I shook my head. "No, actually." My hands trembled as I prepared myself to tell him my secret. "I found a body."

"I know. Folks out hiking, don't realise how dangerous it can be. Weather can just turn." He sighed deeply. "Poor old fella was obviously looking for help, probably couldn't even see the hotel right in front of him through the storm. Literally feet from the door. A terrible thing."

I opened my mouth to correct him, to tell him about the body upstairs in the hidden bedroom, to ask him for help. Just as the beginning of a word escaped my lips, the hotel doors swung open and the police constables, followed by the other paramedic and Delia, stepped out onto the stone porch. She smiled graciously at them and thanked them for their time. They returned the sentiment. The paramedic covertly slipped his e-cigarette into his breast pocket and snapped to attention.

"Best be off." He offered me a brief but firm pat on the shoulder. "You'll be alright. It can help to talk about these things. Don't keep it bottled up."

Before I could answer, he jogged towards the van and began speaking to his colleague. I wanted to open my mouth and scream after him, to beg him to come back, to show him the body upstairs. Or perhaps he could just take me away with him.

I felt my lips form the words "Please don't leave me."

The vehicles started to rumble, and a moment later they had vanished down the drive, but not before I saw the kind paramedic wave at me in his wing mirror.

My eyes pricked with hot tears as I stumbled back into the hotel, grasping the e-cigarette in my fist for the small comfort it offered me. I walked past reception, where Henry nodded politely at me, and then glanced to the bar, where the men sat quietly, heads hovering low over drinks. I wanted to scream.

"Delia has given us the afternoon off," Henry stated from behind his desk. "Says it's been a terrible shock for us all."

Ignoring him, I turned to the stairs and broke into a run, the smooth soles of my shoes sliding against wool carpet. On the first floor, where I knew the finest rooms remained unoccupied but beautifully maintained, I burst into the corridor. The scent of fresh paint filled my nostrils, and I saw the slightly uneven patch of wall that Ollie had plastered over. As though driven by instinct, I hammered my fists into the material, hearing it crack and split. I let out long, anguished sobs as I dug my fingers into the gaps. I ripped out chunks, covering myself in a delicate powder, filling the air with a fine white cloud. Behind the plaster was a great, black, cavernous space, wooden support beams crossing otherwise empty darkness. As the dust settled around me, I stared breathlessly through the large hole in front of me, light-headed and swaying precariously. If I climbed inside and lost my balance, I could fall, and I couldn't see how far it went down; the dimensions and structure of the hotel were impossible to rationalise just now. With a deep, shuddering breath, I lifted one foot and pushed it into the hole. When my sole touched one of the horizontal wooden beams it slipped, knocking against the plaster beside it, sending a hollow bang echoing through the cavernous space. I removed my shoes and placed them neatly against the wall beneath the hole. My socks came off too, and I tucked them inside the brogues. They were the only trace of me that would remain. Then again, I realised the socks and shoes weren't even mine; not really. They were just standard hotel uniform. Nobody would know that they were mine.

My bare feet curled around the beam as I ducked inside, hands gripping the wood around me and securing my balance. The light only extended through the hole so far; after a point I would need to travel by touch alone. Despite being cold and damp, I felt a peculiar comfort being confined in that strange, dark place, as though I was a child in a hidey hole. A comfort that dissipated whenever I looked down.

I moved deeper into the darkness, clutching the e-cigarette, which was warm from the heat of my enclosed palm, and pausing intermittently to reassure myself that it was still there. The fear of dropping it down into the unknown abyss was chilling.

Clambering one-handed, I realised that I could no longer be sure what direction I was climbing in, whether up or down. I thought about the climbers trapped in an avalanche, spitting on their hands to help them find their way up when they became disorientated. I knew that wouldn't help me; not in here.

# CHAPTER 48

There were other men who lived in the walls. I couldn't say for certain that they were men, as I couldn't actually see them and they never spoke or engaged with me, other than those rare occasions when I brushed against them in the darkness. I heard them sometimes, moving nimbly, practiced. I didn't imagine they bumped into one another, having been in the walls for so long they could weave between the rafters and beams with ease. Meanwhile, my clumsy limbs would get tangled between beams, and when I squeezed in and out of tight spaces I'd bump my head or scrape my knees and elbows as I did so. I started to wonder if my eyes had adjusted to the dark or if I was just imagining things, but sometimes I convinced myself that I could see outlines in the deep darkness like shimmers in petrol on black tarmac, and when those outlines moved, sometimes I called out, wondering if it was one of the men, if they might just answer me. They never did.

I nested like a bird, finding soft places that I assumed were clumps of insulating material stuffed between tightly fitted planks, preventing me from slipping through. None of it made sense; the vast, dark spaces in the walls extended beyond all logical proportions. Sometimes when I slept, I would roll over and wake up just as my body was about to tip over an edge. It felt like waking from a dream with the sensation that I was falling, my body in free fall, out of control, until I lurched back into consciousness, realising I was never really falling. There was a name for that – hypnic jerks. When I remembered that, I announced it proudly into the darkness.

"Hypnic jerks!" I shouted, seeking solace in my own voice bouncing back at me, a comfort of some kind. There was a rustling close by as men scurried away, frightened by the unexpected noise. Grinning to myself, I sucked on the e-cigarette and nestled back into the insulation.

When I began to worry about dehydration, I followed a gentle dripping until I came to a leaking pipe, stumbling blindly on it in the dark. A small crack leaked out a very small dribble of water, but it was my own private water fountain. I had heard about Legionnaires' disease before; it formed in stagnant water and could make a person very sick. I found myself feeling a little light-headed and feverish, but I was certain it was psychosomatic. Perhaps I was just hungry. I couldn't recall the last time I had eaten.

The first time I came across food was because I was awoken by a smell. I scrabbled around carefully until my hands closed around a small mound of biscuits. I crammed them in my mouth, elated by the burst of sweetness. I didn't even realise that someone was helping me until some time later when I noticed the pattern: I would wake up and find food nearby. The best was waking to a chunk of honey-glazed gammon, both salty and sweet. I licked my fingers for hours afterwards, hoping to recapture the taste. It was still slightly warm when I ate it, as though it had been in the oven relatively recently. Whoever was feeding me must have stolen it from the kitchen. I had stopped trying to sleep once per day and napped whenever I became tired. Being awake and then being asleep had been my measure of a day, but I wasn't entirely convinced that my pattern had been matching the actual days. Sometimes I wasn't entirely sure whether I was even sleeping anymore. Suspended in darkness, even my dreams had become dark. Complete sensory deprivation left me unsure of whether I was up or down, conscious or not. There was a peacefulness to it, oddly, and I was unafraid.

I became increasingly curious about whoever was helping me, willing them to introduce themselves. However, they only seemed to appear once they were convinced I was asleep, quietly laying out the food by my side and slinking away. Sometimes I imagined it was Henry, slipping away from his position at the front desk after convincing Delia that he was under her spell. I hoped his addled memories of his past, filled with magpies and gold, were just a front and he was actually planning another escape. Although I was quite happy to remain in the walls, I truly did wish the best for him, and the thought of him returning to his wife and children made me smile. I wondered if Delia knew that I was hiding in the walls. Maybe she would creep in while I slept, scuttling between the beams and rafters like a giant spider, clutching her findings from the kitchen in pincers and laying them next to my sleeping body which was wrapped in insulation like a web. Fat prey made for a better meal. The thought of it disturbed my sleep, making me peer fearfully into the darkness, paranoid that I was actually asleep and she was already there, crouched by my side with eight unblinking eyes.

I started pretending to sleep, hoping that I could catch them out – whoever was helping me. Perhaps they were a friend. I had to be careful, as one wrong move could frighten them away. If they were quicker at moving through the darkness than me then I risked losing them forever. So, instead I laid in wait. Keeping my eyes shut, I listened out for their approach. Patiently. Time after time. Until – there! – a slight creak in the beams. Barely loud enough for me to notice if I wasn't paying close attention. I felt them by my side, the sound of them holding their breath almost audible, and sensed them place the food by my side. I wondered greedily what was being served. And waited for them to leave.

This time: a bundle of lemon muffins in paper casings, an entire baguette, a wheel of soft cheese and various other cold or lukewarm items.

I remained patient, listening to them, learning their routine and eating their offerings gratefully.

Eventually I knew everything I could about them. I recognised their short, rapid breath and how long it took them to rise again after they had crouched by my side. I was convinced by that point that it wasn't Delia, and this brought me both comfort and a fresh excitement, something to nervously look forward to when I discovered their identity.

At their next appearance I tried to smell what they were carrying from a distance. I hoped for meat, fantasising about a whole chicken, skin crisp and salty. I would gnaw it like a wild animal. The wooden beams creaked as they came closer, their weight pressing down on the support of my nest as they eased themselves forward. I waited.

They breathed, short and sharp, tired from weaving through the walls, and then they paused over my body as they always did, checking that I was asleep. I kept my breath steady. Then, ever so slowly, they bent down by my side, hands extending so close that I could have sworn I felt the warmth of them next to me. Either my senses had sharpened in the darkness or I was imagining it.

Not yet, I told myself. I waited until they were comfortably stooped, until the food bumped gently on the surface beside me, and only then I lunged. I thrust my arm out, hand open and ready to snatch. I found what I believed to be a shirt collar and gripped tightly. Barely a gasp came from the stranger; they seemed to freeze for a moment before stumbling back and landing at the edge of my nest. I knew that I had them then; their advantage of agility was gone as soon as their feet were off the ground. I had them.

"What are you doing?" My voice came out unfamiliar, neither accusatory nor frightened. It reminded me of something computer generated, as though I had forgotten about tone and how to use it. I clambered on top of them, mindful of the nearby edge of my nest, and pinned them down. Their body felt weak and weightless.

They made a noise.

"What?" I said, shaking their collar more firmly, their legs wriggling unpleasantly beneath me. "What do you want?"

Eventually he spoke, a masculine voice, distant and rasping like it hadn't been used in a long time: "Nothing." He stopped struggling and lay breathlessly beneath me. My hands moved up, exploring his face which was thick with wiry hair and sharp where bones pressed against flesh. He felt old and papery.

"Why are you helping me?" I let my voice get quieter, private. A conversation for ourselves rather than echoes for the walls.

"You helped me – *yes*, helped me," he replied, words clumsy and disjointed as he let out a stifled cough. "She would have burned me."

I paused, exploring my tangled memory. After a moment I saw it: Delia in the living room, the knowing smile on her face as she struck the match and leaned towards the hearth, the filthy hand that waved frantically to get my attention.

"You!" I exclaimed. "You're the man in the fireplace?"

I sensed him nod.

"You've lived here all this time?"

He nodded again. We remained still for a short period. I breathed out, let my hands relax just a little.

"If I let you go, do you promise not to run?"

He nodded.

Slowly, ready to snatch him if I sensed he was about to scurry away, I let my grip loosen and pulled my hands away. Eventually, I moved back, allowing the man to gather himself. I heard him dust himself off, patting his front. It was funny how, after a while in the darkness, you could see noises as well as you might see an image. The brush of skin against fabric, being able to hear that it was coming from the chest where the heart beat faintly.

"What's your name?" I asked eventually.

He shook his head slowly.

"I don't remember."

# CHAPTER 49

We sat side by side in the darkness for a time; it was impossible to say for how long. Quiet, we listened to each other breathe, as though we were waiting for signs of dishonesty or bad intentions – a sudden intake of breath or a hesitation. Eventually, I reached blindly over to the small bundle that had been placed by my side, relieved to find that it hadn't been knocked over in the commotion. It was sweet and sticky.

"What is it?" I asked.

"Strawberry tart," the man replied. "The fat chef makes good cakes."

"He does." I nodded in agreement, recognising the taste and licking thick cream from my fingers. "Want a piece?"

"No, I ate already. Full of food, the kitchen."

"So, do you get food from the kitchen at night?" I asked. "Is that what you were doing that night I saw you in the chimney?"

"Yes." I sensed him nod rapidly again, his movement causing tiny vibrations in the beams beneath us. "Don't stay too long, though. The kitchen is where she can trap you. She knows some of us still need to eat. Always check where she is before you go to the kitchen; make sure she can't catch you. Nuts and crisps…" his voice trailed as he paused to think. "Nuts and crisps from the bar are nice, but my stomach doesn't feel good after." I listened to his clothes rustle as he gestured. "Tonight was a good night – a whole pie. The chef has seen me, I think, but he doesn't stop me."

"Alistair," I murmured through a mouthful of sugary crust. "He's nice. He's part of the baking club, makes a lot of cakes."

The man let out a hoarse laugh, catching himself at the sound of it and coughing as though he had inhaled his first cigarette.

"Baking club," he repeated, as though amused by the concept.

I made a querying sound, unsure of the meaning of his tone, but he didn't react. We were both distracted by a brief shuffle in the distance, a rodent-like scurry vanishing into the inkiness.

"How many men live in these walls?"

"Don't know," the man replied, not seeming at all perturbed. "I hear them sometimes – mostly she catches them though. It frightens them at first, the loneliness and the darkness, but you get used to it, and after a while it's nice to know that nobody can see you. Yes, nice and safe to be hidden."

"And they *all* live off the kitchen stores?"

"*No, no, no.* They don't eat anymore." He chuckled, a noise I didn't like. "They just exist now. They've forgotten how to talk– very sad, very sad. They all talked at first. I have to be careful not to end up like them too." I felt him tap his head with a finger, a dull thudding sound. "Don't go *too* deep in the dark; *no, no, no* – not *too* deep."

"Then how do they survive if they don't eat?"

I sensed him smile. It was impossible to describe how I knew; I could somehow feel the corners of his lips tug upwards and the wrinkle of his cheeks scrunching.

"*How?*" He rolled the word in his mouth. "*How* – I used to ask *how* a lot too. Yes – *how*. *How* can this dark place behind the walls be so big? *How* did I let myself get here? *How* are those women who live in the snow old and young at the same time? *How* did I stop questioning it? *How, how, how?*" His voice became less erratic as he asked the questions from his memories, as though he was playing a different role, the role of a man who could articulate himself.

I felt my hands explore my surroundings, wondering how far the beams extended into the darkness. When I thought about it, I ought to have been wedged between plaster and stone; the amount of space we had behind the walls didn't make any sense when I considered the structure of the hotel.

"It's her. She does it to us." His voice became low. "Don't let her catch you."

"What does she do if she catches you?"

"Don't know; nobody knows. She calls the car, the black car with the old driver, and she sends us away when she's done with us. We disappear into the night and nobody sees us ever again. At least most of them get a party before they go." He gave an empty chuckle. "There'll be no retirement party for me – *no, no, no* – not if I'm caught, not now. It'll be quick and discreet. I used to think I wanted to escape. I told myself that it was what I wanted, but I think I'm quite content in the walls now – yes, quite content."

"I found a corpse in one of the rooms, a man who died a long time ago. Do you think he's one of them? Do you think she kills the men?"

"Maybe." He began chewing his nails. I could hear the sound of his fingers against his teeth.

"And Edward – he died too."

"Yes, very sad. I liked Edward."

"Did she kill him?"

"Don't think so." The man removed his fingers from his mouth to speak clearly. "Edward was her favourite. Don't think she could kill him – *no, no, no* – not Edward. I used to feel very jealous. I'd listen, you see, listen to their conversations. Long conversations about all sorts, and silences that don't feel like silences. He wasn't under her spell. He really did love her; yes, really loved her." He paused. "But no, she wouldn't kill him, wouldn't kill Edward. He wanted to come back. The women outside were watching him crawl back, just watching. They didn't help. They thought love made Delia weak." He was murmuring now. "I'd have helped him – yes! I'd have helped him if I could. But those women, I couldn't go outside – *no, no, no* – not outside with them. *Monsters.*"

"But they're her friends!" I insisted. "If she loved him, why would they let that happen to their friend?"

"I don't know what '*friend*' is."

"But you helped me. Aren't *we* friends?" My voice was embarrassingly hopeful.

"No, not friends," he replied simply. "You helped me, I helped you – not friends. I don't know if I like you yet. I hope I do though."

I paused to consider it, wondering if that was truly the case. When I thought of Henry, the first thing that came to mind was that he was my friend, but the more I thought about it, the more I realised that we had a shared goal – to escape the hotel. Henry was too afraid to do it alone and, at the very worst, another body provided warmth in the cold. Outside that, there was really very little genuine fondness there. He looked down on me and found my aspirations pitiful, and I considered him to be arrogant and condescending.

When I was a child, I wasn't very good at making friends. Children's parents were awkward around my mum because they all knew what was going on and they were all friends with Annie. Sometimes I was invited to birthday parties, but the connections lasted the afternoon and were forgotten again by Monday morning in school. As I grew older, my friendships became tailored to what suited me and, once that was achieved, they were forgotten about. They didn't care because the connection had never really been that meaningful to begin with. I made friends with the brothers of girlfriends, and we would stop speaking after the relationship ended, or with the person who organised the parties at their place and eventually moved away. Once there were no more parties, there was no more friendship.

Eleanor had real friends; the kind she messaged regularly and spoke about as though they were an integral part of her life. She would casually tell me what they had been up to as though it was relevant to us; that was something I never really understood.

As I sat in the darkness thinking about it, I wondered if it had seemed so strange to me because I had never actually had a real friend.

Suddenly I desperately wanted it. I wanted a meaningful connection with someone whose activities were of relevance to me, whose problems were shared and who when I wanted to sit quietly would be by my side, wordlessly offering comfort. Instead, I sat alone in the dark next to someone who was just as lonely as me.

As time passed, I tried to coax information out of this man in the walls, attempting to bring us closer to something that could possibly become a friendship. His voice was alien even to him, with emotions mixed up and stilted as though he had nearly forgotten how they worked. One moment I would think he was about to be kind and understanding, but the next he would sound angry.

When I asked him about his past, before he arrived at the hotel, he mumbled to himself incoherently, becoming irritated by his loosening grasp on reality.

"I try and remember sometimes." He huffed breathlessly from the exertion of thinking, his hands tapping irritably against the wood. "I get these thoughts – like, snippets – but they're not right, they're not real. Or at least I don't think they can be."

"How do you mean?"

"In my memories I was a woodchopper in an enchanted forest." His voice lost its erratic jumpiness as he told his story. "I was hired by the king to chop down the trees, to make space for the villagers to grow their crops. But no axeman had ever succeeded in bringing down the trees, because they were guarded by a creature who lived in the branches. Every time an axe cut into one of her trees, she would cast a spell so that the axeman would turn the blade on himself. Well, I was smarter than those other men. I went to see the forest creature, a funny-looking thing in clothes that she had fashioned out of plants and other foliage. Her hair twisted like yellow vines, curling down her back and entwined with flowers. I tricked her, saying that in the village our currency was leaves, which made her the richest creature in all the land. At first that didn't interest her, but when I explained that, with her leaf money, she could purchase anything she wanted – and that included seeds for planting more trees – she slipped down from her perch and gathered as many as she could before heading to the village. She wanted to buy seeds and expand her beloved forest. Of course, they laughed her out of the market when she spread her decaying leaves across their counters." He sighed regretfully. "By the time she had made it back, I had chopped down her entire forest. She was devastated and enraged beyond anything I had ever seen before; she wept for them like you would weep for the loss of your home and family." I sensed him hesitate, almost feeling the hairs rise on his body. "That same night, I awoke to a crackling sound, and outside my home she had dragged the dead branches from her forest and formed a bonfire around my house. She set it alight, trapping me inside. I could see her through my window standing behind the flames, watching me with sadness in her eyes as she waited for me to burn."

"But you got away somehow," I interrupted. "You got out of the fire and you ran away with a strange woman – a beautiful woman with dark hair and a snaggled tooth."

The man in the walls laughed in surprise.

"Yes! How did you know the ending of my story? Did I tell it already? I forget."

"Because all the stories end that way." I felt something grip my stomach, my breath catching in my throat as it dawned on me. "Everyone manages to run away in their fairy tales – and the woman they run away with, it's always the same one. It's always Delia."

# CHAPTER 50

The more time I spent in the darkness, the more I recognised what the sounds of the hotel meant and where to find them. When I descended amid the beams, carefully lowering my body bit by bit – lacking the confidence of that man in the walls, who seemed able to simply drop and land intuitively on a slender plank, never losing his balance or stumbling – I could hear a low rumble that I recognised as the laundry room. A slight tremor crept through the walls and made the wooden supports shudder ever so slightly. Sometimes I thought I might even be able to smell it, the soft scent of detergent, which was a pleasure to inhale in comparison to my own damp muskiness.

Sometimes I heard low chatter and distance clattering, which I assumed came from the kitchen. I asked the man in the walls if he would show me his route out and into the body of the hotel, so that I could peruse the vast shelves of food and the giant fridges. The thought of it made my mouth water. The man in the walls refused, advising that I wasn't quick or wary enough for that – not yet. He didn't want to risk Delia catching me and teasing out the information of his whereabouts, even though I promised not to tell. He said that if she knew his map of the walls, with all his secret exits, he would never be able to come out again and he would become trapped in the walls where he would gradually lose his appetite, his voice and his sense of self. Eventually he would become one of the hollow souls who haunt the walls. He said he would rather be sent to his death by

Delia. I didn't press him any further, loathe to allow anything to happen to him, the closest thing I had to a friend. Although we hadn't been together long, I couldn't bear the thought of the darkness without him. He offered a strange, familiar comfort that I hadn't felt in a long time.

There was one area in the walls where, if I clambered through the narrowest beams and into a small, box-like cranny, I could hear wailing. Pressing myself up against damp plaster, so that my cheek and ear became wet against the cold moisture, it sounded almost animal-like. Long, mournful cries that echoed eerily. Something about it made me think of whales in captivity, those sad calls that were muted by the water, bouncing from wall to wall.

"It's her!" I gestured blindly for the man in the walls. "It's Delia."

"Shh," he hissed, his voice further back. "Don't let her hear you."

I couldn't tell where in the hotel she was; perhaps in one of the bedrooms. I shuddered at the thought of her in the hidden child's bedroom, in the bed where the body lay, pressed against the bones as she grieved.

"She's weeping for Edward," he whispered. "Very sad. She's very sad."

"But she's the one who sent him away."

"Maybe she changed her mind. Yes, changed her mind."

"I used to think it was just me," I said quietly, slipping away from the ledge and back towards the wooden beam, keen to get away from the walls, fearing that her hand might plunge through the plaster and snatch me. "I thought she loved me and that everyone else here just worked for her. I didn't even notice when I started working for her. It's as though I just slipped into it without even realising."

"We all thought that. That's what happens. Sometimes we keep thinking it, even as we're sent away."

"If Edward knew, why didn't he do something? If he loved her so much, how could he just watch her with other men, having her way with them?"

"Maybe he was scared to lose her?" The man began creeping upwards and I followed, ensuring that my feet didn't bump against the plaster that thinly separated us from Delia.

"That's insane," I muttered, rolling my eyes despite the fact I knew he couldn't see me. Then I thought of my mother watching my father leave at night, her quiet grimace as he returned the following morning with the trace of another woman on his unchanged clothes, and the way we would sit for breakfast as a family pretending that everything was just fine.

I pictured Eleanor looking adoringly up at me, aware of the disparity in our physical appearances and enamoured by the romance of marrying a writer. I thought of a future with her as she grew old, as the lines in her plump face began to deepen and the sadness started to show – sadness that she had been lied to from the beginning, and that she would never have the family she had always dreamed of. Instead of small children, her time would have been occupied soothing my ego and meeting my expenses with her salary and inheritance. She would progress to head of a department somewhere or a team leader, working more hours than she had ever intended to maintain our lifestyle, while I professed to fulfil my dreams. All the while her heart would be aching as she watched the children she helped run and play around her, children she would never have. As her family passed away, we would come into an inheritance that I would fritter away in pursuit of the lifestyle I wanted. She would never say anything to me, because she would be too frightened to lose the precious life I had convinced her she had with me, not realising that it never had and would never exist.

My breath caught in my throat as I thought of her smiling face, her splashing in the freezing sea with the family she loved dearly – the family I sought to exploit. I saw a happy woman, and suddenly that seemed more precious than the life she could offer me. All my notions of leaving the hotel and returning to her now horrified me as I foresaw exactly what I would do to her, denying her the future she dreamed of and failing to share her grief at the eventual demise of her family. I felt disgusted by the glee I would feel as the will was declared. In that moment, I hated myself for what could have been and I felt my body crumple beneath me.

I tumbled down, bumping against beams, plaster filling the air around me, upsetting dust and debris that had gone undisturbed for decades. I felt myself choke, trying to call out for the man in the walls to help me, my eyes stinging as I plummeted in the blackness, arms clawing at empty space. I wondered if, when I met the ground, I would even know I was dead. If death was the great darkness I had always believed it to be, then perhaps I was already there.

# CHAPTER 51

Through the pain and the disorientation, everything seemed to become clearer. The rooms of the hotel – the real spaces – were suddenly closer than before, as though I could reach out and touch them. I listened to a commotion behind the plaster, which started off as a low pitter-patter of footsteps and hushed male voices. I lay motionless in the darkness, beneath the dust and loose wood that had broken off in the fall, and listened carefully. When I opened my mouth and called out for the man in the walls, there was no reply. I wondered if he assumed I was dead. If that was the case, I hoped he mourned for me as I would mourn for him. If I were to die, hidden away inside the walls of an old, remote building, it gave me some small comfort to think that at least one person might grieve my loss, perhaps conduct some kind of service to bid me farewell. If he didn't, then by the time anyone found me I would be no more than a crumpled skeleton like the corpse on the bed, a stranger who would elicit little more than token sympathy. "What a terrible way to die," they would say as if by rote, while clumsily excavating my remains. "I hope he didn't suffer," they would add unthinkingly, as my exposed bones clattered to the floor. All they would feel would be the thrill of exhuming a corpse during a routine construction job.

Something was going on in the hotel, something that was frightening the men. I could sense their fear. I recognised the sound of them working, fussing about and tending to the needs of the hotel, the cleaning. I must have been close to the main entrance because I could hear Henry's voice offering empty good mornings and good evenings to whoever passed him. I heard them speak in hushed tones to one another.

"She hasn't come out of her office in days."

"Ollie tried to knock and she screamed at him to go away."

"I've never seen her like this."

"None of the orders have been signed off and we're running low on food. Alistair's doing what he can, but the meals are becoming sparser."

As time passed, they became increasingly nervous, and the information they relayed became less gossip-orientated and instead punctuated with real concern and eventually fear.

"Why are there no guests?" one of them asked. "Why does it always snow?"

I wondered to myself if they were starting to understand. Was the spell breaking?

A warmth had gathered around the back of my head, which had become sticky. I imagined I had bumped it on the way down. The blood would have matted my hair. Not bothering to touch it, I continued to lie still, occasionally moving my fingers to reassure myself that I was still conscious.

I used to be very good at staying still. It had been a form of meditation, I suppose. After my morning run and my shifts at the restaurant, which involved constantly moving and being on my feet, I would like to stop and simply observe. There was a little café in the middle of a bookshop where I would perch at one of the tables and order a small black coffee. I had never liked coffee all that much, let alone black coffee, all that much, but I used to watch the university students breeze in and out in their cliques with their black coffees, mindful that their choice of drink was being judged alongside everything else. They dressed to give the impression that they were impoverished students, but the frayed and faded clothing hung off them so perfectly, discoloured in just the right places to let everyone know that they had paid for it to look that way. I watched them place their orders, a cake and a coffee totalling five pounds, maybe more, and they spoke to the girl at the till with the kind of familiarity that suggested that they were there every day. Approximately thirty-five pounds a week on coffee and cake. One-hundred-and-forty pounds a month. I sat very still as I watched them, ordering a black coffee too as if I was somehow part of their group. I sipped the bitterness, and I let my mouth twitch into a smile when they laughed, as though I was in on their jokes too.

I was jealous. I was jealous of their wealth, their access to education and the way they could spend one-hundred-and-forty pounds a month on coffee and cake despite not working. My father had never been a believer in further education. The students grew up and I grew up alongside them, jumping errat-ically from job to job in the city, never truly satisfied, although I was under no illusion that the type of jobs that we jumped from were very different and for very different reasons. While they buzzed with enthusiasm in the café, nattering about their new ventures, I sat motionless, simply watching and listening. Biding my time before my shifts.

Initially, Eleanor hadn't stood out to me, one of many in a group of well-dressed coffee sippers. It was one of her more confident and better-looking friends who approached me, the sort who glided over as though she had been carried on the autumn breeze and hadn't even considered that rejection or humiliation were a possibility. Her mouth spread into a wide smile.

"Hi," she said, placing a hand on the coffee table, leaning forward as though she was sharing a secret. "Look, my friend has seen you here a few times and she's wondering if you might want to get a coffee just the two of you sometime?"

I had peered past her to the table, identifying the one that looked most mortified – the mousiest in the group of otherwise attractive women. Her palm was clasped over her mouth and her freckle-speckled cheeks had gone an angry shade of red. She was bundled into a thick duffel coat, as though prepared to run away, and her surrounding friends were keen-eyed and giggly. Their table was littered with designer handbags, which had no doubt replaced the MacBooks of their student days, and most of them wore suits instead of old bohemian chic shirts, skirts and battered satchels. When I looked directly at her and smiled – a charming, one-sided smile, nodding slowly – her friends cheered.

Eleanor once said to me that the first thing she noticed about me was how still I was, as though I had been sculpted for the café's aesthetic. In among the movement and the rush, she would see me smooth-faced and cross-legged, quietly observing what was going on around me.

"You're not part of any of it," she said fondly. "You're your own world entirely."

That had sounded romantic and artistic back then, but as I lay in the darkness and the dirt I began to wonder. I thought of myself back then, my naturally flattering stubble and defined jawline, chestnut hair that fell in exactly the right position above lean shoulders. I didn't even have to *move* and I would be admired. Now, greyed by age and dust, my once fine jaw was hidden by the drooping jowls of time and my body was heavy and sagging. Where the blood had gathered at the back of my head, I already knew the whitening hair was thinning and threatening to reveal the unflattering pink of a scalp. I wondered if Eleanor would still have desired me in this condition, if she would have looked at me with the same adoration, blushing at my gestures of affection, wondering if she actually deserved them. Without my looks, I was nothing, still or not.

My thoughts were interrupted by loud, startled cries and protests from within the hotel.

"You can't!" came the first cry.

There was a thundering – a stampede down the stairs and the roll of wheels. Suitcases.

"Get out, all of you!" I heard Delia scream, a horrible, wild scream that wound its way through the corridors and seeped through the pores of the walls. "Just go!"

"Delia, please!" Someone tried to plead with her. "Where are we going?"

I heard her march past the wall where I lay, breathless with rage and grief. Each exhalation seemed tight in her throat, as though she was unable to take in a full breath.

"I don't care. The taxis are on their way."

They were leaving; the men were all being sent away. I opened my mouth to cry out a warning, to beg them not to get into the cars, but barely a whisper escaped my lips. The sound of my thudding heart and heavy breathing was lost in the commotion, the sound of suitcases being dragged across the floor, of startled voices asking one another where they were going. None of them seemed entirely sure. I knew that the front door had opened when I heard the storm break into the building, startling the staff as it swirled around them. I heard them hesitate.

"*Get out!*" Delia screamed again, her voice reverberating frighteningly and silencing any objectors. They scuttled like rodents, the soles of their shoes clipping the slate floor, the crunch as they ventured outside. I let out a silent moan, the faint brush of breath on my lips. When I moved, every part of my body ached and my head stuck painfully to the ground, matted in metallic stickiness. Desperately alone, I wasn't sure whether I wanted to warn them not to leave or for them to take me with them. Perhaps I simply didn't want to be alone.

Now I was alone in the walls. Nobody knew I was there and nobody seemed to care that I was gone. As the upheaval in the hotel gradually quietened, with staff leaving one by one, an eerie silence filled the place. None of them wondered where I was or why I wasn't leaving with them. My friendships were transient; my father and his family would think it typical of me to vanish without a word, and my fiancée would assume I had chosen to never come back. The more times they said it the more people would believe it, until nobody questioned it anymore. Not even the man in the walls had come down to find me. There was no one in the world whose life would be changed by my disappearance, nobody who would think about me long enough to come and find me. I was destined to be alone. Once I had been the beautiful young creature in the café who sat motionless, enviously observing the lives of others and waiting for the offer of a better existence. Now, trapped in the walls of an old, snow-covered hotel, I lay cold and still, seeing the approach of the lonely end that I would never admit to deserving.

# CHAPTER 52

I was not going to die alone in the dark. Self-pity was all well and good until the realisation struck that there was nobody there to acknowledge it and share the pity. I would not – I *could* not – disappear into the darkness like my mother had done.

I flexed my hands, and a small, choking noise gargled unpleasantly from my throat. As I started to move properly, I realised that perhaps I wasn't as badly injured as I had thought. The dust cleared from my throat in a wet cough and I felt the soft murmur of my voice rise to the surface. My spine, which I had previously assumed was fractured and had left me motionless, creaked hopefully as I attempted to stretch. A burst of pain exploded above my coccyx, causing me to gasp and wheeze. However, I could move. Painful as it was, I let my arms and legs begin to stir, the source of the pain firmly located at the base of my spine. Perhaps only a cracked coccyx. I extended my hands to either side, surprised to find walls; it was as narrow as I would have expected behind the plaster. There was no longer the abundance of space, the inexplicable dimensions; the strange universe plunged in darkness had vanished. It was just an ordinary wall cavity.

Pulling myself up into a sitting position, I pressed my back against the cool, damp stone and dug the heels of my bare feet into the plaster. I tested for the weakest point, tapping tentatively until I heard a delicately hollow bump. I kicked with the full force of my leg, gritting my teeth against the sting of nerves and twisted soft tissue, and my heel exploded through the plaster. A burst of light filled the narrow space and, though it felt blinding, I couldn't imagine it was actually all that bright. My eyes were shut tight, having been accustomed to the dark. Even through my eyelids I could see the soft glow, which lit up red capillaries and skin. I blinked, at first rapidly and then more slowly, allowing myself more exposure to the light, until I could make out where I was, albeit with my eyes scrunched into narrow slits.

My surroundings looked unexpectedly ordinary. In the darkness I had pictured a maze of wooden beams and expanding darkness, as though I was suspended in outer space, and if I ventured far enough I would begin to see the twinkle of stars and the colourful glints of planets. However, I saw just a stone wall approximately a foot and a half from plasterboard. In the light, I could no longer hear or sense the scuttling of the hiding men, and there most certainly didn't seem to be the space for me to clamber freely and stretch out to nest at night. Straining my neck, I peered upwards and, if anything, the space became even narrower higher up.

I kicked again, coughing and spluttering amid the plaster dust and general dirt and decay surrounding me. The bursts of light illuminated spiderwebs that had tangled in my clothes and hair, pale and spindly like sticky strands of candy floss. I brushed them away in disgust, always afraid of a spider's bite, though I had never experienced one before. Did native spiders even bite? Sensing one scuttle around my exposed neck, I cried out and scrambled towards the damaged plaster, hands and arms first, breaking weakened spots and forcing my head and shoulders through, reborn into the light.

I slumped against the stone floor, leaving behind me a gaping wound in the yellow wall and a trail of grey dirt and dust. My eyes stung from the light and the grains of dirt, making the entrance to the hotel blur around me, only identifiable by the feel of the floor and the flash of yellow interrupted by the bright bursts of tropical birds, gawking in delight with their fixed expressions.

I levered myself up onto all fours, wary of trusting my lower half with my full weight, paranoid that it might snap and crumble beneath me leaving me broken and helpless, a pile of bones and flesh. I pictured my flesh decaying, leaving only a skeleton in a filthy white shirt and grey trousers. I wondered if she would move me, dragging my shrivelled corpse to the bedroom and laying me on the bed, my final resting place before she bricked up the doorway, sealing me inside a tomb of my very own, soon to be little more than an arrangement of bones.

The thought of my unidentifiable body confined to the hotel rooms compelled me into a standing position. I sensed my bones creak and crunch into their correct positions as I steadied myself, hands spread around me for balance like I was standing on ice. Once I was confident that nothing was going to snap inside me, I took a step towards the front door, my bruised body aching. The hotel had a strange feeling to it, an emptiness that I hadn't felt before. Even during the night, as the majority of the staff slept, there had always been the sense of people dwelling in the building, as though you could feel the gentle rise and fall of their breath pulsating from the rooms. There was a warmth to it. In their absence, there was an almost indiscernible chill, a hollow warning that I was very much alone.

My hands gripped the doorknob and I wrenched the door open, struck by the familiar slap of a blizzard from outside. Looking down, I saw that my feet were bare, and the thin cotton of my shirt had already started to dampen and freeze against my chest. I wouldn't last an hour in the cold. Recalling my failed escape with Henry, I remembered the dreadful tiredness and the cold that seeped into my impractical shoes, numbing my feet and mimicking the sensation of pain in my leg nerves. I remembered how, had the witches not taken us back, we would have wound up like Edward, frozen in the snow, limbs outstretched as we tried to drag ourselves to freedom.

I swore under my breath. Perhaps if I could get into Delia's office I could use her phone and call the police. This time I would tell them about the body in the bedroom, and then they would take me away. I pictured a warm police station buzzing with activity, a kindly officer draping a fleecy blanket over my shoulders and offering me a hot cup of tea in one of those paper cups which would thaw my frozen hands. The papers would want my story, my ordeal. Perhaps I would be offered a book deal. I pictured book signings at my favourite book shops as the crowds gathered, desperate to know what had happened at Delia's hotel.

What did happen at Delia's hotel? It wasn't really a hotel, more like a huge house staffed by men to tend to the needs of its owner. We had cooked and cleaned, provided entertainment where required, and placed aside any dreams or aspirations that we may once have harboured, in order to serve her.

"She was good to you, though, wasn't she?" the critics might ask, heads cocked to one side. "Your accommodation and meals were all paid for. She didn't exactly force you to work, did she? You chose to go there, you chose to work for her and you wanted for nothing for all those years."

I would shake my head despairingly.

"No," I would insist. "It wasn't like that. She manipulated us – she made us think we were in love with her, and we stopped looking out for ourselves and our own happiness. For God's sake, Edward died because of it!"

"Edward should have known better. Delia didn't do that. He did it to himself."

"Delia sounds like a strong woman," another would say, their tone elevated in admiration. "She knew what she wanted and she got it. I mean, what did she actually do to you? Was she ever violent towards you?" They would poise with their notebooks, preparing for scandal.

"No, not directly, but—"

"You just sound bitter. Have some self-respect and get on with your life," they would say, snapping their notebooks shut.

The imaginary conversation whirled in my head as I tried to make sense of what had happened in the hotel.

"Body in the bedroom," I whispered, determined to keep reminding myself, the memory threatening to flutter away. "There's a body in the bedroom. Delia is a murderer."

I shut the door against the force of the storm and resolved to find the telephone, even if it meant smashing down the office door. Pressing my hands against the glass until it clicked shut, I was greeted again by the eerie silence of the hotel, and was chilled by the thought that she was surely still inside.

The darkening sky of the early afternoon meant that I caught a glimpse of my reflection in the glass of the door. At first my grey-and-white image appeared to blend in with the sky and snow outside, as though the world was black and white. Then I saw the flash of blue in my eyes and the tinge of pink on my dry lips. Raising my hands, I clasped them against my sunken cheeks, peering closer at the labyrinth of burst capillaries around my nose which appeared more bulbous than I recalled, and the way the papery flesh around my eyes sunk in colourless folds as though I was made of rumpled fabric. As I frowned at myself, the lines in my forehead deepened, dragging my sagging features together in a loose grimace. Irrationally, I wondered if it was the plaster dust from the walls, and I swatted desperately at myself, trying to brush off any residue that might be disguising colour and hiding my youth. There was no dust, just the slight pinkening of the skin where I had slapped desperately, and within seconds that too had returned to the ashen grey of an elderly man, a man I didn't recognise. In my mind's eye, I was tall and proud, with enviably strong features that resembled portraits of handsome nobility. I had the healthy flush of youth and eyes that glittered with aspiration and desire. The eyes of the old man in front of me were diluted to a watery colourlessness, sad and drooping. Undesirable. Where I was once able to sit in a public space and watch the world gravitate towards me, envious and lusting glances in equal measure cast my way, this old man would sit alone, blending into the inattentive crowd. Women of all ages would pass him as though he was invisible. Young women would hide their disdain for his pallid, papery skin and stooped appearance, and the older woman would breeze past him in their cheerful gangs, either engrossed in conversations with friends or hands clasped with their weathered counter-part, equally stooped and warped by age, but brightened by the intangible radiance of a long-established love. Perhaps, if the old man in the reflection cried out, or maybe even tripped and fell over, people might turn to look at him, they might help him up if they thought he needed it. But before long they would forget his face forever, and when they recanted the tale to their friends, they would massage their own sense of self-worth by describing how *they* helped the poor old man, how *they* got him to his feet and dusted him down. They wouldn't bother adding whether the old man was alright or not, since he was little more than a prop supporting their good deed. He didn't matter.

Crying out in dismay, I dropped my hands from my face, resenting the tears that fell and cleared my vision. I turned away from my reflection in disgust, and as I did so, I saw, just over its shoulder, the figure of Delia.

She was standing behind me in a white nightdress, still and silent. Her dark hair tumbled over bare shoulders, unbrushed and limp. Her appearance was the same as it had always been, but there was something ugly about her reflection, something imperceptible that I couldn't attribute to anything in particular. In fact, her features were as beautiful as they had always been, like a porcelain doll. A perfect, dreadful doll that made me want to run into the blizzard and risk a slow, cold death rather than turn and face her.

"Eric." Her voice was low, lips barely moving in the reflec-tion. "Come and sit by the fire."

# CHAPTER 53

Gesturing vaguely, she turned her back to me and began walking towards the drawing room. Her bare feet made a light padding noise against the stone, the thin gown floating around her ankles. It surprised me to note that she wasn't shivering.

There was a part of me that had expected her to lunge as I turned around, her hands curled and claw-like, poised to pounce. Instead, her body was slouched, and she appeared thin rather than slender, her bones sharp beneath sagging skin. There was a slightly blue tinge to her flesh, amplified by the white of her antiquated nightdress, which, with all its trims and lacey frills, seemed somehow obscene draped over her frail body.

I followed her to the living room, where the fire burned contentedly. She reached for a log and tossed it on the glowing embers where it crackled and eventually caught light, popping behind the metal grate. Crossing her legs, she lowered herself into a childlike seated position on the worn rug, charcoal remnants scattered around her. Resting her elbows on her exposed and knobbly knees, she leaned towards the fire and shut her eyes against the heat.

"Why didn't you leave?" she asked eventually. "Everyone else has."

Hesitating, I moved to one of the leather armchairs a short distance from her and lowered myself into it. I sank into the loose springs, which were no longer able to support me, until the frame of the chair dug uncomfortably into my rear.

"I didn't know," I replied eventually. "I was stuck in the…" I was unsure how much she knew about the men in the walls and their hiding spots. I was loathe to betray the man who had helped me. "In another part of the hotel." It wasn't a lie. "And nobody told me they were leaving."

She nodded.

"You should have left with them."

"Where did they go?"

"I don't know." She shrugged, the bones of her shoulders stretching her skin. "I don't care."

We sat in silence for a moment before I cleared my throat and spoke.

"So, I take it you're not running the hotel anymore?"

Her head twisted over her shoulder and she peered at me, letting out a bark of a laugh.

"Really, Eric?" She half smiled, somewhere between pitying and patronising. "We both knew that this was never a hotel, didn't we?"

263

# CHAPTER 54

I glanced behind me, assessing the time it would take me to run from my chair to the door. Delia smiled.

"Run if you like." She turned back to the fire. "I won't chase you."

"What do you mean when you say it was never a hotel?" I watched her carefully, and tested my stiff limbs, waiting for her to scuttle towards me unexpectedly – the spider moving nimbly across its web.

"You never wondered why there were never any guests?"

"Well, I did, of course, but we were renovating, and the winters were too bad for guests to get here."

"You never questioned why it was always winter?" She seemed to take pleasure in my discomfort. "Or why I never aged, even though the men around me have grown old and tired?"

I stared at her in silence, my lips pursed tightly.

"With Edward gone, everything seems so pointless now. Everything I ever wanted to achieve is redundant." Toying with a piece of charcoal between her fingers, she rubbed the black into her palms. "I have no incentive to go on. Have you ever felt that way, Eric?"

I didn't answer.

"No?" She smiled, this time sadly, eyes glittering. "Maybe that should make me happy. It's a horrible feeling." Her blackened finger rose to her eye, smudging a tear aside. It left a grey trail across her sunken eye socket. "Edward changed, you know, from when he first arrived here. At first, I thought I would hate him just the same as I hated the rest of you, but he changed. He taught me what it meant to love again. He was kind, and I realised that what I had mistaken for cruelty in him was actually just the obliviousness of youth. He was a good man." She snatched another log and rolled it on top of the pile on the grate. "The logs will run out soon," she murmured. "This place will become very cold. Everything will decay, just as it was always meant to. I suggest you leave before then."

"I don't understand." I leaned forward, hands tightening against the fabric of my trousers, which were still damp from the spaces in the walls. "Why us?"

Her laugh tinkled.

"Oh, Eric." She shook her head, smiling to herself. "None of this was ever about you. It was *them* – all those women who had convinced themselves that they loved you and would give up everything for you. I could see what their futures held, and I didn't want that for them." Her face became pained. "I didn't want them to suffer like I did."

I followed her gaze to the window, looking out at the heavy white sky, the snow falling almost hypnotically.

"Those fairy tales they told by the fire at night – I loved listening to them, seeing how little those men had learned during their time here. They were true in a sense, or at least they held the men's truths, the way they fell victim to the wicked ways of women. They had been here so long, Eric, that they had lost their grip on reality – but that's what happens, isn't it? Men forget what the truth is, and they turn it into a story that suits them. *We* are always to blame." Uncrossing her legs, she hugged her knees to her body, making her look very small and vulnerable. "Edward used to tell that story, the one about the sea monster. He remembered how he had married that girl, that free spirit living her life as she pleased. Suddenly she was shackled by marriage, and by overbearing in-laws who expected her to become something she was never meant to be. I watched her from the sidelines, and I could see what she was becoming, a shell of her former self, while Edward was away at sea and would come back oblivious to how much his wife was changing – ready to have his dinner served right on time. It made me angry watching them, and I knew what that girl would become if I didn't do something, so I took Edward away. For a time, as his story warped in his head, he told the tale of the sea monster that wore the skin of his wife, a dreadful, wicked creature. However, she was just a lonely girl who became very sad – she was never a monster. After a time, Edward realised what he had done to her; he was the first to understand the truth. I originally planned to let him go once he had learned the error of his ways, but I fell in love with him. I taught him to be better. I wanted to keep him." She dropped her chin onto her chest, tucked behind her knees as though ashamed of herself. "Then there was Sandy and his story of the vampire. That vampire was nothing more than a girl who enjoyed spending time with her friends. He was so jealous that he didn't let her out, he kept her confined at home, a place he thought most appropriate for a woman. He managed to convince himself that *she* was the monster. And then there's Ollie, who used to take home a different woman each night and discard them once he was through with them, shattering hearts and self-esteem without a care in the world – and yet he thought *he* was the victim when the consequences of his actions caught up with him." She paused, licking her lips, which had dried out in the heat of the fire. "Or Henry, who told the story about the magpie that lured him in. *He* was the married man. It was *his* wrongdoing – that woman, the magpie in his story, she was nothing more than an innocent who found herself infatuated by everything he professed to offer. However, he would have given her nothing, and tarnished her career in the process." Lifting a brow, she gestured at me. "Tell me your story, Eric – go on."

I hesitated for a second.

"I was an axeman in an enchanted forest, and there was a fairy who lived in the trees and…" My voice trailed away. "No, that's not right – that can't be right; that wasn't my story – that was the story of the man in the walls."

Delia continued to watch me with her lingering smile.

"There's nobody in the walls," she said softly. "There never was."

"There must be – I saw him! Or, maybe not *saw* him, but… *no, no, no.*" I heard myself babbling, shaking my head, feeling my temples throb as I grew angry and confused. "You kidnapped us! You took us here against our will."

Delia laughed, this time unnervingly shrilly.

"No, not at all." The snaggled canine protruded more prominently from her thin face, which suddenly had a gaunt, skeletal look about it. "You all came willingly, leaving your supposed loves behind when you thought there was a better deal to be had."

Her smile widened eerily, and she shuffled around to face me, her back to the fire and her knees tucked up against her chest again. There was a silence between us as the wind howled, sending a shudder through the building. Excitement flashed in Delia's widening eyes, the sky was darkened by the late afternoon and the room beginning to glow orange in the light of the flames.

"Would you like to hear a story, Eric?" she asked eagerly. "Would you like to hear *my* story?"

# CHAPTER 55:

## DELIA'S FAIRY TALE

O nce upon a time there was a girl who lived with her family in a beautiful stately home in the countryside. She led a happy and immensely privileged life surrounded by all the toys, dolls and doting nannies that she could hope for. Her favourite room in the house was her bedroom, a lavish space with bright-pink decorative wallpaper and a beautiful canopy bed that made her feel like a princess. During the day, the girl spent her time out in the gardens, wandering as far as she dared from the house.

In those days, rural lands were rich with myths and often-frightening stories. The girl loved them, and she would beg the servants to tell her of the ogres that hid by the streams and caves, of the cackling witches that hunted in the night. Instead of being afraid, the girl was fascinated, and often on her walks she would call out for the fairy creatures to show themselves to her, to be her friends. Sometimes the girl thought she could see the witches watching her from her bedroom window, their eyes reflecting the stars in the darkness below. She waved, but they never waved back. The girl's mother discouraged such fantasy, banning it outright after a certain point, considering the girl too old to indulge in children's stories and daydreams – it was particularly embarrassing, she bemoaned, when they had guests over.

It had always been important to the girl's mother that she was well put together. Her mother always said that a lady should look her best at all times and that little girls were no exception. How else would she find a husband? The little girl allowed her hair to be bound tightly in fabric each night to create doll-like ringlets, and she would sit carefully in extravagant dresses with puffed sleeves and lace trim, not allowing one single crease. Everyone complimented her; they told her that she looked like a doll, just as a little girl ought to. Her mother would sigh at the little snaggle tooth that poked out from her lip, and she tried to teach the girl to smile in a different way that would disguise it. But when the girl smiled properly – particularly if tickled by her father – there was no hiding the wonky little tooth. She would never admit it to her mother, but the girl didn't really want a husband. She was happy with her mother and her father and their wonderful home in their wonderful fairy-tale kingdom. She hoped that nothing would ever change.

Of course, things do change. Things change in a heartbeat. The girl's mother and father fell ill to a terrible flu that ravaged their bodies and left them mere husks of their former selves. The girl wasn't allowed to see them as they died, for fear that the sickness would spread through the household. Their bodies were carefully removed, wrapped tightly in linen and taken to be buried deep in a place where the sickness would never escape. As they wrapped the corpses, the girl caught a glimpse of her mother through a crack in the door, horrified by the sunken features and the limp hair, the pallid skin. Her mother wouldn't have wanted anyone to remember her that way.

By the time of her parents' deaths, the girl was barely out of childhood and not yet an adult. She found herself bewildered by the grim-faced men who let themselves into her house, offering advice, suggesting she sign documents and calculating the worth of her father's estate. As it turned out, his liquid assets were not as much as he had indicated and, before long, the staff in the house began to trickle away, leaving the girl cold and alone. All by herself, she was lost, the corridors endlessly long, and she sought comfort in the howl of the wind which whistled through the walls like people would, people living in the walls. Sometimes, in her darkest moments, she would whisper to the walls, hoping that they might respond, might reassure her that she wasn't alone. But they never did. Sometimes she fantasised about breaking through the walls and crawling inside, into the darkness where she could disappear, such was her despair.

One day, a man came to visit the girl in her sad and empty home. He was a businessman who had done some dealings with her father when he was alive. The girl eyed him cautiously, alarmed by the way he breezed with confidence into her drawing room and sat by the barren fireplace. He raised a brow at the lack of servants to light it. She was used to guests who waited to be addressed by her, the bow of a head or a gracious curtsy. This man took her hand without asking, planting a kiss against the fine bones of her wrist which had become more pronounced in her hunger over the past few months, especially since the cooks had left. He took a seat and crossed his legs, interlocking his fingers and taking a deep breath before making his proposition.

The man was self-made, a savvy businessman who earned his fortune overseas through sheer cunning. However, money had only enabled him to get so far in life, and he was ambitious; what he lacked was a name and status.

"You and I could be good for one another." His voice was smooth, that of an accomplished salesman. "I feel so sorry for you, all alone in this great big house – like a ghost!" He laughed, even though it wasn't a joke. "I know how it would pain your father to see you in this state, and I hope you know that I had a great deal of respect for him – he was a good man. I have the wealth to support you, to allow you to keep your family home. You have the status and the contacts I need to advance myself to the point I wish to reach in life. We can help each other. Your father would want that." Sensing her doubt, he rose and placed a cool hand on her cheek. The girl resisted the urge to recoil.

"I've spoken to the accountants and it's not good," he sighed. "Poor, sweet girl. If things don't improve for you, they're going to take your home and everything you own. You'll be destitute and all alone." His eyes sparkled. "I could get it all back for you."

The wedding took place shortly after the proposition. It was the kind of wedding that the girl's mother had always wanted for her. However, the girl's heart was empty as she stood at the altar, her exquisite white gown trailing the church floors. When she looked around, she saw none of her friends from school or the neighbouring families whose children she had been brought up with. Instead, there were stuffy-looking men in taut suits with po-faced wives who peered down narrow noses, critically examining every detail of the day. The businessman spent little time with the girl on their wedding day; instead, he circulated among the guests he had tactically invited. On the night of her wedding, she could have sworn that, as the guests danced and drank in their dining hall, she could see the familiar eyes of the witches from her childhood watching her through the window, outside in the darkness. As she approached, she thought she saw a weathered hand reach out from behind the glass, just for a second, before it was whipped away, the eyes vanishing with it into the night. She scolded herself, reminded of her mother's warnings that a young lady shouldn't indulge in such outlandish fantasies.

The servants and the cooks reappeared in the home and the fires were lit, fighting off the damp that had crept in over the years the girl had been alone. However, nothing really ever felt warm. Her home hosted lavish parties, with guests who trampled across her parents' beautiful rugs and spilt drinks, who laughed and shouted and whose drunken glances at the girl made her distrust them. Her husband took centre stage at these parties, promoting himself shamelessly, taking little pleasure in genuine fun or friendship. The girl's home became a stranger to her.

One day, the girl's husband hosted a luncheon at the house. Some of the guests – friends and associates – turned up with suitcases and guns for a weekend of shooting in the country. Their rooms had been prepared by diligent servants.

The girl was seated nowhere near her husband; he explained that he needed to surround himself with people who were useful to him. Instead, she sat near the end of the long table next to a young man whose face was unfamiliar to her; he had the slightly bewildered expression of someone who was out of their comfort zone. As it turned out, he had recently obtained a junior position at a bank in the city and his boss had invited him along for the weekend, as the girl's husband was one of their clients. He spoke softly and expressed little interest in networking, instead wanting to know about the girl. She told him about her childhood growing up in the house and about her parents. The young man had lost his parents at a young age too, and he offered her the first words that had been a comfort to her. However, it wasn't his kind and inquisitive nature that first drew her to him; it was his scent. She had caught it as soon as she sat down, and it reminded her of summer days by the stream as a child. He smelled of dewy grass and earth, delightfully so, and she wondered how it was that something as simple as a scent could have such power over her. She smiled at him, and he smiled back.

The girl fell deeply in love with the young man, who became a regular at their parties and events. They spent late nights hidden in the shadows of empty corridors or creeping into unoccupied rooms, wrapping each other in their arms and vowing that one day they would be together.

Not long after one of their clandestine visits, he wrote to her from the city, bearing his soul to her in a scrawl of ink, telling her that he couldn't stand the long periods of time spent apart. He invited her to run away with him and enclosed a train ticket. His letter never did reach the girl because, little did she know, her husband read all her mail before it got to her. Initially this had been to ensure that he was on top of her financial affairs, but after everything had been wound up he continued to monitor her communications.

One night, her husband snatched her from their marital bed, dragging her by her hair as she screamed in fright. The servants didn't dare intervene, watching her stumbling down the corridor. He snarled at her, asking her if she realised how humiliating it would be to have his wife run out on him like that, if she knew what it would do to his reputation.

He dragged her to the landing on the stairs where her childhood bedroom had been. It had never been decorated, still childish and pink, with an elaborate child's bed cloaked in a white canopy. He threw her against the mattress, gesturing at the letter in a jagged envelope by the letter opener on the bedside table. When the girl read it, she wept and confessed her feelings for the young man, begging her husband to let her go – after all, legally he would be entitled to everything that had once belonged to her, and she had no desire to fight for it. He refused to let her go and instead slammed the door and locked it behind him. He left no lamps or candles, and the girl was plunged into darkness.

The girl remained alone in the room for many weeks, and the nights became longer as winter washed in like a dark wave. Servants slipped in with small meals and drinks, but they kept their eyes low, refusing to meet her gaze or communicate with her. They had been instructed to keep her in solitude. The girl's heart ached for her lover, and she dreamed of him coming to rescue her from this prison. At first she was comforted by this thought, but as time passed and the likelihood of it happening became increasingly improbable, her heart began to ache and she despaired. The door was too thick to break through, and the window was too high to smash the glass and scale down. None of the servants answered her cries. She started whispering to the walls, brushing the smooth paper with the tips of her fingers as she imagined voices speaking back to her. Once again, she dreamed of giving in to the darkness behind the walls.

One evening, as the girl had become accustomed to living mostly in darkness, she heard the fumbling and twisting of a key outside. The door to the bedroom swung open and her husband stood in the dark doorway, a lamp in his hand illuminating his gleefully wicked expression.

He told her that, after the girl had failed to show up at the train station, the young man had presumed that she didn't share his feelings. He had continued with his life, an aura of sadness about him, which his boss had reported as being of concern. The girl's husband had told the young man's boss that all he needed was a distraction and that he could think of the perfect thing. They introduced the young man to the daughter of a mutual friend, a charming young lady who would make the perfect wife for him. They were engaged to be married, and the girl's husband had been at the wedding that very night, citing sickness for the girl's absence. Triumphantly, he announced that the young man hadn't so much as asked after her; in fact, he seemed too overjoyed with his new bride to notice the girl's absence.

The girl began to wail, and at first her husband took satisfaction in this, but then he told her to be quiet. Her cries were irritating him. When she didn't stop, he shoved her hard and yelled at her to pull herself together, threatening to leave her locked up forever if she continued like that. He stank of wine, whisky and cigarettes, just like the guests he invited to their parties, who left their scent lingering in the girl's home. Filled with an uncontrollable rage, the girl reached for the bedside table where the letter opener had lain untouched for many months, and she stabbed her husband in the chest. His mouth opened in a little "O" shape, more surprised than anything else. Of course, the girl regretted it immediately, and began to scream as blood oozed through his white shirt and spilt across the bed's white linen. Her screams attracted the attention of one of the servants, who had been tidying up for the night, and he ran to the room, clasping his hand over his mouth at the sight of his master dying on the bed before him. The girl pleaded that it was an accident and she stumbled from the body towards the door, insisting that they call a doctor, that she would tell the police the truth.

The servant was a shrewd man who had always considered himself worthy of greater things in life; he had simply been waiting for the opportunity. Before the girl could flee from the room, he snatched her arms firmly and held her steady.

"They'll hang you," he said firmly, gesturing at the body. "Look. He's already dead."

The girl sobbed, collapsing to the floor. The servant told her not to fear; he would help her, on one condition.

The servant would pack his master's things for a hunting trip and spread the word around the staff that the master planned to be away all weekend. When he didn't return, it would be assumed that he had gone ill-prepared and perished in the winter hills. The servant would leave traces of him for the police to find. In the meantime, they would leave the body in the room. They would brick up the wall, dividing the room in two and papering over it so that no one need ever know that the room even existed.

The servant would do this on one condition. The girl was to marry him, so that he could lay claim to her fortune. True to her word, one year after her husband was presumed dead, she married the servant, who promptly became master of the house.

The servant was never cruel to the girl – not directly. They lived largely as acquaintances, nodding benignly to one another over prepared meals, occasionally sharing an evening drink by the fire. The staff gossiped about his many affairs, the women he brought back with him after indulgent weekends in the city, but, of course, they weren't aware that the entire relationship was a sham and that the girl didn't care what he did. Sometimes she even talked to the women he brought back with him and indulged fantasies that he might have them stay and they could be friends.

"You know that you use me," she said to him over dinner one evening. They sat at a great distance from one another at the long dining-room table. By that point, the girl was losing her eyesight to age, and she had to squint to see him smile at her, shrugging.

"Everyone uses everyone," he replied with a hint of sadness, as though it was an unpleasant truth to which he had resigned himself.

Being considerably older than her, the servant died long before she did, and the girl lived on, a long and heartbreakingly lonely existence. Her loneliness was immortalised by a self-portrait that she commissioned and hung in her drawing room. She would touch the image of the sagging cheeks and the thin line of the lips dragged down by a frown, and she would wonder how the happy little girl had become this. There was nothing doll-like left to her; nobody would ever want her like that.

As she grew steadily older and her body began to fail her, the time came for her to say goodbye to her long and woeful life, so she took to her bed and awaited the inevitable.

It was winter when she prepared to die, a particularly cold one that chilled the rooms and sent whispering winds throughout the walls of her home. She was briefly reminded of a time in her childhood after her parents died, a time she thought had been the loneliest of her life, but, now that she thought of it, wasn't.

That was when the witches came for her.

They crept through the entrance one evening, stealthily, as though they travelled on the blizzard itself, and they ascended the stairs to the girl's bedroom. She lay, an old greying woman wrapped in her bedsheets, shivering in the chill of the night. Her once blue eyes, which had turned milky with blindness, widened as the witches approached her bed. Over a dozen blurred creatures stood before her in long flowing gowns that could never have protected them from the cold. Despite her near-full blindness, she could see their eyes sparkle, just like the ones she had seen from her window as a child. They were all elderly women, moving with surprising agility. One with pale strawberry blonde hair, which would once have been a vibrant red, leaned in close and touched the girl's forehead, stroking tenderly. She whispered in the girl's ear, telling her stories of witch trials and burnings. She told her that a long time ago they were forced to flee their homes in a place where the cities now stood. The witches had fled north and made their home in the hills, a place to hide from the fate that awaited them at the hands of men.

"They wanted to burn us." The witch's voice crackled with age. "They wanted to drag us from our homes and punish us for being different, for not conforming to their expectations." She cackled, a husky rasp, and ran her fingers through her wispy red hair. "My hair – at first they loved me for it, and then they said I deserved to burn for it. Flawed features, old age, being outspoken, childlessness – anything that men didn't like could see us burned." Her eyes widened, swirling with greens, greys and blues like planets. "So, we ran away. We hid where no one would ever decide our fate for us."

"You don't have to die," another witch whispered, approaching the bed. "We have been watching you. We offer you a choice."

The offer was made: die alone or join the witches.

Later that evening she would die alone, her dying croaks unheard, most of the servants having left and the others downstairs out of earshot. By the time they came up with her dinner, her body would be cold. Nobody would really remember the girl, and even if they did they would think of her as the pretty young wife of the businessman who had vanished in the hills on a hunting trip decades earlier. The conversation would veer to the businessman and his various accolades. Occasionally, she would feature in the dreams of her former lover, now an old man, but he would remember her only with fleeting fondness, a distant memory that bore no relevance to the life he had built for himself and his family.

Or, that evening, the girl would join the witches in their snowy world. She would have eternal youth and beauty, if she so wished, and she would finally be free from the control of others, running wild in the nights, conforming to nothing but her own standards. She would become the hunter, one of the pack.

For the longest time, the girl had harboured a darkness deep within her, a white-hot rage that boiled low in her belly when she thought of the men who had taken her fortune or who had used her for their own gain, locking her up like a dog when she didn't obey. She thought of the letter opener between the ribs of her former husband, who lay behind a wall of bricks, and that rage became even hotter as she considered how she had been driven to that point. Then she recalled – a long-buried memory – those dark nights in solitude, the madness that had begun to creep up on her with each passing day. She was suddenly rabid with rage.

The witches eased her out of bed and led her over to her dressing table where they lowered her onto her stool, gently supporting her back so she could sit upright. The girl felt suddenly weepy at the tenderness of their touch, which was absent of the strategic grasps of men or the humiliating practicality of the staff, who rolled her ageing body from bed to chair, uncomfortably averting their gaze and hastily removing her clothes. Glancing at the witches, the girl was too tired to shed any tears, but they nodded at her, silently acknowledging that they understood.

As she looked at herself in the mirror, the witches gathered around, hands interlinked and bodies swaying in an invisible breeze. The girl's vision became gradually clearer, and she watched the white wispiness of her hair become dense and black, tumbling over her shoulders which straightened, the skin swelling and masking the harsh bones with a layer of youthful fat. Her breasts rose, becoming pert again, and her chest and hips – with one loud crack – snapped back into their former places. She watched her facial features begin to shrink, her nose becoming more button-like, and her eyes widening, doll-like.

"Stop," she said, surprised by the clarity of her voice. "This is how I want to remain." She touched the snaggled canine that protruded sharply when she drew back her lips and smiled. She didn't want them to fix that. Her fingers brushed her slightly pointed ears, which had not yet been fully pinned against her head. "The absence of all flaws will not be what makes me so desirable," she breathed, recalling the intoxicating scent of grass and earth that had lingered with her for decades since she had last been in the presence of her one and only love. "Scent will be the trap; it's far more powerful."

Intrigued by her request, the witches gifted her the power she requested, and they continued to manipulate their own features, playing with their faces and body parts until they had tweaked them to their liking, until they were no longer old and haggard but impossibly beautiful creatures. They stepped back, smiling, and welcomed the girl with open arms. Rising, the girl tested her legs, wobbling slightly like a new-born deer before finding her feet.

The girl dismissed her servants the following day. She planned on leaving the hotel forever and running free with the witches in their snowy world, where they would gleefully torment tres-passers and dance beneath the stars. They would play with their appearances and lure unsuspecting hunters beyond the bound-ary and into their endless winter-world. However, just as the servants were leaving, she watched a couple, a maid and the cook, dragging their suitcases across the stone-floored entrance. She saw something that only a witch could see.

The maid, a rosy-cheeked creature who seemed colour-ful despite her dowdy uniform, had a sparkle about her that made the girl smile fondly. However, as she watched her more closely, she began to see more; she saw things that she didn't want to see. She could see what awaited the maid in her future. Before too long, the unmarried maid would carry the child of the cook, who, upon finding out, would make his excuses and vanish from her life. She would only be able to hide her secret for so long before her future employer, a stony-faced mistress, sent her away in disgrace. Reluctantly, her family would take her in, humiliated at the thought of her being unmarried and with child. They would come to an agreement that the baby would be passed off as her sister's and the whole sordid affair would be brushed under the carpet. After that, the maid could return to her life as planned and they would never speak of it again. However, the maid's life would never be the same. Her heart would ache for that baby for the rest of her life, and one day she would see the cook on the street with a family of his own, smiling obliviously, and she would be filled with a hateful poison that ran so deep that she would never recover. The girl knew what that kind of poison did to a person, and it pained her to think that this was what awaited the smiling maid.

"Wait." The girl strode through the door in the guise of a long-lost niece who was taking over the estate. Brushing the maid out of the way, she turned her focus to the cook and let a small smile cross her lips. She oozed the scent of fresh rosemary, a smell that reminded the cook of the gardens of his youth and the preparation of Sunday lunches. She watched as he succumbed to it, a fly in a web. His eyes drifted over her body, taking note of her appearance, breathing in every inch of her, and, to the girl's disgust, barely even attempting to hide his desire.

"I'm going to require a chef," she said boldly, ignoring the hurt in the maid's eyes. "A chef for my new business venture."

The cook nodded, not even bothering to enquire any further, willing to do anything to stay in the girl's company.

"I will be opening a hotel," she announced boldly. "And it will be wonderful."

In the distance, as the wind howled and the snow fell heavier than ever, the girl could sense the witches pause in their wild frolicking, standing alert, peering through the storm towards the house and, after a moment's consideration, smiling.

# CHAPTER 56

The room became increasingly dark, despite the flickering orange of the fire, which cast bold shapes on the walls. I sat in silence for several minutes after Delia's story, watching the glossy black of her hair as she gazed into the flames.

"But it's just a fairy tale," I said eventually. "Just like the others. It's not real. There aren't really witches and spells." I hesitated. "You're a murderer, and making up stories won't change that."

I sensed her smile, watching her pointed ears rise.

"Maybe," she said quietly. "Maybe not. But whatever the case, you should leave. It's getting dark and I imagine my friends will be here soon." She glanced at the depleting log basket. "The logs will all be gone soon, and we'll need to find other things to burn to keep warm. You really ought to go. My friends are very particular about the company we keep. They only tolerated you because I asked them to. Without me protecting you, who knows what they'll do. You're fair game now."

Feeling a familiar flash of panic, I shook my head.

"But where will I go?" My voice came out quietly, barely a squeak, and didn't sound anything like me. "What do you expect me to do? I don't have anything. I'll die out there."

"I called you a car," she replied stonily, rising to her feet and moving towards one of the mahogany tables by the window. Her fingers fumbled with the little bronze key on the narrow drawer and it creaked open awkwardly, swollen from cold and damp.

"When?"

"When I realised you were still here," she said simply. "Here, take this." She emerged with a wad of notes wrapped in an elastic band. She thrust them into my hand, a wad of twenties probably not amounting to any more than several hundred pounds.

"No." I shook my head, despite holding the money. "Where did you send the other men? I know that something bad happens when they leave in those cars. I've seen how scared they are." I sensed myself becoming breathless, panicked. "Edward died trying to make it back from wherever you sent him."

Delia stared blankly at me, and I noticed an unusual milkiness to her eyes, a cloudy film over the blue like a sign of blindness.

"You can't toy with our lives like this!" I cried. Rising to my feet, I moved towards her, hoping to breathe her in and become filled with the wave of warmth and love, like a drug that would put me at ease and return me to blissful ignorance. However, as I moved closer to her, I smelled nothing. Inhaling through my nostrils, I found that there was something deeply disconcerting about it; after all, everyone had a smell. It was as though she didn't exist. Tears pricked the corner of my eyes. "Why are you doing this to me?"

"I used to think I was right," she said quietly, her voice slow and thoughtful but wavering at the end of sentences. "I thought I was doing the right thing for so long. It wasn't you I saw in the Christmas market that day, it was *her*. The lovely woman in the orange mittens who smiled adoringly at you, and I hated seeing that, because I knew exactly what awaited her. It's a curse, you see, being able to see tragedy the way I can. I watched that woman grow older, tirelessly supporting you in *your* quest for happiness, a thing you were never going to find, while losing *her* own sense of self. You were never going to find it because happiness doesn't exist for you, Eric, and it never will; it's always just around the corner, with something or someone you perceive to be better, richer, more beautiful. The saddest part about it all is that that girl *was* happy – blissfully so, in fact – and she would have been blissfully happy without you in her life too. She had friends and a loving family, but, if she stayed with you, over time that happiness would fade. You would turn your nose up at her friends, who you considered bland, but really you were envious of their happiness, and she would listen to you, and eventually she would be poisoned against them. You would isolate her from her family, pulling away out of jealousy and insecurity. You would lie to her about your mutual dreams for a family. "One day," you would say, "one day." But one day would never come and it would be too late. She would grow old, and her brightness would fade, her kind nature darkening into a resentment of others, and she would hate herself for it. Others would hate her for it too, and she would be alone." I watched as Delia's eyes glittered. "I saw that lady as an old woman with drawn features and a resignation about her, washed clean of that brightness and warmth, and it devastated me." Her eyes narrowed and she took a step closer to me. "So, I took you away, just like I took all the others. I was so angry. I wanted to make it right, to even the scales a bit, but…" Her voice trembled. "Now I don't know if I did the right thing. When I first brought Edward here, I thought he was so selfish and cavalier, clueless about what he might have done had I not intervened. But maybe *I* made a mistake. Maybe he was actually loving and kind and it was *me* who used *him*." A fat tear rolled down her cheek. "And now, that wonderful, loving man is dead and it's my fault. He just wanted to get back to me, and for once I couldn't see what was going to happen. I was completely unaware to what his future held, blinded by my own stubbornness." With a heavy sniff, she moved towards the wall and pressed her hands against it. "I keep hoping I'll hear him behind these walls. The way I used to hear the voices when I was young, and so lonely for the longest time." She rested her ear against the paintwork. "I hope that I'll hear his voice, and that I'll be able to claw through the plaster and pull him out, and we'll be together again – but, really, all I ever hear is the echo of my own voice. Perhaps I'll climb inside and try to find him. When I'm ready." Turning back to me, her mouth twisted into a wry smile. "I think I loved it, you know. I loved the power and control that I had over you all. You know what that feels like, don't you? It's like you have the world in the palm of your hand and everything revolves around you. I didn't think it was *cruel*, because none of you starved – you were all warm and comfortable enough. The loneliness and rejection you suffered was justice." She wiped a tear away, gathering herself. "But I was the only judge, and maybe everything I've done here has been wrong. I don't know anymore." She shook her head and waved her hand dismissively. "Anyway, I want you gone."

"Gone like the man behind the bricked-up wall?" The words came out hatefully, each one spat to the floor before her. "Your *husband?*"

She continued to stare with an unfocused gaze.

"You *used* me!"

"Everyone uses everyone," she replied simply, turning to the window where she peered blindly out at the dimming horizon. "They're on their way." Her voice was quiet as she reached out and touched my arm with a gnarled hand. "Come on."

She pushed me lightly towards the door, and I found myself stumbling along beside her, one foot in front of the other being as much as I could manage. We walked out into the reception area, towards the glass door through which shone two bright beams of light, causing me to wince. I continued shaking my head as she turned the handle and guided me out into the cold. My feet vanished into the snow.

"No." My voice sounded pathetic, even to me. "I don't want to go. I don't want to get in."

Delia nodded at the taxi driver, whose face was obscured by a low hat. He returned a single nod.

In the distance, I could make out small, dark shapes drifting over the horizon. At first they looked like a row of tombstones, but, as they became bigger and better formed, I could see the outline of the women, their hair billowing in the wind. I watched Delia wave at them before she glanced back at me.

"Goodbye, Eric." Her tone was brusque and final. The taxi door opened automatically, and she ushered me inside without pausing to look at me. I tried to catch her eye, just for a moment, so that I might memorise her face, but she slammed the taxi door behind me and took a step back. I found myself sinking sideways onto the leather seat, trapped in the small space between locked doors and Pyrex glass that separated me and the driver.

"*No!*" I felt the well of panic rise in my throat, wondering how I could have let her push me inside the taxi so easily, wishing I had fought harder to stay. My hand grasped for the handle, but I already knew that the taxi was locked from the inside. "I don't want to go!"

The taxi reversed back through the snow, rumbling over uneven ground, jostling me about.

"Seatbelt," the driver barked through the glass. Obediently, I sat up properly and leaned over to fasten my belt. The taxi turned away from the hotel and picked up speed down the drive. I twisted round sharply against the force of the belt to look out the rear window, clasping my hands around the headrest to steady myself, and watched Delia standing on the drive. Her white nightdress was barely visible in the falling snow, and her long, exposed limbs hung at her sides in the cold, unmoving, like she was a doll suspended by strings. She wasn't watching me, but looking into the distance as her friends approached. Behind her, the hotel that I had called home for as long as I could remember looked different from the hotel in my memory. I recalled that first time coming down the drive, wide-eyed with wonder at the gingerbread mansion, its thick icing of snow blanketed plumply over the roof and windows, which glowed orange like bright candies pressed into sugary walls.

Instead, all I saw was decaying brick that had crumbled like biscuit, and grey glass broken in parts. The snow was patchy across the roof, having fallen away in great chunks, leaving black and grey slate, or dark holes among the rafters. The grounds around the hotel had clearly become overgrown at some point before dying back, leaving little more than snow-dusted husks of hedges and plants. There was nothing of the warmth that I recalled, just cold decay like somewhere left derelict for years. My eyes followed the thick tyre marks in the ground, winding snakelike away into the distance, and the hotel became smaller and smaller, and blurred in the storm.

"No!" I cried. "Delia!" My fists slammed forward, hammering at the glass. "Don't do this to me! Don't leave me!"

The car bumped over the road, moving in the direction of the approaching witches, who appeared to glide effortlessly across the snow, their long arms hanging by their sides and swaying in the storm. I screamed a warning to the driver as we came closer, their forms becoming clearer. Warped by the blizzard, their faces blurred, flashing between eerily perfect youth and the deep lines of age with their features drawn into unpleasant half smiles.

My screams continued as we came close to them, my body rigid with fear, and I pictured the doors opening and me being flung out into the snow like a carcass for a pack of hungry wolves. However, instead of stopping, the taxi simply drove past them, and the women barely acknowledged me, continuing to glide in the direction of the hotel where they would greet their old friend.

I heard the driver chuckle as we drove into the night.

# CHAPTER 57

The snow melted on the bench beneath me, soaking through the fabric of the cheap coat that I had picked up in one of the multi-floor clothing shops on Princes Street. I had counted out the notes carefully from the wad, which was exactly five hundred and eighty, and anxiously calculated how long the remainder would last me. The woman at the till didn't make eye contact, nor did she smile, but she did wish me a "happy holiday." Looking around me at the decorations that lined the walls, all glistening plastics and precariously placed stuffed Santas, I asked her what day it was. She looked at me oddly and told me that it was Christmas. I replied that I had never known shops to be open on Christmas Day, and she shrugged, muttering that "All the big ones are these days."

*These days.* I bristled.

Outside, the snow had fallen in patches, melting away outside shop doors where the heating blasted out, leaving glistening black wells of pavement. It was all brighter than I recalled, the long row of buildings alive with screens that flashed moving images instead of motionless adverts, the ones they used to paste to the glass and replace every few months for a fresh campaign. These ones flickered manically, changing every few seconds. Huddling deeper into my coat's faux sheepskin lining, I pulled the toggles tight and buried my face as deep inside the collar as I could.

The sky above me was clear, a bright, crisp winter blue with a cold sun that hadn't yet made up its mind about whether or not it was going to clear the roads and parks of the remaining snow. I found myself wandering down the small hill into Princes Street Gardens, where damp benches lined the path overlooking the grounds below the castle. As I sat down, I was reminded of warm summer days, an ice cream cone in one hand and the other intertwined in the soft fingers of a young woman whose enthusiastic chattering was lost in the noise of bustling shoppers and the horns of angry taxi drivers challenging buses. Glancing behind me at the cold and quiet street, there were long tram structures cutting through the road where the buses used to gather, thick wires suspended between heavy metal structures. I didn't remember anything like that.

The gardens in front of me were a much more picturesque view of Edinburgh, more akin to the Edinburgh I remembered. Open ground, unencroached upon by infrastructure, home to clusters of trees that had turned bald and black in the winter. Their long, dark tendrils reached out like spidery fingers, casting great shadows across the thin but pristine layer of snow. Behind it, the castle stood just as I remembered, looming over the city from Castle Rock, defiantly resisting change and the forces of modernisation that swirled around it. I fixed my gaze on it, seeking a small comfort in something that hadn't changed.

My hands fingered the notes in my pockets, wondering how much a room for the night would cost. Or perhaps there was someone who might remember me and who could offer a sofa for a while – just like they used to when I found myself in tight spots. I wondered if people still threw parties – big, bright, drink-fuelled affairs with tables laden with food. The thought made me both hungry and exhausted. As telephone boxes seemed to be a thing of the past, I was unsure how I would contact anyone, and that was if I even managed to track down their number in the first place. Touching my face uncertainly, I wondered if they would see the Eric whose stillness somehow made him more popular, the Eric they envied, the Eric women giggled nervously around, who would one day write the kind of books that would be discussed in book clubs and become cult classics, because someone as mysterious and alluring as Eric would most certainly write something like that. I wondered if they would see that Eric, or if they would see the sad, lonely, old Eric who had no job, no prospects, no real friends to speak of. My eyes began to blur. I felt frighteningly isolated.

At the sound of a commotion down the path, I blinked heavily and wiped away any sign of weakness from my face, turning to see an oncoming family. They traipsed heavily, three small children stomping in colourful welly boots and waving bright toys excitedly. Behind them, an elderly couple watched them fondly, strolling arm in arm along the path. My gaze paused on the woman, who was tightly bundled in several layers of bright fabrics, curly white hair spiralling out from beneath what appeared to be a handknitted hat. Her face, despite being deeply etched with the lines that come from a lifetime of expression, appeared strangely familiar. She paused and met my eyes.

After a moment observing each other, she dropped her partner's arm and took a step towards me, her mouth twisting into a slightly confused smile.

"*Eric?*" she asked uncertainly. "Eric, is that you?"

I recognised her voice at once, slightly crackled with age but still with the brightness from her youth, with her middle-class Edinburgh twang.

"Eleanor." I found myself almost laughing with relief, removing my hands from my pockets and placing them against my chest.

"I don't believe it." She shook her head and blinked, as though confirming to herself that I really was sat before her. "How are you?"

"Well, thank you," I lied, and rose to my feet. We bobbed uncertainly in front of each other before laughing at our awkwardness. "And you?"

"Oh, very well, thank you," she replied, slightly jittery. Turning to her partner and the three children, who had stopped and were staring at me with heads cocked to one side, she laughed again and waved her mittened hands. "Sorry, this is my family. My husband, Peter." She touched the arm of the old man, who smiled and leaned forward, removing his glove to shake my hand. His skin was warm. "And these are my grandchildren, Ellie – Eleanor actually, her parents named her after me – Rachel and Thomas. We're on a little walk to get them out of the way while their dads are busy in the kitchen making Christmas dinner." She ushered them over and gave them a fond but stern look; understanding at once, they turned to me and said hello. The smallest one, a little boy, brightened with a smile.

"Merry Christmas!" he chirruped, waving a strange robotic doll with moving legs. "This is what I got!"

I nodded uncertainly.

"Wow," I said eventually. "Looks great."

"It is," he confirmed, returning his attention to the toy.

I looked back at Eleanor, whose attention had rested momentarily on her grandchildren before returning to me. Peter ushered the three children together and along the path, as though sensing that there was something more to be said between us.

"And you?" she asked. "Family?"

"Yes." I nodded, before shaking my head. "No, actually – well, not really."

"And what about the books? You know, I always kept an eye out for your name on the shelves, but I didn't see it." She hesitated, looking suddenly appalled with herself, worried that she had offended me. "But you just never know – so many writers use pen names and such these days!"

I did my best to smile.

"I took a break from it for a while."

"That's a shame. You were so talented."

"Thank you." I didn't recall her reading much, other than the odd chapter I had produced during our time together. The memory she held of me was the Eric I had sold to her. "You know…" I paused to take a deep, steadying breath. "I'm so sorry about how things ended between us. It was awful how I left."

Eleanor became flustered, shaking her head and waving a mitten at me. "It was so long ago," she said, maintaining her unwavering cheeriness. "I barely remember now." Her smiled returned. "And besides, life goes on. We both found our own different paths."

Nodding slowly, I glanced up to the sky, at a lone, heavy cloud that pulled a shadow over us. A chill had replaced the warm glow of the winter sun. I heard one of the children begin to moan. Eleanor's husband called back and said something about walking ahead to avoid a toddler meltdown. As they moved further away from us, she turned back to me.

"I forgive you. I think I forgave you a long time ago."

"Thank you." Her forgiveness didn't make me feel any better; if anything, it made me feel worse, as though my part in her life was less significant than I had thought. "It must have been awful for you, seeing me just leave with that woman. That was wrong of me."

Frowning curiously, Eleanor hesitated before speaking.

"It was just strange, more than anything," she said slowly. "Who was that old lady? I contacted your father when you never came back, but he said you didn't have any elderly relatives, or anyone he could think of."

I froze, my words jumbled in my mouth.

"I don't know." I shook my head. "I don't remember."

Shrugging her plump shoulders, Eleanor resumed her bright smile and leaned forward, placing a wool-protected hand against my arm. There was the gentlest, softest padding sound as we made contact. A soft dusting of snow began to drift between us, landing on Eleanor's face and melting into glistening beads that travelled through the deep wrinkles of her skin. We looked into each other's eyes for a lingering moment, and I wondered, just for that moment, what might happen. I hoped.

"Well, it was a long time ago." Withdrawing her hand, she patted her face where the snowflakes had melted, and she gave an exaggerated shiver. "Gosh, chilly, isn't it? I'd better be off." She took a step away from me, ready to join her family several yards ahead, before glancing back once at me and smiling. "It really was good to see you, Eric. Merry Christmas."

I opened my mouth to wish her a Merry Christmas in return, but my words were lost and she had already walked away, marching briskly to escape the shadow of the cloud above us, the snow that had begun to fall with increasing heaviness. She caught up with her family without a second glance back at me, wrapping her arm in her husband's, bundling close to escape the weather together. I considered getting up and running from it too, running from it all in the hope that it wouldn't catch up with me. A little sing-song voice in my head goaded me. *Run, run, as fast as you can.*

I didn't move. Instead, I remained on the bench – still – a fine white powdering of snow gathering on my hood and shoulders, on my thighs and feet. I glanced uncertainly around me at passers-by, hoping that I might draw their attention as I used to do so naturally, effortlessly. But nobody turned to look at me. Nobody paused in appreciation. And, slowly, without really noticing it at first, I began to disappear beneath the weight of the falling snow.

# ACKNOWLEDGEMENTS

I would like to thank Haunt Publishing for bringing this book to life. Thank you Rebecca Wojturska for believing in my story from the very beginning and taking it to where it is now, and to Ross Stewart, a fantastic editor, for your skill and expertise.

I would also like to thank Zuzanna Kwiecien for a wonderful cover design.

And last but not least, thank you Tom. Your endless encouragement, reading of my drafts and listening to my ideas means the world to me.

# THE CREDITS

Creating a book takes a massive team effort. Haunt and Joanna Corrance would like to thank everyone who worked behind the scenes on *The Gingerbread Men*.

**Managing Director and Editor**
Rebecca Wojturska

**Copyeditor**
Ross Stewart

**Proofreader**
Kirstyn Smith

**Designer**
Zuzanna Kwiecien

**Typesetter**
Laura Jones

**Contracts Consultant**
Caro Clarke

# ABOUT THE AUTHOR

Joanna is an author and solicitor living in the Scottish Highlands. She has always been fascinated by Gothic horror and
dark speculative fiction, and her debut science fiction novella,
*John's Eyes*, was published by Luna Press Publishing in 2020. As
a child, Joanna would tell spooky bedtime stories most nights at
her little sister's request and her family have a tradition of telling
ghost stories in front of the fire on Christmas Day. She loves to
write about the strange and the frightening, telling stories that
linger long after reading.

Printed in the USA
CPSIA information can be obtained
at www.ICGtesting.com
LVHW030251061123
763089LV00008B/337

9 781916 234789